3 PLAYS
BY MART CROWLEY

3 PLAYS
BY MART CROWLEY

The Boys in the Band
A Breeze From the Gulf
For Reasons That Remain Unclear

ALYSON PUBLICATIONS
LOS ANGELES

ISBN 1-55583-357-8

The Boys in the Band first published by Farrar, Straus & Giroux: 1968
A Breeze From the Gulf first published by Farrar, Straus & Giroux: 1974

THIS COLLECTION IS FOR
BRIDGET ASCHENBERG

CONTENTS

INTRODUCTION

I think I made my first stabs at creative writing when I was about twelve or thirteen. I can't remember the plot of the thing, but it had to do with a big, dark mansion with big, dark secrets. There might have been a hint of something based on fact, but for the most part I'm sure it was all made up, obviously influenced by the gothic novels and movies that left an impression on me.

By the time I was in college and taking a playwriting course, I realized that just my imagination was not quite enough. Something was missing, something was empty, something was false. And it was not until I thought I'd fallen in love for the first time in my life that I was moved to write a play which told the "truth," theatricalized within the disciplines I was being taught. Up to that point, I'd always marveled at writers who had such a wealth of *material* and lamented that I had none and had nothing to say. I knew the old adage that you must write what you know, but I also knew I didn't know very much, except for the personal things which had happened to me. And then the obvious hit me: My experience was my material.

There was never a real birthday party attended by nine actual men, which was then literally transcribed into *The Boys in the Band.* However, just before I began to write the play, I had, indeed, attended a party for a friend's birthday, and it gave me the idea of how to frame what had already been on my mind (originally, I'd thought of setting it in a gay bar). All of the characters are based on people I either knew well or are amalgams of several I'd known to varying degrees, plus a large order of myself thrown into the mix. Each and every one of the "boys" reflects, inevitably, a different aspect of my own persona as much as anyone else, real or imagined.

A Breeze From the Gulf is based on my relationship with my parents from the beginning of my life to the ends of theirs. But it is merely based on my family, as the events of the play do not occur as they took place, nor in the same locales, nor in the same time frame. It's all been pushed and pulled, fictionalized and dramatized and, yes, personalized. After all, it's only my subjective side of things, and who knows whether that's true or not. I know for certain my mother and father had points of view toward me that were quite a different story.

No confrontation ever took place in a hotel room in Rome over some indelible interaction which happened *For Reasons That Remain Unclear.* The man I knew wasn't a priest but a religious of a different sort, and he was dead long before I was ever equipped to probe that disturbing part of my past. No doubt it is the way I fantasized coming face-to-face with him and the way I dreamt I'd exorcise my demons. And by finally being able to consider what happened and invent a way to put it down, I think I accomplished that. At least, for myself. I can honestly say I am at peace now about some of the more obsessive events of my life, just by having tried to use them in a creative way as my material. To more than a considerable extent, with the work and with the laughs, has come a release from the unhappiness and the resentment.

—*Mart Crowley*

FOREWORD

For Mart Crowley, each of these plays is dramatized autobiography. In *The Boys in the Band* (1968) the character called Michael is a portrait of the artist as a (relatively) young man, thirty years old and living in New York. *A Breeze From the Gulf* (1973) flashes back to Michael's adolescence and early manhood in a small Mississippi town. *For Reasons That Remain Unclear* (1993) finds him in Rome, aged forty-five and renamed Patrick. Together the plays form a kind of trilogy as well as a psychological jigsaw puzzle with a "Rosebud" as its final piece.

At the time, *The Boys in the Band* was rightly considered groundbreaking, "the frankest treatment of homosexuality I have ever seen on the stage," according to Clive Barnes in *The New York Times*. It was time-framed by two other groundbreaking events, opening just seven months after the first issue of *The Advocate* and fourteen months before the Stonewall rebellion. Ten years later, with gay liberation well under way and coming out transformed from a personal to a political decision, militants condemned *The Boys* as too "negative." Then, in the '90s, the pendulum swung again. It was not only OK for *Angels in America* to portray Roy Cohn as the meanest and most dangerous queen of them all but also to celebrate the twenty-fifth anniversary of *The Boys*. Produced at a little theater in Hollywood, it was perceived as an exact account of the prevailing mood of gay life in the '60s and a wonderfully accurate period piece.

But in fact it's no more a period piece than, say, *Suddenly Last Summer,* which also disappeared under a cloud of political incorrectness, only to be revived in the '90s as a TV movie and then in an off-Broadway production. In 1993 a mainly youngish audience responded to the wit of *The Boys* as if that birthday party had been held only last week, and a year later the characters in Terrence McNally's *Love! Valour! Compassion!* were carrying on in much the same way. In McNally's play, which owes not a little to Crowley's (the all-gay party stretched to an all-gay weekend), only the fact that one of the group is dying of AIDS creates an occasional hiatus in the general bitching, camping, and intrigue. Not since Bette Davis in *Dark Victory* has anyone died so nobly on stage or screen; yet most of the critics found it "moving," although twenty-five years earlier they found the far less sentimental telephone game in *The Boys* "sentimental."

All this, of course, is politics. Except for the Christian Coalition and their deluded allies, believers in "family values" who bomb abortion clinics, gay is, if not good, a force to be reckoned with. But in the '60s gay was still widely regarded as bad, or at best a neurosis, and the only genuine emotion *The Boys* could be allowed was guilt. According to a 1967 *New York Times* report on the growing "infiltration" of the arts by gay men, "No homosexual has a vision that is decent enough to make him a writer." And even as late as 1985, Quentin

Crisp announced: "Because homosexual men are pathologically incapable of making love with their friends or making friends of their lovers, it is not possible to write a satisfactory play about their world." This is also politics, of course, from a onetime rebel turned conservative, the most picturesque and entertaining member of a gay right wing. Its more typical members are the militants who decide, like the former Soviet Union's cultural commissars, which "deviant" works (and their authors) should be sent to Siberia. For many years they played down the fact that drag queens, who supposedly projected the "wrong" image for the cause, were in the forefront of the Stonewall rebellion. But when drag queens finally came into their own, as standard-bearers of an independent lifestyle, they were "rehabilitated." Although not, I'm afraid, really appreciated. A revolutionary with a sense of humor is hard to find.

The political view tries to nail down a work of the imagination in the coffin of its period. But *The Boys* triumphantly survives both the view and the period. Today it seems immediate as ever because it's a fairly savage comedy about a potentially tragic situation: the conflict between personal instinct and the dictates of society. In one sense Michael, Donald, Emory, and the rest could be members of any underground group, even a terrorist one, to judge from Michael's attack on the closeted Alan in Act 2. But their weapon of choice is humor, humor as an act of self-defense. They're role-players who play their roles (Guilty Catholic, Angry Jew, Flaming Queen, All-American Mixed-Up Kid) to the hilt, and at the same time are trapped in them. Occasionally self-pitying, they are more often self-critical, and they have few illusions. (Michael: "Well, one thing you can say for masturbation...you certainly don't have to look your best.") It's a very funny play because of its sharp wit and a very sad play because the wit is often sharp enough to be painful. One of its famous lines, "Show me a happy homosexual and I'll show you a gay corpse," comes from Michael, the central character with a Catholic upbringing and the burden of God as well as society on his shoulders. A drunk but a mean one, he is denounced near the end of the play as "a sad and pathetic man. You're a homosexual and you don't want to be. But there is nothing you can do about it. Not all your prayers to your God, not all the analysis you can buy in all the years you've got left to live."

This was the playwright's unsparing view of himself in 1968. Five years later, in *A Breeze From the Gulf,* he shows us Michael from age fifteen to age twenty-five, and the "feminizing" mother that he mentioned in *The Boys in the Band,* "who made me sleep in the same bed with her until I was fourteen years old," who "didn't want to prepare me for life or how to be out in the world on my own." Blowsy and genteel, helpless and ruthless, Lorraine is drifting slowly into a drug-addicted haze, and Teddy, Michael's father, is a sweet and crazy drunk. "I don't understand any of it. I never did" are his last words as he lies dying in Michael's arms. "We had only moments of happiness—and they were always on the Gulf Coast—but they were enough to make up for a lifetime" are Lorraine's next-to-last, as she leaves to end her life in a sanatorium.

The comedy of the play is that Lorraine truly believes this; the tragedy, that she makes Michael believe it. As she says, "You can just about win anybody over if you are warm and charmin'," and in spite of their ugly quarrels, of Teddy's passing out in the kitchen yet again and Lorraine's having yet another break-down, they *are* warm and charmin'. They try desperately to love Michael, he tries desperately to love them, but in the end, as he tells Teddy, "All the three of us do is torture each other." The dialogue in *A Breeze* is characteristically sharp but strikes a new note as well. It's a false paradise that Michael has lost, but his sense of loss is still strong, and Crowley conveys this with a kind of bitter poetry.

Although favorably reviewed by Walter Kerr, Clive Barnes, and even John Simon, and although Crowley thought Ruth Ford "wonderful" as Lorraine, *A Breeze* ran only six weeks off-Broadway. Perhaps it wasn't the play that audiences expected after *The Boys*, just as they didn't expect *Camino Real* after *The Rose Tattoo*. In both cases, revival and recognition are long overdue.

Michael in *The Boys* links himself to Michael in *A Breeze* when he describes the mother who "made me into a girlfriend dash lover," and Michael in *A Breeze* links himself to Patrick in *For Reasons That Remain Unclear* when he discusses "Uncle Brian" with his father:

TEDDY
I have never forgiven myself for leaving you alone in the house with him.
MICHAEL
You didn't know he'd do what he did.
TEDDY
I should have. He did the same thing to me. Worse, I think, 'cause I was older. He made me bend over. He didn't do that to you, did he?
MICHAEL
No.

"There are no accidents" is a line that recurs frequently in *The Boys*, and in *For Reasons* it seems more like fate than coincidence when Patrick, a screen-writer on an all-expenses-paid trip to Rome, encounters the priest who sexually abused him at the age of nine. Although Patrick recognizes Conrad, Conrad doesn't recognize Patrick, who invites him for a drink in his hotel room, where the situation gradually unravels. The first half of this long one-acter, which runs about 95 minutes, is a tense, finely sustained game of cat and mouse in which the audience is kept wondering who's the cat and who's the mouse. But when Patrick decides to show his hand, another and more jolting surprise occurs. He doesn't take the high moral ground on pedophilia but accuses Conrad of "Emotional betrayal. Sexual betrayal..." Conrad was "the first person to teach me what I thought was love," but when he decided it was a "sin" and abruptly broke off the relationship, Patrick was left "wrecked inside forever": "Left with nothing but apathy, indifference, a detachment toward everything that is given any emotional credence in this world. The thought of a human being about whom I might genuinely care makes me ill.... And left with that numbing emptiness, I fill it with a pathological commitment to luxury, a life of living beyond my means, an obsession for expensive, inanimate possessions of quality which cannot betray me."

Another unsparing self-portrait, but at the end of the play, in a powerfully dramatic parody of the confessional, Conrad begs for forgiveness, and Patrick grants it. Being able to forgive brings a sense of release, symbolized by "a surreal blaze of white light" and a wind that invade the hotel room while the sound of church bells in the distance grows louder. It's a reversal of the end of *The Boys*, when Michael goes off to midnight mass in the role of penitent but knows that tomorrow will still be "a day of nerves, nerves, and more nerves"; and a variation on the scene toward the end of *A Breeze* when Michael asks his dying father "to say the act of contrition with me," and they mumble it together.

Writing these plays, according to Crowley's introduction, was a kind of exorcism, and he feels "at peace now about some of the more obsessive events of my life." It's worth remembering, by the way, that thirty years ago intelligent and talented gay men didn't have to be Catholic to feel intense sexual guilt and opt for various "treatments" supposed to convert them to heterosexuality. (See Martin Duberman's *Cures*.) Medical journals ran horrifyingly serious reports on "Homo-Anonymous" (an invention of the appropriately named Dr. Harms), aversion therapy (posthypnotic suggestion that equated the male body with the smell of urine, shit, and bad breath), electroshock, and other forms of legal gay-bashing.

But the Angelus is still tolling at the end of *For Reasons*, as if to suggest that Catholic power as well as the parental and sexual betrayals of childhood can never be entirely shaken off. Like all the best American "gay" plays, from *Suddenly Last Summer* to *Angels in America*, Crowley's are not "gay" plays in a ghettoized sense. "The creative writer perceives his world once and for all in childhood and adolescence," Graham Greene wrote, "and his whole career is an effort to illustrate his private world in terms of the great public world we all share." He dramatized this idea in a short story, "The Basement Room" (later a movie called *The Fallen Idol*), which has nothing to do with homosexuality. The same idea recurs in these three plays by Mart Crowley, which of course have a lot to do with homosexuality but also with "the great public world" beyond the private world. "What I did is something I'll never forget or comprehend," Conrad remarks in *For Reasons That Remain Unclear*. "You can try, and all you'll get is a giant explosion, like the first blast of the universe," Patrick answers. "In the end, whatever you figure out, whatever you really *crack*, just reassembles into a question mark as soon as you turn your head." It's a "Rosebud," in fact, for both of them and yet another of the play's many surprises.

It's also *not* on the nose or judgmental or flip or "affirmative" but as ambiguous and unsettling as most human relations. *For Reasons* has not been produced in New York since its tryout at the Olney Theatre in 1993, but meanwhile it can at least be read—as part of a body of work from a playwright with a unique tone of voice and theatrical flair.

—*Gavin Lambert*

THE BOYS IN THE BAND

FOR
HOWARD JEFFREY
AND
DOUGLAS MURRAY

The Boys in the Band was first performed in January 1968 at the Playwrights Unit, Vandam Theatre, Charles Gnys, managing director.

The Boys in the Band was first produced on the New York stage by Richard Barr and Charles Woodward Jr. at Theatre Four on April 14, 1968. The play was designed by Peter Harvey and directed by Robert Moore.

The original cast was:

MICHAEL	*Kenneth Nelson*
DONALD	*Frederick Combs*
EMORY	*Cliff Gorman*
LARRY	*Keith Prentice*
HANK	*Laurence Luckinbill*
BERNARD	*Reuben Greene*
COWBOY	*Robert La Tourneaux*
HAROLD	*Leonard Frey*
ALAN	*Peter White*

The play is divided into two acts. The action is continuous and occurs one evening within the time necessary to perform the script.

Characters:

MICHAEL	Thirty, average face, smartly groomed
DONALD	Twenty-eight, medium blond, wholesome American good looks
EMORY	Thirty-three, small, frail, very plain
LARRY	Twenty-nine, extremely handsome
HANK	Thirty-two, tall, solid, athletic, attractive
BERNARD	Twenty-eight, Negro, nice-looking
COWBOY	Twenty-two, light blond, muscle-bound, too pretty
HAROLD	Thirty-two, dark, lean, strong limbs, unusual Semitic face
ALAN	Thirty, aristocratic, Anglo-Saxon features

Act 1

A *smartly appointed duplex apartment in the East Fifties, New York, consisting of a living room and, on a higher level, a bedroom. Bossa nova music blasts from a phonograph.*

> MICHAEL, *wearing a robe, enters from the kitchen, carrying some liquor bottles. He crosses to set them on a bar, looks to see if the room is in order, moves toward the stairs to the bedroom level, doing a few improvised dance steps en route. In the bedroom, he crosses before a mirror, studies his hair—sighs. He picks up comb and a hair dryer, goes to work.*

> *The downstairs front door buzzer sounds. A beat.* MICHAEL *stops, listens, turns off the dryer. More buzzing.* MICHAEL *quickly goes to the living room, turns off the music, opens the door to reveal* DONALD, *dressed in khakis and a Lacoste shirt, carrying an airline zipper bag.*

MICHAEL
Donald! You're about a day and a half early!

DONALD
[*Enters*]
The doctor canceled!

MICHAEL
Canceled! How'd you get inside?

DONALD
The street door was open.

MICHAEL
You wanna drink?

DONALD
[*Going to bedroom to deposit his bag*]
Not until I've had my shower. I want something to work out today—I want to try to relax and enjoy *something*.

MICHAEL
You in a blue funk because of the doctor?

DONALD
[*Returning*]
Christ, no. I was depressed long before I got *there*.

MICHAEL
Why'd the prick cancel?

DONALD
A virus or something. He looked awful.

MICHAEL
[*Holding up a shopping bag*]
Well, this'll pick you up. I went shopping today and bought all kinds of
goodies. Sandalwood soap...

DONALD
[*Removing his socks and shoes*]
I feel better already.

MICHAEL
[*Producing articles*]
...Your very own toothbrush because I'm sick to death of your using mine.

DONALD
How do you think *I* feel.

MICHAEL
You've had worse things in your mouth.
[*Holds up a cylindrical can*]
And, also for you...something called "Control." Notice nowhere is it called
hair spray—just simply "Control." And the words "For Men" are written
about thirty-seven times all over the goddamn can!

DONALD
It's called Butch Assurance.

MICHAEL
Well, it's *still* hair spray—no matter if they call it *"Balls"*!
[*DONALD laughs*]
It's all going on your very own shelf, which is to be labeled: Donald's
Saturday Night Douche Kit. By the way, are you spending the night?

DONALD
Nope. I'm driving back. I still get very itchy when I'm in this town too long.
I'm not that well yet.

MICHAEL
That's what you say every weekend.

DONALD
Maybe after about ten more years of analysis I'll be able to stay one night.

MICHAEL
Maybe after about ten more years of analysis you'll be able to move back to town permanently.

DONALD
If I live that long.

MICHAEL
You will. If you don't kill yourself on the Long Island Expressway some early Sunday morning. I'll never know how you can tank up on martinis and make it back to the Hamptons in one piece.

DONALD
Believe me, it's easier than getting here. Ever had an anxiety attack at sixty miles an hour? Well, tonight I was beside myself to get to the doctor—and just as I finally make it, rush in, throw myself on the couch, and vomit out how depressed I am, he says, "Donald, I have to cancel tonight—I'm just too sick."

MICHAEL
Why didn't you tell him you're sicker than he is.

DONALD
He already knows *that*.
  [*DONALD goes to the bedroom, drops his shoes and socks. MICHAEL follows*]

MICHAEL
Why didn't the prick call you and cancel. Suppose you'd driven all this way for nothing.

DONALD
  [*Removing his shirt*]
Why do you keep calling him a prick?

MICHAEL
Whoever heard of an analyst having a session with a patient for two hours on Saturday evening.

DONALD
He simply prefers to take Mondays off.

8

MICHAEL
Works late on Saturday and takes Monday off—what is he, a psychiatrist or a hairdresser?

DONALD
Actually, he's both. He shrinks my head and combs me out.
[*Lies on the bed*]
Besides, I had to come in town to a birthday party anyway. Right?

MICHAEL
You had to remind me. If there's one thing I'm not ready for, it's five screaming queens singing "Happy Birthday."

DONALD
Who's coming?

MICHAEL
They're really all Harold's friends. It's *his* birthday and I want everything to be just the way he'd want it. I don't want to have to listen to him kvetch about how nobody ever does anything for anybody but themselves.

DONALD
Himself.

MICHAEL
Himself. I think you know everybody anyway—they're the same old tired fairies you've seen around since the day one. Actually, there'll be seven, counting Harold and you and me.

DONALD
Are you calling me a screaming queen or a tired fairy?

MICHAEL
Oh, I beg your pardon—six tired screaming fairy queens and one anxious queer.

DONALD
You don't think Harold'll mind my being here, do you? Technically, I'm *your* friend, not his.

MICHAEL
If she doesn't like it, she can twirl on it. Listen, I'll be out of your way in just a second. I've only got one more thing to do.

DONALD
Surgery, so early in the evening?

MICHAEL
Sunt! That's French, with a cedilla.
[*Gives him a crooked third finger, goes to mirror*]
I've just got to comb my hair for the thirty-seventh time. Hair—that's singular.
My hair, without exaggeration, is clearly falling on the floor. And *fast*, baby!

DONALD
You're totally paranoid. You've got plenty of hair.

MICHAEL
What you see before you is a masterpiece of deception. My hairline starts
about here.
[*Indicates his crown*]
All this is just tortured forward.

DONALD
Well, I hope, for your sake, no strong wind comes up.

MICHAEL
If one does, I'll be in terrible trouble. I will then have a bald head and shoul-
der-length fringe.
[*Runs his fingers through his hair, holds it away from his scalp, dips the top
of his head so that DONALD can see. DONALD is silent*]
Not good, huh?

DONALD
Not the best.

MICHAEL
It's called, "getting old." Ah, life is such a grand design—spring, summer,
fall, winter, death. Who*ever* could have thought it up?

DONALD
No one *we* know, that's for sure.

MICHAEL
[*Turns to study himself in the mirror, sighs*]
Well, one thing you can say for masturbation...you certainly don't have to
look your best.
[*Slips out of the robe, flings it at DONALD. DONALD laughs, takes the robe,
exits to the bath. MICHAEL takes a sweater out of a chest, pulls it on*]

MICHAEL
What are you so depressed about? I mean, other than the usual *everything*.
[*A beat*]

DONALD
[*Reluctantly*]
I really don't want to get into it.

MICHAEL
Well, if you're not going to tell me, how can we have a conversation *in depth*—a warm, rewarding, meaningful friendship?

DONALD
Up yours!

MICHAEL
[*Southern accent*]
Why, Cap'n Butler, how you talk!
[*Pause.* DONALD *appears in the doorway holding a glass of water and a small bottle of pills.* MICHAEL *looks up*]

DONALD
It's just that today I finally realized that I was *raised* to be a failure. I was *groomed* for it.
[*A beat*]

MICHAEL
You know, there was a time when you could have said that to me and I wouldn't have known what the hell you were talking about.

DONALD
[*Takes some pills*]
Naturally, it all goes back to Evelyn and Walt.

MICHAEL
Naturally. When doesn't it go back to Mom and Pop? Unfortunately, we all had an Evelyn and a Walt. The crumbs! Don't you love that word—crumb? Oh, I love it! It's a real Barbara Stanwyck word.
[*A la Stanwyck's frozen-lipped Brooklyn accent*]
"Cau'll me a keab, you kr-rumm."

DONALD
Well, I see all vestiges of sanity for this evening are now officially shot to hell.

MICHAEL
Oh, Donald, you're so serious tonight! You're fun-starved, baby, and I'm eating for two!

[*Sings*]
"Forget your troubles, c'mon get happy! You better chase all your blues away. Shout, 'Hallelujah!' c'mon get happy..."
   [*Sees* DONALD *isn't buying it*]
—what's more boring than a queen doing a Judy Garland imitation?

DONALD
A queen doing a Bette Davis imitation.

MICHAEL
Meanwhile—back at the Evelyn and Walt Syndrome.

DONALD
America's Square Peg and America's Round Hole.

MICHAEL
Christ, how sick analysts must get of hearing how mommy and daddy made their darlin' into a fairy.

DONALD
It's beyond just that now. Today I finally began to see how some of the other pieces of the puzzle relate to them.— Like why I never finished anything I started in my life...my neurotic compulsion to not succeed. I've realized it was always when I failed that Evelyn loved me the most—because it displeased Walt, who wanted perfection. And when I fell short of the mark she was only too happy to make up for it with her love. So I began to identify failing with winning my mother's love. And I began to fail on purpose to get it. I didn't finish Cornell—I couldn't keep a job in this town. I simply retreated to a room over a garage and scrubbing floors in order to keep alive. Failure is the only thing with which I feel at home. Because it is what I was taught at home.

MICHAEL
Killer whales is what they are. Killer whales. How many whales could a killer whale kill...

DONALD
A lot, especially if they get them when they were babies.
   [*Pause.* MICHAEL *suddenly tears off his sweater, throws it in the air, letting it land where it may, whips out another, pulls it on as he starts down the stairs for the living room.* DONALD *follows*]
Hey! Where're you going?

MICHAEL
To make drinks! I think we need about thirty-seven!

DONALD
Where'd you get *that* sweater?

MICHAEL
This clever little shop on the right bank called Hermes.

DONALD
I work my ass off for forty-five lousy dollars a week *scrubbing* floors and you waltz around throwing cashmere sweaters on them.

MICHAEL
The one on the floor in the bedroom is vicuña.

DONALD
I *beg* your pardon.

MICHAEL
You could get a job doing something else. Nobody holds a gun to your head to be a charwoman. That is, how you say, your neurosis.

DONALD
Gee, and I thought it's why I was born.

MICHAEL
Besides, just because I *wear* expensive clothes doesn't necessarily mean they're paid for.

DONALD
That is, how you say, *your* neurosis.

MICHAEL
I'm a spoiled brat, so what do I know about being mature. The only thing mature means to me is *Victor* Mature, who was in all those pictures with Betty Grable.
    [*Sings à la Grable*]
"I can't begin to tell you, how much you mean to me..."
Betty sang that in 1945. '45?— '43. No, '43 was *Coney Island*, which was remade in '50 as *Wabash Avenue*. Yes, *Dolly Sisters* was in '45.

DONALD
How did I manage to miss these momentous events in the American cinema? I can understand people having an affinity for the stage—but movies are such garbage, who can take them seriously?

MICHAEL
Well, I'm sorry if your sense of art is offended. Odd as it may seem, there wasn't any Shubert Theatre in Hot Coffee, Mississippi!

DONALD
However—thanks to the silver screen, your neurosis has got style. It takes a certain flair to squander one's unemployment check at Pavillion.

MICHAEL
What's so snappy about being head over heels in debt. The only thing smart about it is the ingenious ways I dodge the bill collectors.

DONALD
Yeah. Come to think of it, you're the type that gives faggots a bad name.

MICHAEL
And you, Donald, *you* are a credit to the homosexual. A reliable, hardworking, floor-scrubbing, bill-paying fag who don't owe nothin' to nobody.

DONALD
I am a model fairy.
[*MICHAEL has taken some ribbon and paper and begun to wrap* HAROLD'S *birthday gift*]

MICHAEL
You think it's just nifty how I've always flitted from Beverly Hills to Rome to Acapulco to Amsterdam, picking up a lot of one-night stands and a lot of custom-made duds along the trail, but I'm here to tell you that the only place in all those miles—the only place I've ever been *happy*—was on the goddamn plane.
[*Puffs up the bow on the package, continues*]
Bored with Scandinavia, try Greece. Fed up with dark meat, try light. Hate tequila, what about slivovitz? Tired of boys, what about girls—or how about boys and girls mixed and in what combination? And if you're sick of people, what about poppers? Or pot or pills or the hard stuff. And can you think of anything else the bad baby would like to indulge his spoiled-rotten, stupid, empty, boring, selfish, self-centered self in? Is that what you think has style, Donald? Huh? Is that what you think you've missed out on—my hysterical escapes from country to country, party to party, bar to bar, bed to bed, hangover to hangover, and all of it, hand to mouth!
[*A beat*]
Run, charge, run, buy, borrow, make, spend, run, squander, beg, run, run, run, waste, waste, *waste!*

[*A beat*]
And why? And why?

DONALD
Why, Michael? Why?

MICHAEL
I really don't want to get into it.

DONALD
Then how can we have a conversation in depth?

MICHAEL
Oh, you know it all by heart anyway. Same song, second verse. Because my Evelyn refused to let me grow up. She was determined to keep me a child forever and she did one helluva job of it. And my Walt stood by and let her do it.
[*A beat*]
What you see before you is a thirty-year-old infant. And it was all done in the name of love—what *she* labeled love and probably sincerely believed to be love, when what she was really doing was feeding her own need—satisfying her own loneliness.
[*A beat*]
She made me into a girlfriend dash lover.
[*A beat*]
We went to all those goddamn cornball movies together. I picked out her clothes for her and told her what to wear and she'd take me to the beauty parlor with her and we'd both get our hair bleached and a permanent and a manicure.
[*A beat*]
And Walt let this happen.
[*A beat*]
And she convinced me that I was a sickly child who couldn't run and play and sweat and get knocked around—oh, no! I was frail and pale and, to hear her tell it, practically female. I can't tell you the thousands of times she said to me, "I declare, Michael, you should have been a girl." And I guess I should have—I was frail and pale and bleached and curled and bedded down with hot-water bottles and my dolls and my paper dolls, and my doll clothes and my dollhouses!
[*Quick beat*]
And Walt bought them for me!

[*Beat. With increasing speed*]
And she nursed me and put Vicks salve on my chest and cold cream on my face and told me what beautiful eyes I had and what pretty lips I had. She bathed me in the same tub with her until I grew too big for the two of us to fit. She made me sleep in the same bed with her until I was fourteen years old—until I finally flatly refused to spend one more night there. She didn't want to prepare me for life or how to be out in the world on my own or I might have left her. But I left anyway. This goddamn cripple finally wrenched free and limped away. And here I am—unequipped, undisciplined, untrained, unprepared, and unable to live!

[*A beat*]
And do you know until this day she still says, "I don't care if you're seventy years old, you'll always be my baby." And can I tell you how that drives me mad! Will that bitch never understand that what I'll always *be* is her son—but that I haven't been her baby for twenty-five years!

[*A beat*]
And don't get me wrong. I know it's easy to cop out and blame Evelyn and Walt and say it was *their* fault. That we were simply the helpless put-upon victims. But in the end, we are responsible for ourselves. And I guess—I'm not sure—but I want to believe it—that in their own pathetic, *dangerous* way, they just loved us too much.

[*A beat*]
Finis. Applause.

[*DONALD hesitates, walks over to* MICHAEL, *puts his arms around him, and holds him. It is a totally warm and caring gesture*]
There's nothing quite as good as feeling sorry for yourself, is there?

DONALD
Nothing.

MICHAEL
[*A la Bette Davis*]
I adore cheap sentiment.
[*Breaks away*]
OK, I'm taking orders for drinks. What'll it be?

DONALD
An extra-dry-Beefeater-martini-on-the-rocks-with-a-twist.

MICHAEL
Coming up.

16

[*DONALD exits up the stairs into the bath;* MICHAEL *into the kitchen. Momentarily,* MICHAEL *returns, carrying an ice bucket in one hand and a silver tray of cracked crab in the other, singing "Acapulco" or "Down Argentine Way" or some other forgotten Grable tune. The telephone rings*]

MICHAEL
[*Answering it*]
Backstage, *New Moon.*
[*A beat*]
Alan? My God, I don't believe it. How *are* you? *Where* are you? In town! Great! When'd you get in? Is Fran with you? Oh. What? No. No, I'm tied up tonight. No, tonight's no good for me.— You mean, *now?* Well, Alan, ole boy, it's a friend's birthday and I'm having a few people.— No, you wouldn't exactly call it a birthday party—well, yes, actually I guess you would. I mean, what else would you call it? A *wake,* maybe. I'm sorry I can't ask you to join us—but—well, kiddo, it just wouldn't work out.— No, it's not place cards or anything. It's just that—well, I'd hate to just see you for ten minutes and...Alan? Alan? What's the matter?— Are you—are you crying?— Oh, Alan, what's wrong?— Alan, listen, come on over. No, no, it's perfectly all right. Well, just hurry up. I mean, come on by and have a drink, OK? Alan...are you all right? OK. Yeah. Same old address. Yeah. Bye.
[*Slowly hangs up, stares blankly into space.* DONALD *appears, bathed and changed. He strikes a pose*]

DONALD
Well. Am I stunning?
[MICHAEL *looks up*]

MICHAEL
[*Tonelessly*]
You're absolutely stunning.— You *look* like shit, but I'm absolutely stunned.

DONALD
[*Crestfallen*]
Your grapes are, how you say, sour.

MICHAEL
Listen, you won't believe what just happened.

DONALD
Where's my drink?

17

MICHAEL
I didn't make it—I've been on the phone.
[*DONALD goes to the bar, makes himself a martini*]
My old roommate from Georgetown just called.

DONALD
Alan what's-his-name?

MICHAEL
McCarthy. He's up here from Washington on business or something and he's on his way over here.

DONALD
Well, I hope he knows the lyrics to "Happy Birthday."

MICHAEL
Listen, asshole, what am I going to do? He's *straight*. And *Square City!*
[*"Top Drawer" accent through clenched teeth*]
I mean, he's rally vury proper. Auffully good family.

DONALD
[*Same accent*]
That's *so* important.

MICHAEL
[*Regular speech*]
I mean, they look down on people in the *theater*—so whatta you think he'll feel about this *freak show* I've got booked for dinner?

DONALD
[*Sipping his drink*]
Christ, is that good.

MICHAEL
Want some cracked crab?

DONALD
Not just yet. Why'd you invite him over?

MICHAEL
He invited himself. He said he had to see me tonight. *Immediately*. He absolutely lost his spring on the phone—started crying.

DONALD
Maybe he's feeling sorry for himself too.

18

MICHAEL
Great heaves and sobs. Really boo-hoo-hoo-time—and that's not his style at all. I mean, he's so pulled-together he wouldn't show any emotion if he were in a plane crash. What am I going to do?

DONALD
What the hell do you care what he thinks.

MICHAEL
Well, I don't really, but...

DONALD
Or are you suddenly ashamed of your friends?

MICHAEL
Donald, *you* are the only person I know of whom I am truly ashamed. Some people *do* have different standards from yours and mine, you know. And if we don't acknowledge them, we're just as narrow-minded and backward as we think they are.

DONALD
You know what you are, Michael? You're a *real* person.

MICHAEL
Thank you and fuck you.
    [*MICHAEL crosses to take a piece of crab and nibble on it*]
Want some?

DONALD
No, thanks. How could you ever have been friends with a bore like that?

MICHAEL
Believe it or not, there was a time in my life when I didn't go around *announcing* that I was a faggot.

DONALD
That must have been before speech replaced sign language.

MICHAEL
Don't give me any static on that score. I didn't come out until I left college.

DONALD
It seems to me that the first time we tricked we met in a gay bar on Third Avenue during your *junior* year.

19

MICHAEL
Cunt.

DONALD
I thought you'd never say it.

MICHAEL
Sure you don't want any cracked crab?

DONALD
Not yet! If you don't mind!

MICHAEL
Well, it can only be getting colder. What time is it?

DONALD
I don't know. Early.

MICHAEL
Where the hell is Alan?

DONALD
Do you want some more club soda?

MICHAEL
What?

DONALD
There's nothing but club soda in that glass. It's not gin—like mine. You want some more?

MICHAEL
No.

DONALD
I've been watching you for several Saturdays now. You've actually stopped drinking, haven't you?

MICHAEL
And smoking too.

DONALD
And smoking too. How long's it been?

MICHAEL
Five weeks.

DONALD
That's amazing.

MICHAEL
I've found God.

DONALD
It *is* amazing—for you.

MICHAEL
Or is God dead?

DONALD
Yes, thank God. And don't get panicky just because I'm paying you a compliment. I can tell the difference.

MICHAEL
You always said that I held my liquor better than anybody you ever saw.

DONALD
I could always tell when you were getting high—one way.

MICHAEL
I'd get hostile.

DONALD
You seem happier or something now—and that shows.

MICHAEL
[*Quietly*]
Thanks.

DONALD
What made you stop—the analyst?

MICHAEL
He certainly had a lot to do with it. Mainly, I just didn't think I could survive another hangover, that's all. I don't think I could get through that morning-after ick attack.

DONALD
Morning-after what?

MICHAEL
Icks! Anxiety! Guilt! Unfathomable guilt—either real or imagined—from
that split second your eyes pop open and you say, "Oh, my God, what did I
do last night!" and ZAP, total recall!

DONALD
Tell me about it!

MICHAEL
Then, the coffee, aspirin, Alka-Seltzer, Darvon, Daprisal, and a quick call to
I.A.—Icks Anonymous.

DONALD
"Good morning, I.A."

MICHAEL
"Hi! Was I too bad last night? Did I do anything wrong? I didn't do anything
terrible, did I?"

DONALD
[*Laughing*]
How many times! How many times!

MICHAEL
And from then on, that struggle to live till lunch, when you have a double
Bloody Mary—that is, if you've *waited* until lunch—and then you're half
pissed again and useless for the rest of the afternoon. And the only sure cure
is to go to bed for about thirty-seven hours, but who ever does that? Instead,
you hang on till cocktail time, and by then you're ready for what the night
holds—which hopefully is another party, where the whole goddamn cycle
starts over!
[*A beat*]
Well, I've been on that merry-go-round long enough and I either had to get
off or die of centrifugal force.

DONALD
And just how does a clear head stack up with the dull fog of alcohol?

MICHAEL
Well, all those things you've always heard are true. Nothing can compare
with the experience of one's faculties functioning at their maximum natural
capacity. The only thing is...I'd *kill* for a drink.
[*The wall-panel buzzer sounds*]

DONALD
Joe College has finally arrived.

MICHAEL
Suddenly, I have such an ick!
[*Presses the wall-panel button*]
Now listen, Donald…

DONALD
[*Quick*]
Michael, don't insult me by giving me any lecture on acceptable social
behavior. I promise to sit with my legs spread apart and keep my voice in
a deep register.

MICHAEL
Donald, you are a real *card-carrying cunt.*
[*The apartment door buzzes several times. MICHAEL goes to it, pauses briefly
before it, tears it open to reveal EMORY, LARRY, and HANK. EMORY is in
Bermuda shorts and a sweater. LARRY has on a turtleneck and sandals. HANK
is in a dark Ivy League suit with a vest and has on cordovan shoes. LARRY
and HANK carry birthday gifts. EMORY carries a large covered dish*]

EMORY
[*Bursting in*]
ALL RIGHT THIS IS A RAID! EVERYBODY'S UNDER ARREST!
[*This entrance is followed by a loud raucous laugh as EMORY throws his
arms around MICHAEL and gives him a big kiss on the cheek.
Referring to dish*]
Hello, darlin! Connie Casserole. Oh, Mary, don't ask.

MICHAEL
[*Weary already*]
Hello, Emory. Put it in the kitchen.
[*EMORY spots DONALD*]

EMORY
Who is this exotic woman over here?

MICHAEL
Hi, Hank. Larry.
[*They say, "Hi," shake hands, enter. MICHAEL looks out in the hall, comes
back into the room, closes the door*]

DONALD
Hi, Emory.

EMORY
My dear, I thought you had perished! Where have you been hiding your classically chiseled features?

DONALD
[*To* EMORY]
I don't live in the city anymore.

MICHAEL
[*To* LARRY *and* HANK, *referring to the gifts*]
Here, I'll take those. Where's yours, Emory?

EMORY
It's arriving later.
[EMORY *exits to the kitchen.* LARRY *and* DONALD's *eyes have met.* HANK *has handed* MICHAEL *his gift—*LARRY *is too preoccupied*]

HANK
Larry!— Larry!

LARRY
What!

HANK
Give Michael the gift!

LARRY
Oh. Here.
[*To* HANK]
Louder. So my mother in Philadelphia can hear you.

HANK
Well, you were just standing there in a trance.

MICHAEL
[*To* LARRY *and* HANK *as* EMORY *reenters*]
You both know Donald, don't you?

DONALD
Sure. Nice to see you.
[*To* HANK]
Hi.

HANK
[*Shaking hands*]
Nice to meet you.

MICHAEL
Oh, I thought you'd met.

DONALD
Well...

LARRY
We haven't exactly me but we've... Hi.

DONALD
Hi.

HANK
But you've what?

LARRY
...*Seen*...each other before.

MICHAEL
Well, *that* sounds murky.

HANK
You've never met but you've seen each other.

LARRY
What was wrong with the way *I* said it?

HANK
Where?

EMORY
[*Loud aside to* MICHAEL]
I think they're going to have their first fight.

LARRY
The first one since we got out of the taxi.

MICHAEL
[*Referring to* EMORY]
Where'd you find this trash?

LARRY
Downstairs leaning against a lamppost.

EMORY
With an orchid behind my ear and big wet lips painted over the lipline.

25

MICHAEL
Just like Maria Montez.

DONALD
Oh, *please!*

EMORY
[*To DONALD*]
What have you got against Maria—she was a good woman.

MICHAEL
Listen, everybody, this old college friend of mine is in town and he's stopping by for a fast drink on his way to dinner somewhere. But, listen, he's *straight*, so...

LARRY
Straight! If it's the one I met, he's about as straight as the Yellow Brick Road.

MICHAEL
No, you met Justin Stuart.

HANK
I don't remember anybody named Justin Stuart.

LARRY
Of course you don't, dope. *I* met him.

MICHAEL
Well, this is someone else.

DONALD
Alan McCarthy. A very close total stranger.

MICHAEL
It's not that I care what he would think of me, really—it's just that *he's* not ready for it. And he never will be. You understand that, don't you, Hank?

HANK
Oh, sure.

LARRY
You honestly think he doesn't know about you?

MICHAEL
If there's the slightest suspicion, he's never let on one bit.

EMORY
What's he had, a lobotomy?
[*He exits up the stairs into the bath*]

MICHAEL
I was super-careful when I was in college and I still am whenever I see him.
I don't know why, but I am.

DONALD
Tilt.

MICHAEL
You may think it was a crock of shit, Donald, but to him I'm sure we were
close friends. The closest. To pop that balloon now just wouldn't be fair to
him. Isn't that right?

LARRY
Whatever's fair.

MICHAEL
Well, of course. And if that's phony of me, Donald, then that's phony of me
and make something of it.

DONALD
I pass.

MICHAEL
Well, even you have to admit it's much simpler to deal with the world
according to its rules and then go right ahead and do what you damn well
please. You do understand *that*, don't you?

DONALD
Now that you've put it in layman's terms.

MICHAEL
I was just like Alan when I was in college. Very large in the dating depart-
ment. Wore nothing but those constipated Ivy League clothes and those
ten-pound cordovan shoes.
[*To HANK*]
No offense.

HANK
Quite all right.

MICHAEL
I butched it up quite a bit. And I didn't think I was lying to myself. I really thought I was straight.

EMORY
[*Coming downstairs tucking a Kleenex into his sleeve*]
Who do you have to fuck to get a drink around here?

MICHAEL
Will you *light* somewhere?
[*EMORY sits on steps*]
Or I thought I thought I was straight. I know I didn't come out till after I'd graduated.

DONALD
What about all those weekends up from school?

MICHAEL
I still wasn't out. I was still in the "Christ-was-I-drunk-last-night syndrome."

LARRY
The *what?*

MICHAEL
The Christ-was-I-drunk-last-night syndrome. You know, when you made it with some guy in school and the next day when you had to face each other there was always a lot of shit-kicking crap about, "Man, was I drunk last night! Christ, I don't remember a thing!"
[*Everyone laughs*]

DONALD
You were just guilty because you were Catholic, that's all.

MICHAEL
That's not true. The Christ-was-I-drunk-last-night syndrome knows no religion. It has to do with immaturity. Although I will admit there's a high percentage of it among Mormons.

EMORY
Trollop.

MICHAEL
We all somehow managed to justify our actions in those days. I later found out that even Justin Stuart, my closest friend...

DONALD
Other than Alan McCarthy.

MICHAEL
[*A look to* DONALD]
…was doing the same thing. Only Justin was going to Boston on weekends.
[EMORY *and* LARRY *laugh*]

LARRY
[*To* HANK]
Sound familiar?

MICHAEL
Yes, long before Justin and I or God only knows how many others *came out*,
we used to get drunk and "horse around" a bit. You see, in the Christ-was-I-
drunk-last-night syndrome, you really *are* drunk. That part of it is true. It's
just that you also *do remember everything.*
[*General laughter*]
Oh, God, I used to have to get loaded to go in a gay bar!

DONALD
Well, times certainly have changed.

MICHAEL
They *have.* Lately I've gotten to despise the bars. Everybody just standing
around and standing around—it's like one eternal intermission.

HANK
[*To* LARRY]
Sound familiar?

EMORY
I can't stand the bars either. All that cat-and-mouse business—you hang
around *staring* at each other all night and wind up going home alone.

MICHAEL
And pissed.

LARRY
A lot of guys have to get loaded to have sex.
[*Quick look to* HANK, *who is unamused*]
So I've been told.

MICHAEL
If you remember, Donald, the first time we made it I was so drunk I could hardly stand up.

DONALD
You were so drunk you could hardly *get* it up.

MICHAEL
        [*Mock innocence*]
Christ, I was so drunk I don't remember.

DONALD
Bullshit, you remember.

MICHAEL
        [*Sings to* DONALD]
"Just friends, lovers no more..."

EMORY
You may as well be. Everybody thinks you are anyway.

DONALD
We never *were—really.*

MICHAEL
We didn't have time to be—we got to know each other too fast.
        [*Door buzzer sounds*]
Oh, Jesus, it's Alan! Now, please, everybody, do me a favor and cool it for the few minutes he's here.

EMORY
Anything for a sis, Mary.

MICHAEL
That's *exactly* what I'm talking about, Emory. *No camping!*

EMORY
Sorry.
        [*Deep, deep voice to* DONALD]
Think the Giants are gonna with the pennant this year?

DONALD
[*Deep, deep voice*]
Fuckin' A, Mac.
[*MICHAEL goes to the door, opens it to reveal BERNARD, dressed in a shirt and tie and sport jacket. He carries a birthday gift and two bottles of red wine*]

EMORY
[*Big scream*]
Oh, it's only another queen!

BERNARD
And it ain't the Red one, either.

EMORY
It's the queen of spades!
[*BERNARD enters. MICHAEL looks out in the hall*]

MICHAEL
Bernard, is the downstairs door open?

BERNARD
It was, but I closed it.

MICHAEL
Good.
[*BERNARD starts to put wine on bar*]

MICHAEL
[*Referring to the two bottles of red wine*]
I'll take those. You can put your present with the others.
[*MICHAEL closes the door. BERNARD hands him the gift. The phone rings*]

BERNARD
Hi, Larry. Hi, Hank.

MICHAEL
Christ of the Andes! Donald, will you bartend please.
[*MICHAEL gives DONALD the wine bottles, goes to the phone*]

BERNARD
[*Extending his hand to DONALD*]
Hello, Donald. Good to see you.

DONALD
Bernard.

MICHAEL
[*Answers phone*]
Hello? Alan?

EMORY
Hi, Bernardette. Anybody ever tell you you'd look divine in a hammock, surrounded by louvres and ceiling fans and lots and lots of lush tropical ferns?

BERNARD
[*To EMORY*]
You're *such* a fag. You take the cake.

EMORY
Oh, what *about* the cake—whose job was that?

LARRY
Mine. I ordered one to be delivered.

EMORY
How many candles did you say put on it—eighty?

MICHAEL
…What? Wait a minute. There's too much noise. Let me go to another phone.
[*Presses the hold button, hangs up, dashes toward stairs*]

LARRY
Michael, did the cake come?

MICHAEL
No.

DONALD
[*To MICHAEL as he passes*]
What's up?

MICHAEL
Do *I* know?

LARRY
Jesus, I'd better call. OK if I use the private line?

MICHAEL
[*Going upstairs*]
Sure.
[*Stops dead on stairs, turns*]
Listen, everybody, there's some cracked crab there. Help yourselves.
[*DONALD shakes his head. MICHAEL continues up the stairs to the bedroom. LARRY crosses to the phone, presses the free-line button, picks up receiver, dials information*]

DONALD
Is everybody ready for a drink?
[*HANK and BERNARD say, "Yeah"*]

EMORY
[*Flipping up his sweater*]
Ready! I'll be your topless cocktail waitress.

BERNARD
Please spare us the sight of your sagging tits.

EMORY
[*To HANK, LARRY*]
What're you having, kids?

MICHAEL
[*Having picked up the bedside phone*]
...Yes, Alan...

LARRY
Vodka and tonic.
[*Into phone*]
Could I have the number for the Marseilles Bakery in Manhattan.

EMORY
A vod and ton and a...

HANK
Is there any beer?

EMORY
Beer! Who drinks beer before dinner?

BERNARD
Beer drinkers.

DONALD
That's telling him.

MICHAEL
...No, Alan, don't be silly. What's there to apologize for?

EMORY
Truck drivers do. Or...or wallpaperers. Not schoolteachers. They have
sherry.

HANK
This one has beer.

EMORY
Well, maybe schoolteachers in *public* schools.
    [*To LARRY*]
How can a sensitive artist like you live with an insensitive bull like that?

LARRY
    [*Hanging up the phone and redialing*]
I can't.

BERNARD
Emory, you'd live with Hank in a minute, if he'd ask you. In fifty-eight seconds. Lord knows, you're *sss*ensitive.

EMORY
Why don't you have a piece of watermelon and hush up!

MICHAEL
...Alan, don't be ridiculous.

DONALD
Here you go, Hank.

HANK
Thanks.

LARRY
Shit. They don't answer.

DONALD
What're you having, Emory?

BERNARD
A Pink Lady.

EMORY
A vodka martini on the rocks, please.

LARRY
[*Hangs up*]
Well, let's just hope.
[*DONALD hands LARRY his drink—their eyes meet again. A faint smile crosses LARRY's lips. DONALD returns to the bar to make EMORY's drink*]

MICHAEL
Lunch tomorrow will be great. One o'clock—the Oak Room at the Plaza OK? Fine.

BERNARD
[*To DONALD*]
Donald, read any new libraries lately?

DONALD
One or three. I did the complete works of Doris Lessing this week. I've been depressed.

MICHAEL
Alan, forget it, will you? Right. Bye.
[*Hangs up, starts to leave the room—stops. Quickly pulls off the sweater he is wearing, takes out another, crosses to the stairs*]

DONALD
You must not work in Circulation anymore.

BERNARD
Oh, I'm still there—every day.

DONALD
Well, since I moved, I only come in on Saturday evenings.
[*Moves his stack of books off the bar*]

HANK
Looks like you stock up for the week.
[*MICHAEL rises and crosses to steps landing*]

BERNARD
Are you kidding—that'll last him two days.

EMORY
It would last *me* two years. I still haven't finished *Atlas Shrugged*, which I started in 1912.

MICHAEL
[*To* DONALD]
Well, he's not coming.

DONALD
It's just as well now.

BERNARD
Some people eat, some people drink, some take dope…

DONALD
I read.

MICHAEL
And read and read and read. It's a wonder your eyes don't turn back in your head at the sight of a dust jacket.

HANK
Well, at least he's a constructive escapist.

MICHAEL
Yeah, what do I do—take planes. No, I don't do that anymore. Because I don't have the _money_ to do that anymore. I go to the baths. That's about it.

EMORY
I'm about to do both. I'm flying to the West Coast—

BERNARD
You still have that act with a donkey in Tijuana?

EMORY
I'm going to *San Francisco* on a well-earned vacation.

LARRY
No shopping?

EMORY
Oh, I'll look for a few things for a couple of clients, but I've been so busy lately I really couldn't care less if I never saw another piece of fabric or another stick of furniture as long as I live. I'm going to the Club Baths and I'm not out till they announce the departure of TWA one week later.

BERNARD
[*To* EMORY]
You'll never learn to stay out of the baths, will you? The last time Emily was taking the vapors, this big hairy number strolled in. Emory said, "I'm just resting," and the big hairy number said, "I'm just *ar*resting!" It was the vice!
[*Everybody laughs*]

EMORY
You have to tell everything, don't you!
[*DONALD crosses to give EMORY his drink*]
Thanks, sonny. You live with your parents?

DONALD
Yeah. But it's all right—they're gay.
[*EMORY roars, slaps HANK on the knee. HANK gets up, moves away. DONALD turns to MICHAEL*]
What happened to Alan?

MICHAEL
He suddenly got terrible icks about having broken down on the phone. Kept apologizing over and over. Did a big about-face and reverted to the old Alan right before my very eyes.

DONALD
Ears.

MICHAEL
Ears. Well, the cracked crab obviously did not work out.
[*Starts to take away the tray*]

EMORY
Just put that down if you don't want your hand slapped. I'm about to have some.

MICHAEL
It's really very good.
[*Gives DONALD a look*]
I don't know why everyone has such an aversion to it.

DONALD
Sometimes you remind me of the Chinese water torture. I take that back. Sometimes you remind me of the *relentless* Chinese water torture.

MICHAEL
Bitch.
[*HANK has put on some music*]

BERNARD
Yeah, baby, let's hear that sound.

EMORY
A drumbeat and their eyes sparkle like Cartier's.
[*BERNARD starts to snap his fingers and move in time with the music. MICHAEL joins in*]

HANK
I wonder where Harold is.

EMORY
Yeah, where *is* the frozen fruit?

MICHAEL
[*To DONALD*]
Emory refers to Harold as the frozen fruit because of his former profession as an ice skater.

EMORY
She used to be the Vera Hruba Ralston of the Borscht Circuit.
[*MICHAEL and BERNARD are now dancing freely*]

BERNARD
[*To MICHAEL*]
If your mother could see you now, she'd have a stroke.

MICHAEL
Got a camera on you?
[*The door panel buzzes. EMORY lets out a yelp*]

EMORY
Oh my God, it's Lily Law! Everybody three feet apart!
[*MICHAEL goes to the panel, presses the button. HANK turns down the music. MICHAEL opens the door a short way, pokes his head out*]

BERNARD
It's probably Harold now.
[*MICHAEL leans back in the room*]

MICHAEL
No, it's the delivery boy from the bakery.

LARRY
Thank God.

38

[*MICHAEL goes out into the hall, pulling the door almost closed behind him*]

EMORY
[*Loudly*]
Ask him if he's got any hot-cross buns!

HANK
Come on, Emory, knock it off.

BERNARD
You can take her anywhere but out.

EMORY
[*To HANK*]
You remind me of an old-maid schoolteacher.

HANK
You remind me of a chicken wing.

EMORY
I'm sure you meant that as a compliment.
[*HANK turns the music back up*]

MICHAEL
[*In hall*]
Thank you. Good night.
[*MICHAEL returns with a cake box, closes the door, and takes it into the kitchen*]

LARRY
Hey, Bernard, you remember that thing we used to do on Fire Island?
[*LARRY starts to do a kind of Madison*]

BERNARD
That was "in" so far back I think I've forgotten.

EMORY
I remember.
[*Pops up—starts doing the steps. LARRY and BERNARD start to follow*]

LARRY
Yeah. That's it.
[*MICHAEL enters from the kitchen, falls in line with them*]

MICHAEL
Well, if it isn't the Geriatrics Rockettes.

[*Now they all are doing practically a precision routine.* DONALD *comes to sit on the arm of a chair, sip his drink, and watch in fascination.* HANK *goes to the bar to get another beer. The door buzzer sounds. No one seems to hear it. It buzzes again.* HANK *turns toward the door, hesitates. Looks toward* MICHAEL, *who is now deeply involved in the intricacies of the dance. No one, it seems, has heard the buzzer but* HANK, *who goes to the door, opens it wide to reveal* ALAN. *He is dressed in black tie. The dancers continue, turning and slapping their knees and heels and laughing with abandon. Suddenly* MICHAEL *looks up, stops dead.* DONALD *sees this and turns to see what* MICHAEL *has seen. Slowly he stands up.* MICHAEL *goes to the record player, turns it off abruptly.* EMORY, LARRY, *and* BERNARD *come to out-of-step halts, look to see what's happened*]

MICHAEL
I thought you said you weren't coming.

ALAN
I...well, I'm sorry...

MICHAEL
[*Forced lightly*]
We were just—acting silly...

ALAN
...Actually, when I called I was in a phone booth around the corner. My dinner party is not far from here. And...

MICHAEL
...Emory was just showing us this...silly dance.

ALAN
...Well, then I walked past and your downstairs door was open and...

MICHAEL
This is Emory.
[EMORY *curtsies.* MICHAEL *glares at him*]
Everybody, this is Alan McCarthy. Counterclockwise, Alan: Larry, Emory, Bernard, Donald, and Hank.
[*They all mumble "Hello," "Hi"*]
Would you like a drink?

ALAN
Thanks, no. I...I can't stay...long...really.

MICHAEL
Well, you're here now, so stay. What would you like?

ALAN
Do you have any rye?

MICHAEL
I'm afraid I don't drink it anymore. You'll have to settle for gin or Scotch or vodka.

DONALD
Or beer.

ALAN
Scotch, please.
   [*MICHAEL starts for bar*]

DONALD
I'll get it.
   [*Goes to bar*]

HANK
   [*Forced laugh*]
Guess I'm the only beer drinker.

ALAN
   [*Looking around group*]
Whose…birthday…is it?

LARRY
Harold's.

ALAN
   [*Looking from face to face*]
Harold?

BERNARD
He's not here yet.

EMORY
She's never been on time…
   [*MICHAEL shoots EMORY a withering glance*]
He's never been on time in his…

41

MICHAEL
Alan's from Washington. We went to college together. Georgetown.
[*A beat. Silence*]

EMORY
Well, isn't that fascinating.
[*DONALD hands ALAN his drink*]

DONALD
If that's too strong, I'll put some water in it.

ALAN
[*Takes a quick gulp*]
It's fine. Thanks. Fine.

HANK
Are you in the government?

ALAN
No. I'm a lawyer. What...what do you do?

HANK
I teach school.

ALAN
Oh. I would have taken you for an athlete of some sort. You look like you might play sports...of some sort.

HANK
Well, I'm no professional but I was on the basketball team in college and I play quite a bit of tennis.

ALAN
I play tennis too.

HANK
Great game.

ALAN
Yes. Great.
[*A beat. Silence*]
What...do you teach?

HANK
Math.

ALAN
Math?

HANK
Yes.

ALAN
Math. Well.

EMORY
Kinda makes you want to rush out and buy a slide rule, doesn't it?

MICHAEL
Emory. I'm going to need some help with dinner and you're elected. Come on!

EMORY
I'm *always* elected.

BERNARD
You're a natural-born domestic.

EMORY
Said the African queen! You come on too—you can fan me while I make the
salad dressing.

MICHAEL
[*Glaring. Phony smile*]
RIGHT THIS WAY, EMORY!
[*MICHAEL pushes the swinging door aside for EMORY and BERNARD to enter.
They do and he follows. The door swings closed, and the muffled sound of
MICHAEL's voice can be heard.
Offstage*]
You son of a bitch!

EMORY
[*Offstage*]
What the hell do you want from me?

HANK
Why don't we all sit down?

ALAN
...Sure.
[*HANK and ALAN sit on the couch. LARRY crosses to the bar, refills his drink.
DONALD comes over to refill his*]

LARRY
Hi.

DONALD
…Hi.

ALAN
I really feel terrible—barging in on you fellows this way.

LARRY
[*To DONALD*]
How've you been?

DONALD
Fine, thanks.

HANK
[*To ALAN*]
…Oh, that's OK.

DONALD
[*To LARRY*]
…And you?

LARRY ·
Oh…just fine.

ALAN
[*To HANK*]
You're married?
[*LARRY hears this, turns to look in the direction of the couch. MICHAEL enters from the kitchen*]

HANK
[*Watching LARRY and DONALD*]
What?

ALAN
I see you're married.
[*Points to HANK's wedding band*]

HANK
Oh.

MICHAEL
[*Glaring at* DONALD]
Yes. Hank's married.

ALAN
You have any kids?

HANK
Yes. Two. A boy nine, and a girl seven. You should see my boy play tennis—
really puts his dad to shame.

DONALD
[*Avoiding* MICHAEL's *eyes*]
I better get some ice.
[*Exits to the kitchen*]

ALAN
[*To* HANK]
I have two kids too. Both girls.

HANK
Great.

MICHAEL
How are the girls, Alan?

ALAN
Oh, just sensational.
[*Shakes his head*]
They're something, those kids. God, I'm nuts about them.

HANK
How long have you been married?

ALAN
Nine years. Can you believe it, Mickey?

MICHAEL
No.

ALAN
Mickey used to go with my wife when we were all in school.

MICHAEL
Can you believe that?

ALAN
[*To HANK*]
You live in the city?

LARRY
Yes, we do.
[*LARRY comes over to couch next to HANK*]

ALAN
Oh.

HANK
I'm in the process of getting a divorce. Larry and I are—roommates.

MICHAEL
Yes.

ALAN
Oh. I'm sorry. Oh, I mean...

HANK
I understand.

ALAN
[*Gets up*]
I...I...I think I'd like another drink...if I may.

MICHAEL
Of course. What was it?

ALAN
I'll do it...if I may.
[*Gets up, starts for the bar. Suddenly there is a loud crash offstage. ALAN jumps, looks toward swinging door*]
What was that?
[*DONALD enters with the ice bucket*]

MICHAEL
Excuse me. Testy temperament out in the kitch!
[*MICHAEL exits through the swinging door. ALAN continues to the bar—starts nervously picking up and putting down bottles, searching for the Scotch*]

HANK
[*To LARRY*]
Larry, where do you know that guy from?

LARRY
What guy?

HANK
That guy.

LARRY
I don't know. Around. The bars.

DONALD
Can I help you, Alan?

ALAN
I...I can't seem to find the Scotch.

DONALD
You've got it in your hand.

ALAN
Oh. Of course. How...stupid of me.
    [*DONALD watches* ALAN *fumble with the Scotch bottle and glass*]

DONALD
Why don't you let me do that?

ALAN
    [*Gratefully hands him both*]
Thanks.

DONALD
Was it water or soda?

ALAN
Just make it straight—over ice.
    [*MICHAEL enters*]

MICHAEL
You see, Alan, I told you it wasn't a good time to talk. But we...

ALAN
It doesn't matter. I'll just finish this and go...
    [*Takes a long swallow*]

LARRY
Where can Harold be?

MICHAEL
Oh, he's always late. You know how neurotic he is about going out in public.
It takes him hours to get ready.

LARRY
Why *is* that?
> [*EMORY breezes in with an apron tied around his waist, carrying a stack of
> plates, which he places on a drop-leaf table. MICHAEL does an eye roll*]

EMORY
Why is what?

LARRY
Why does Harold spend hours getting ready before he can go out?

EMORY
Because she's a sick lady, that's why.
> [*Exits to the kitchen. ALAN finishes his drink*]

MICHAEL
Alan, as I was about to say, we can go in the bedroom and talk.

ALAN
It really doesn't matter.

MICHAEL
Come on. Bring your drink.

ALAN
I...I've finished it.

MICHAEL
Well, make another and bring it upstairs.
> [*DONALD picks up the Scotch bottle and pours into the glass ALAN has in his
> hand. MICHAEL has started for the stairs*]

ALAN
> [*To DONALD*]
Thanks.

DONALD
Don't mention it.

48

ALAN
[*To HANK*]
Excuse me. We'll be down in a minute.

LARRY
He'll still be here.
[*A beat*]

MICHAEL
[*On the stairs*]
Go ahead, Alan. I'll be right there.
[*ALAN turns awkwardly, exits to the bedroom. MICHAEL goes into the kitchen.
A beat*]

HANK
[*To LARRY*]
What was *that* supposed to mean?

LARRY
What was what supposed to mean?

HANK
You know.

LARRY
You want another beer?

HANK
No. You're jealous, aren't you?
[*HANK starts to laugh. LARRY doesn't like it*]

LARRY
I'm Larry. *You're* jealous.
[*Crosses to DONALD*]
Hey, Donald, where've you been hanging out these days? I haven't seen you
in a long time...
[*MICHAEL enters to witness this disapprovingly. He turns, goes up the stairs.
In the bedroom ALAN is sitting on the edge of the bed. MICHAEL enters, pauses
at the mirror to adjust his hair. Downstairs, HANK gets up, exits into the
kitchen. DONALD and LARRY move to a corner of the room, sit facing upstage,
and talk quietly*]

ALAN
[*To MICHAEL*]
This is a marvelous apartment.

49

MICHAEL
It's too expensive. I work to pay rent.

ALAN
What are you doing these days?

MICHAEL
Nothing.

ALAN
Aren't you writing anymore?

MICHAEL
I haven't looked at a typewriter since I sold the very, very wonderful, very, very marvelous *screenplay* which never got produced.

ALAN
That's right. The last time I saw you, you were on your way to California. Or was it Europe?

MICHAEL
Hollywood. Which is not in Europe, nor does it have anything whatsoever to do with California.

ALAN
I've never been there but I would imagine it's awful. Everyone must be terribly cheap.

MICHAEL
No, not everyone.
   [*ALAN laughs. A beat. MICHAEL sits on the bed*]
Alan, I want to try to explain this evening...

ALAN
What's there to explain? Sometimes you just can't invite everybody to every party and some people take it personally. But I'm not one of them. I should apologize for inviting myself.

MICHAEL
That's not exactly what I meant.

ALAN
Your friends all seem like very nice guys. That Hank is really a very attractive fellow.

MICHAEL
...Yes. He is.

ALAN
We have a lot in common. What's his roommate's name?

MICHAEL
Larry.

ALAN
What does *he* do?

MICHAEL
He's a commercial artist.

ALAN
I liked Donald too. The only one I didn't care too much for was—what's his name—Emory?

MICHAEL
Yes. Emory.

ALAN
I just can't stand that kind of talk. It just grates on me.

MICHAEL
What kind of talk, Alan?

ALAN
Oh, you know. His brand of humor, I guess.

MICHAEL
He can be really quite funny sometimes.

ALAN
I suppose so. If you find that sort of thing amusing. He just seems like such a goddamn little pansy.
[*Silence. A pause*]
I'm sorry I said that. I didn't mean to say that. That's such an awful thing to say about *anyone*. But you know what I mean, Michael—you have to admit he *is* effeminate.

MICHAEL
He is a bit.

ALAN
A bit! He's like a…a butterfly in heat! I mean, there's no wonder he was trying to teach you all a dance. He *probably* wanted to dance *with* you!
[*Pause*]
Oh, come on, man, you know me—you know how I feel—your private life is your own affair.

MICHAEL
[*Icy*]
No. I *don't* know that about you.

ALAN
I couldn't care less what people do—as long as they don't do it in public—or—or try to force their ways on the whole damned world.

MICHAEL
Alan, what was it you were crying about on the telephone?

ALAN
Oh, I feel like such a fool about that. I could shoot myself for letting myself act that way. I'm so embarrassed I could die.

MICHAEL
But, Alan, if you were genuinely upset—that's nothing to be embarrassed about.

ALAN
All I can say is—please accept my apology for making such an ass of myself.

MICHAEL
You must have been upset or you wouldn't have said you were and that you wanted to see me—*had* to see me and had to talk to me.

ALAN
Can you forget it? Just pretend it never happened. I know *I* have. OK?

MICHAEL
Is something wrong between you and Fran?

ALAN
Listen, I've really got to go.

MICHAEL
Why are you in New York?

ALAN
I'm dreadfully late for dinner.

MICHAEL
Whose dinner? Where are you going?

ALAN
Is this the loo?

MICHAEL
Yes.

ALAN
Excuse me.
[*Quickly goes into the bathroom, closes the door.* MICHAEL *remains silent—sits on the bed, stares into space. Downstairs,* EMORY *pops in from the kitchen to discover* DONALD *and* LARRY *in quiet, intimate conversation*]

EMORY
What's-going-on-in-here-oh-Mary-don't-ask!
[*Puts a salt cellar and pepper mill on the table.* HANK *enters, carrying a bottle of red wine and a corkscrew. Looks toward* LARRY *and* DONALD. DONALD *sees him, stands up*]

DONALD
Hank, why don't you come and join us?

HANK
That's an interesting suggestion. Whose idea is that?

DONALD
Mine.

LARRY
[*To* HANK]
He means in a conversation.
[BERNARD *enters from the kitchen, carrying four wineglasses*]

EMORY
[*To* BERNARD]
Where're the rest of the wineglasses?

BERNARD
Ahz workin' as fas' as ah can!

EMORY
They have to be told everything. Can't let 'em out of your sight.
[*Breezes out to the kitchen. DONALD leaves LARRY's side and goes to the coffee table, helps himself to the cracked crab. HANK opens the wine, puts it on the table. MICHAEL gets up from the bed and goes down the stairs. Downstairs, HANK crosses to LARRY*]

HANK
I thought maybe you were abiding by the agreement.

LARRY
We have no agreement.

HANK
We *did*.

LARRY
You did. I never agreed to anything!
[*DONALD looks up to see MICHAEL, raises a crab claw toward him*]

DONALD
To your health.

MICHAEL
Up yours.

DONALD
Up my health?

BERNARD
Where's the gent?

MICHAEL
In the gent's room. If you can all hang on five more minutes, he's about to leave.
[*The door buzzes. MICHAEL crosses to it*]

LARRY
Well, at last!
[*MICHAEL opens the door to reveal a muscle-bound young MAN wearing boots, tight Levi's, a calico neckerchief, and a cowboy hat. Around his wrist there is a large card tied with a ribbon*]

COWBOY
[*Singing fast*]
"Happy birthday to you,
Happy birthday to you,
Happy birthday, dear Harold.
Happy birthday to you."
[*And with that, he throws his arms around* MICHAEL *and gives him a big kiss on the lips. Everyone stands in stunned silence*]

MICHAEL
Who the hell are you?
[EMORY *swings in from the kitchen*]

EMORY
She's Harold's present from me and she's *early!*
[*Quick, to* COWBOY]
And that's not even Harold, you *idiot!*

COWBOY
You said whoever answered the door.

EMORY
But *not until midnight!*
[*Quickly, to group*]
He's supposed to be a *midnight cowboy!*

DONALD
He *is* a midnight cowboy.

MICHAEL
He looks right out of a William Inge play to me.

EMORY
[*To* COWBOY]
...Not until midnight and you're supposed to sing to the right person, for Chrissake! I *told* you Harold has very, very tight, tight, black curly hair.
[*Referring to* MICHAEL]
This number's practically bald!

MICHAEL
Thank you and fuck you.

BERNARD
It's a good thing *I* didn't open the door.

EMORY
Not that tight and not that black.

COWBOY
I forgot. Besides, I wanted to get to the bars by midnight.

MICHAEL
He's a class act all the way around.

EMORY
What do you mean—get to the bars! Sweetie, I paid you for the whole night, remember?

COWBOY
I hurt my back doing my exercises and I wanted to get to bed early tonight.

BERNARD
Are you ready for this one?

LARRY
[To COWBOY]
That's too bad, what happened?

COWBOY
I lost my grip doing my chin-ups and I fell on my heels and twisted my back.

EMORY
You shouldn't *wear* heels when you do chin-ups.

COWBOY
[Oblivious]
I shouldn't do chin-ups—I got a weak grip to begin with.

EMORY
A weak grip. In my day it used to be called a limp wrist.

BERNARD
Who can remember that far back?

MICHAEL
Who was it that always used to say, "You show me Oscar Wilde in a cowboy suit, and I'll show you a gay caballero."

DONALD
I don't know. Who *was* it who always used to say that?

56

MICHAEL
[*Katharine Hepburn voice*]
I don't know. Somebody.

LARRY
[*To* COWBOY]
What does your card say?

COWBOY
[*Holds up his wrist*]
Here. Read it.

LARRY
[*Reading card*]
"Dear Harold, bang, bang, you're alive. But roll over and play dead. Happy birthday, Emory."

BERNARD
Ah, sheer poetry, Emmy.

LARRY
And in your usual good taste.

MICHAEL
Yes, so conservative of you to resist a sign in Times Square.

EMORY
[*Glancing toward stairs*]
Cheese it! Here comes the socialite nun.

MICHAEL
Goddammit, Emory!
[ALAN *comes down the stairs into the room. Everybody quiets*]

ALAN
Well, I'm off... Thanks, Michael, for the drink.

MICHAEL
You're entirely welcome, Alan. See you tomorrow?

ALAN
...No. No, I think I'm going to be awfully busy. I may even go back to Washington.

EMORY
Got a heavy date in Lafayette Square?

57

ALAN
What?

HANK
Emory.

EMORY
Forget it.

ALAN
[*Sees* COWBOY]
Are you...Harold?

EMORY
No, he's not Harold. He's *for* Harold.
[*Silence.* ALAN *lets it pass. Turns to* HANK]

ALAN
Good-bye, Hank. It was nice to meet you.

HANK
Same here.
[*They shake hands*]

ALAN
If...if you're ever in Washington—I'd like for you to meet my wife.

LARRY
That'd be fun, wouldn't it, Hank?

EMORY
Yeah, they'd love to meet him—*her.* I have such a problem with pronouns.

ALAN
[*Quick, to* EMORY]
How many esses are there in the word pronoun?

EMORY
How'd you like to kiss my ass—that's got two or more *essessss* in it!

ALAN
How'd you like to blow me!

EMORY
What's the matter with your *wife*, she got lockjaw?

ALAN
   [*Lashes out*]
Faggot, fairy, pansy...
   [*Lunges at* EMORY]
...queer, cocksucker! I'll kill you, you goddamn little mincing swish! You
goddamn freak! FREAK! FREAK!
   [*Pandemonium.* ALAN *beats* EMORY *to the floor before anyone recovers from
   surprise and reacts*]

EMORY
Oh, my God, somebody help me! Bernard! He's killing me!
   [BERNARD *and* HANK *rush forward.* EMORY *is screaming. Blood gushes from
   his nose*]

HANK
Alan! ALAN! ALAN!

EMORY
Get him off me! Get him off me! Oh, my God, he's broken my nose! I'm
BLEEDING TO DEATH!
   [*Larry has gone to shut the door. With one great, athletic move,* HANK *force-
   fully tears* ALAN *off* EMORY *and drags him backward across the room.*
   BERNARD *bends over* EMORY, *puts his arm around him, and lifts him*]

BERNARD
Somebody get some ice! And a cloth!
   [LARRY *runs to the bar, grabs the bar towel and the ice bucket, rushes to put it
   on the floor beside* BERNARD *and* EMORY. BERNARD *quickly wraps some ice in
   the towel, holds it to* EMORY's *mouth*]

EMORY
Oh, my face!

BERNARD
He busted your lip, that's all. It'll be all right.
   [HANK *has gotten* ALAN *down on the floor on the opposite side of the room.*
   ALAN *relinquishes the struggle, collapses against* HANK, *moaning and beating
   his fists rhythmically against* HANK's *chest.* MICHAEL *is still standing in the
   same spot in the center of the room, immobile.* DONALD *crosses past the
   COWBOY*]

DONALD
[*To* COWBOY]
Would you mind waiting over there with the gifts?
[*COWBOY moves over to where the gift-wrapped packages have been put.* DON-
ALD *continues past to observe the mayhem, turns up his glass, takes a long
swallow. The door buzzes,* DONALD *turns toward* MICHAEL, *waits.* MICHAEL
doesn't move. DONALD *goes to the door, opens it to reveal* HAROLD]
Well, Harold! Happy birthday. You're just in time for the floor show, which,
as you see, is on the floor.
[*To* COWBOY]
Hey, you, *this* is Harold!
[HAROLD *looks blankly toward* MICHAEL. MICHAEL *looks back blankly*]

COWBOY
[*Crossing to* HAROLD]
"Happy birthday to you,
Happy birthday to you,
Happy birthday, dear Harold.
Happy birthday to you."
[*Throws his arms around* HAROLD *and gives him a big kiss.* DONALD *looks
toward* MICHAEL, *who observes this stoically.* HAROLD *breaks away from*
COWBOY, *reads the card, begins to laugh.* MICHAEL *turns to survey the room.*
DONALD *watches him. Slowly* MICHAEL *begins to move. Walks over to the bar,
pours a glass of gin, raises it to his lips, downs it all.* DONALD *watches silently
as* HAROLD *laughs and laughs and laughs*]

C U R T A I N

Act 2

A *moment later.* HAROLD *is still laughing.* MICHAEL, *still at the bar, lowers his glass, turns to* HAROLD.

MICHAEL
What's so fucking funny?

HAROLD
[*Unintimidated. Quick hand to hip*]
Life. Life is a goddamn laff-riot. You remember life.

MICHAEL
You're stoned. It shows in your arm.

LARRY
Happy birthday, Harold.

MICHAEL
[*To* HAROLD]
You're stoned and you're late! You were supposed to arrive at this location at approximately eight-thirty dash nine o'clock!

HAROLD
What I *am*, Michael, is a thirty-two-year-old, ugly, pockmarked Jew fairy—and if it takes me a while to pull myself together and if I smoke a little grass before I can get up the nerve to show this face to the world, it's nobody's goddamn business but my own.
[*Instant switch to chatty tone*]
And how are *you* this evening?
[HANK *lifts* ALAN *to the couch.* MICHAEL *turns away from* HAROLD, *pours himself another drink.* DONALD *watches.* HAROLD *sweeps past* MICHAEL *over to where* BERNARD *is helping* EMORY *up off the floor.* LARRY *returns the bucket to the bar.* MICHAEL *puts some ice in his drink*]

EMORY
Happy birthday, Hallie.

HAROLD
What happened to *you?*

EMORY
[*Groans*]
Don't ask!

HAROLD
Your lips are turning blue; you look like you been rimming a snowman.

EMORY
That piss-elegant kooze hit me!
    [*Indicates* ALAN. HAROLD *looks toward the couch.* ALAN *has slumped his head forward into his own lap*]

MICHAEL
Careful, Emory, that kind of talk just makes him s'nervous.
    [ALAN *covers his ears with his hands*]

HAROLD
Who is she? Who was she? Who does she hope to be?

EMORY
Who knows, who cares!

HANK
His name is Alan McCarthy.

MICHAEL
Do forgive me for not formally introducing you.

HAROLD
    [*Sarcastically, to* MICHAEL]
Not the famous college *chum*.

MICHAEL
    [*Takes an ice cube out of his glass, throws it at* HAROLD]
Do a figure eight on that.

HAROLD
Well, well, well. I finally get to meet dear ole Alan after all these years. And in black tie too. Is this my surprise from you, Michael?

LARRY
I think Alan is the one who got the surprise.

DONALD
And, if you'll notice, he's absolutely speechless.

EMORY
I *hope* she's in *shock!* She's a beast!

COWBOY
[*Indicating* ALAN]
Is it his birthday too?

EMORY
[*Indicates* COWBOY *to* HAROLD]
That's your surprise.

LARRY
Speaking of beasts.

EMORY
From me to you, darlin'. How do you like it?

HAROLD
Oh, I suppose he has an interesting face and body—but it turns me right off
because he can't talk intelligently about art.

EMORY
Yeah, ain't it a shame.

HAROLD
I could never *love* anyone like that.

EMORY
Never. *Who could?*

HAROLD
I could and *you* could, that's who could! Oh, Mary, she's *gorgeous!*

EMORY
She may be dumb, but she's all yours!

HAROLD
In affairs of the heart, there are no rules! Where'd you ever find him?

EMORY
Rae knew where.

MICHAEL
[*To* DONALD]
Rae is Rae Clark. That's R-A-E. She's Emory's dyke friend who sings at a
place in the Village. She wears pinstriped suits and bills herself "Miss Rae
Clark—Songs Tailored to Your Taste."

EMORY
Miss Rae Clark. Songs tailored to your taste!

MICHAEL
Have you ever heard of anything so crummy in your life?

EMORY
Rae's a fabulous chanteuse. I adore the way she does "Down in the Depths
on the Ninetieth Floor."

MICHAEL
The faggot national anthem.
[*Exits to the kitchen singing "Down in the Depths" in a butch baritone*]

HAROLD
[*To EMORY*]
All I can say is thank God for Miss Rae Clark. I think my present is a super-
surprise. I'm so thrilled to get it I'd kiss you but I don't want to get blood all
over me.

EMORY
Ohhh, look at my sweater!

HAROLD
Wait'll you see your face.

BERNARD
Come on, Emory, let's clean you up. Happy birthday, Harold.

HAROLD
[*Smiles*]
Thanks, love.

EMORY
My sweater is ruined!

MICHAEL
[*From the kitchen*]
Take one of mine in the bedroom.

DONALD
The one on the floor is vicuña.

BERNARD
[*To EMORY*]
You'll feel better after I bathe your face.

64

EMORY
Cheer-up-things-could-get-worse-I-did-and-they-did.
[*BERNARD leads EMORY up the stairs*]

HAROLD
Just another birthday party with the folks.
[*MICHAEL returns with a wine bottle and a green-crystal white-wine glass, pouring en route*]

MICHAEL
Here's a cold bottle of Pouilly-Fuissé I bought especially for you, kiddo.

HAROLD
Pussycat, all is forgiven. You can stay. No. You can stay, but not all is forgiven. Cheers.

MICHAEL
I didn't want it this way, Hallie.

HAROLD
[*Indicating ALAN*]
Who asked Mr. Right to celebrate my birthday?

DONALD
There are no accidents.

HAROLD
[*Referring to DONALD*]
And who asked *him?*

MICHAEL
Guilty again. When I make problems for myself, I go the whole route.

HAROLD
Always got to have your crutch, haven't you?

DONALD
I'm *not* leaving.
[*Goes to the bar, makes himself another martini*]

HAROLD
Nobody ever thinks completely of somebody else. They always please themselves; they always cheat, if only a little bit.

LARRY
[*Referring to* ALAN]
Why is he sitting there with his hands over his ears?

DONALD
I think he has an ick.
[DONALD *looks at* MICHAEL. MICHAEL *returns the look, steely*]

HANK
[*To* ALAN]
Can I get you a drink?

LARRY
How can he hear you, dummy, with his hands over his ears?

HAROLD
He can hear every word. In fact, he wouldn't miss a word if it killed him.
[ALAN *removes his hands from his ears*]
What'd I tell you?

ALAN
I...I...feel sick. I think...I'm going to...throw up.

HAROLD
Say that again and I won't have to take my appetite depressant.
[ALAN *looks desperately toward* HANK]

HANK
Hang on.
[HANK *pulls* ALAN's *arm around his neck, lifts him up, takes him up the stairs*]

HAROLD
Easy does it. One step at a time.
[BERNARD *and* EMORY *come out of the bath*]

BERNARD
There. Feel better?

EMORY
Oh, Mary, what would I do without you?
[EMORY *looks at himself in the mirror*]
I am not ready for my close-up, Mr. De Mille. Nor will I be for the next two weeks.
[BERNARD *picks up* MICHAEL's *sweater off the floor.* HANK *and* ALAN *are midway up the stairs*]

ALAN
I'm going to throw up! Let me go! Let me go!
[*Tears loose of* HANK, *bolts up the remainder of the stairs. He and* EMORY *meet head-on.* EMORY *screams*]

EMORY
Oh, my God, he's after me again!
[EMORY *recoils as* ALAN *whizzes past into the bathroom, slamming the door behind him.* HANK *has reached the bedroom*]

HANK
He's sick.

BERNARD
Yeah, sick in the head. Here, Emory, put this on.

EMORY
Oh, Mary, take me home. My nerves can't stand any more of this tonight.
[EMORY *takes the vicuña sweater from* BERNARD, *starts to put it on. Downstairs,* HAROLD *flamboyantly takes out a cigarette, takes a kitchen match from a striker, steps up on the seat of the couch, and sits on the back of it*]

HAROLD
TURNING ON!
[*With that, he strikes the match on the sole of his shoe and lights up. Through a strained throat*]
Anybody care to join me?
[*Waves the cigarette in a slow pass*]

MICHAEL
Many thanks, no.
[HAROLD *passes it to* LARRY, *who nods negatively*]

DONALD
No, thank you.

HAROLD
[*To* COWBOY]
How about you, Tex?

COWBOY
Yeah.
[COWBOY *takes the cigarette, makes some audible inhalations through his teeth*]

MICHAEL
I find the sound of the ritual alone utterly humiliating.
[*Turns away, goes to the bar, makes another drink*]

LARRY
I hate the smell poppers leave on your fingers.

HAROLD
Why don't you get up and wash your hands?
[*EMORY and BERNARD come down the stairs*]

EMORY
Michael, I left the casserole in the oven. You can take it out anytime.

MICHAEL
You're not going.

EMORY
I couldn't eat now anyway.

HAROLD
Well, *I'm* absolutely ravenous. I'm going to eat until I have a fat attack.

MICHAEL
[*To* EMORY]
I said, you're *not going.*

HAROLD
[*To* MICHAEL]
Having a cocktail this evening, are we? In my honor?

EMORY
It's your favorite dinner, Hallie. I made it myself.

BERNARD
Who fixed the casserole?

EMORY
Well, *I* made the sauce!

BERNARD
Well, *I* made the salad!

LARRY
Girls, please.

MICHAEL
Please *what!*

HAROLD
Beware the hostile fag. When he's sober, he's dangerous. When he drinks, he's lethal.

MICHAEL
[*Referring to* HAROLD]
Attention must *not* be paid.

HAROLD
I'm starved, Em, I'm ready for some of your Alice B. Toklas' opium-baked lasagna.

EMORY
Are you really? Oh, that makes me so pleased maybe I'll just serve it before I leave.

MICHAEL
You're not leaving.

BERNARD
I'll help.

LARRY
I better help too. We don't need a nosebleed in the lasagna.

BERNARD
When the sauce is on it, you wouldn't be able to tell the difference anyway.
[*EMORY, BERNARD, and LARRY exit to the kitchen*]

MICHAEL
[*Proclamation*]
Nobody's going anywhere!

HAROLD
You are going to have schmertz tomorrow you wouldn't believe.

MICHAEL
May I kiss the hem of your schmata, Doctor Freud?

COWBOY
What are you two talking about? I don't understand.

69

DONALD
He's working through his Oedipus complex, sugar. With a machete.

COWBOY
Huh?
[HANK *comes down the stairs*]

HANK
Michael, is there any air spray?

HAROLD
Hair spray! You're supposed to be holding his head, not doing his hair.

HANK
Air spray, not *hair* spray.

MICHAEL
There's a can of floral spray right on top of the john.

HANK
Thanks.
[HANK *goes back upstairs*]

HAROLD
Aren't you going to say "If it was a snake, it would have bitten you"?

MICHAEL
[*Indicating* COWBOY]
That is something only your friend would say.

HAROLD
[*To* MICHAEL]
I am turning on and you are just turning.
[*To* DONALD]
I keep my grass in the medicine cabinet. In a Band-Aid box. Somebody told me it's the safest place. If the cops arrive, you can always lock yourself in the bathroom and flush it down the john.

DONALD
Very cagey.

HAROLD
It makes more sense than where I *was* keeping it—in an oregano jar in the spice rack. I kept forgetting and accidentally turning my hateful mother on with the salad.
[*A beat*]
But I think she liked it. No matter what meal she comes over for—even if it's breakfast—she says, "Let's have a salad!"

COWBOY
[*To* MICHAEL]
Why do you say I would say "If it was a snake, it would have bitten you"? I think that's what I *would* have said.

MICHAEL
Of course you would have, baby. That's the kind of remark your pint-size brain thinks of. You are definitely the type who still moves his lips when he reads and who sits in a steam room and says things like "Hot enough for you?"

COWBOY
I never use the steam room when I go to the gym. It's bad after a workout. It flattens you down.

MICHAEL
Just after you've broken your back to blow yourself up like a poisoned dog.

COWBOY
Yeah.

MICHAEL
You're right, Harold. Not only can he not talk intelligently about art, he can't even follow from one sentence to the next.

HAROLD
But he's beautiful. He has *unnatural* natural beauty.
[*Quick palm upheld*]
Not that that means anything.

MICHAEL
It doesn't mean *everything.*

HAROLD
Keep telling yourself that as your hair drops out in handfuls.
[*Quick palm upheld*]
Not that it's not *natural* for one's hair to recede as one reaches seniority. Not that those wonderful lines that have begun creasing our countenances don't make all the difference in the world because they add so much *character.*

MICHAEL
Faggots are worse than women about their age. They think their lives are over at thirty. Physical beauty is not that goddamned important!

HAROLD
Of course not. How could it be—it's only in the eye of the beholder.

MICHAEL
And it's only skin deep—don't forget that one.

HAROLD
Oh, no, I haven't forgotten that one at all. It's only skin deep and it's *transitory* too. It's *terribly* transitory. I mean, how long does it last—thirty or forty or fifty years at the most—depending on how well you take care of yourself. And not counting, of course, that you might die before it runs out anyway. Yes, it's too bad about this poor boy's face. It's tragic. He's absolutely cursed!
[*Takes* COWBOY's *face in his hands*]
How can *his* beauty ever compare with *my* soul? And although I have never seen my soul, I understand from my mother's rabbi that it's a knockout. I, however, cannot seem to locate it for a gander. And if I could, I'd sell it in a flash for some skin-deep, transitory, meaningless beauty!
[ALAN *walks weakly into the bedroom and sits on the bed. Downstairs,* LARRY *enters from the kitchen with salad plates.* HANK *comes into the bedroom and turns out the lamps.* ALAN *lies down. Now only the light from the bathroom and the stairwell illuminate the room*]

MICHAEL
[*Makes sign of the cross with his drink in hand*]
Forgive him, Father, for he know not what he do.
[HANK *stands still in the half darkness*]

HAROLD
Michael, you kill me. You don't know what side of the fence you're on. If somebody says something pro-religion, you're against them. If somebody denies God, you're against *them.* One might say that you have some problem in that area. You can't live with it and you can't live without it.
[EMORY *barges through the swinging door, carrying the casserole*]

EMORY
Hot stuff! Comin' through!

MICHAEL
[*To* EMORY]
One could murder you with very little effort.

HAROLD
[*To* MICHAEL]
You hang on to that great insurance policy called The Church.

MICHAEL
That's right. I believe in God, and if it turns out that there really isn't one,
OK. Nothing lost. But if it turns out that there *is*—I'm covered.
[BERNARD *enters, carrying a huge salad bowl. He puts it down, lights table candles*]

EMORY
[*To* MICHAEL]
Harriet Hypocrite, that's who you are.

MICHAEL
Right. I'm one of those truly rotten Catholics who gets drunk, sins all night
and goes to Mass the next morning.

EMORY
Gilda Guilt. It depends on what you think sin is.

MICHAEL
Would you just shut up your goddamn minty mouth and get back to the
goddamn kitchen!

EMORY
Say anything you want—*just don't hit me!*
[*Exits. A beat*]

MICHAEL
Actually, I suppose Emory has a point—I only go to confession before I get
on a plane.

BERNARD
Do you think God's power only exists at thirty thousand feet?

MICHAEL
It must. On the ground, I *am* God. In the air, I'm just one more scared son of
a bitch.
[*A beat*]

BERNARD
I'm scared on the ground.

COWBOY
Me too.
[*A beat*]
That is, when I'm not high on pot or up on acid.
[*HANK comes down the stairs*]

LARRY
[*To HANK*]
Well, is it bigger than a breadstick?

HANK
[*Ignores last remark. To MICHAEL*]
He's lying down for a minute.

HAROLD
How does the bathroom smell?

HANK
Better.

MICHAEL
Before it smelled like somebody puked. Now it smells like somebody puked in a gardenia patch.

LARRY
And how does the big hero feel?

HANK
Lay off, will you?
[*EMORY enters with a basket of napkin-covered rolls, deposits them on the table*]

EMORY
Dinner is served!
[*HAROLD comes to the buffet table*]

HAROLD
Emory, it looks absolutely fabulous.

EMORY
I'd make somebody a good wife.
[*EMORY serves pasta. BERNARD serves the salad, pours wine. MICHAEL goes to the bar, makes another drink*]

I could cook and do an apartment and entertain…
> [*Grabs a long-stem rose from an arrangement on the table, clenches it between his teeth, snaps his fingers and strikes a pose*]

Kiss me quick, I'm Carmen!
> [*HAROLD just looks at him blankly, passes on. EMORY takes the flower out of his mouth*]

One really needs castanets for that sort of thing.

MICHAEL
And a getaway car.
> [*HANK comes up to the table*]

EMORY
What would you like, big boy?

LARRY
Alan McCarthy, and don't hold the mayo.

EMORY
I can't keep up with you two—
> [*Indicating HANK, then LARRY*]

—I thought you were mad at him—now he's bitchin' you. What gives?

LARRY
Never mind.
> [*COWBOY comes over to the table. EMORY gives him a plate of food. BERNARD gives him salad and a glass of wine. HANK moves to the couch, sits, and puts his plate and glass on the coffee table. HAROLD moves to sit on the stairs and eat*]

COWBOY
What is it?

LARRY
Lasagna.

COWBOY
It looks like spaghetti and meatballs sorta flattened out.

DONALD
It's been in the steam room.

COWBOY
It has?

MICHAEL
[*Contemptuously*]
It looks like spaghetti and meatballs sorta flattened out. Ah, yes, Harold—
truly enviable.

HAROLD
As opposed to you, who knows so much about *haute cuisine*.
[*A beat*]
Raconteur, gourmet, troll.
[*LARRY takes a plate of food, goes to sit on the back of the couch from behind it*]

COWBOY
It's good.

HAROLD
[*Quick*]
You like it, eat it.

MICHAEL
Stuff your mouth so that you can't say anything.
[*DONALD takes a plate*]

HAROLD
Turning.

BERNARD
[*To DONALD*]
Wine?

DONALD
No, thanks.

MICHAEL
Aw, go on, kiddo, force yourself. Have a little *vin ordinaire* to wash down all
that depressed pasta.

HAROLD
Sommelier, connoisseur, pig.
[*DONALD takes the glass of wine, moves up by the bar, puts the glass of wine
on it, leans against the wall, eats his food. EMORY hands BERNARD a plate*]

BERNARD
[*To EMORY*]
Aren't you going to have any?

EMORY
No. My lip hurts too much to eat.

MICHAEL
    [*Crosses to table, picks up knife*]
I hear if you puts a knife under de bed it cuts de pain.

HAROLD
    [*To* MICHAEL]
I hear if you put a knife under your chin it cuts your throat.

EMORY
Anybody going to take a plate up to Alan?

MICHAEL
The punching bag has now dissolved into Flo Nightingale.

LARRY
Hank?

HANK
I don't think he'd have any appetite.
    [ALAN, *as if he's heard his name, gets up from the bed, moves slowly to the top of the stairwell.* BERNARD *takes his plate, moves near the stairs, sits on the floor.* MICHAEL *raps the knife on an empty wineglass*]

MICHAEL
Ladies and gentlemen. Correction: Ladies and ladies, I would like to announce that you have just eaten Sebastian Venable.

COWBOY
Just eaten *what?*

MICHAEL
Not *what*, stupid. *Who.* A character in a play. A fairy who was eaten alive. I mean the chop-chop variety.

COWBOY
Jesus.

HANK
Did Edward Albee write that play?

MICHAEL
No. Tennessee Williams.

HANK
Oh, yeah.

MICHAEL
Albee wrote *Who's Afraid of Virginia Woolf?*

LARRY
Dummy.

HANK
I know that. I just thought maybe he wrote that other one too.

LARRY
Well, you made a mistake.

HANK
So I made a mistake.

LARRY
That's right, you made a mistake.

HANK
What's the difference? You can't add.

COWBOY
Edward who?

MICHAEL
    [*To EMORY*]
How much did you pay for him?

EMORY
He was a steal.

MICHAEL
He's a ham sandwich—fifty cents anytime of the day or night.

HAROLD
King of the Pig People.
    [*MICHAEL gives him a look. DONALD returns his plate to the table*]

EMORY
    [*To DONALD*]
Would you like some more?

DONALD
No, thank you, Emory. It was very good.

EMORY
Did you like it?

COWBOY
I'm not a steal. I cost twenty dollars.
    [*BERNARD returns his plate*]

EMORY
More?

BERNARD
    [*Nods negatively*]
It was delicious—even if I did make it myself.

EMORY
Isn't anybody having seconds?

HAROLD
I'm having seconds and thirds and maybe even fifths.
    [*Gets up off the stairs, comes toward the table*]
I'm absolutely desperate to keep the weight up.
    [*BERNARD bends to whisper something in EMORY's ear. EMORY nods affirmatively and BERNARD crosses to COWBOY and whispers in his ear. A beat. COWBOY returns his plate to the buffet and follows EMORY and BERNARD into the kitchen*]

MICHAEL
    [*Parodying HAROLD*]
You're *absolutely* paranoid about *absolutely* everything.

HAROLD
Oh, yeah, well, why don't you *not* tell me about it.

MICHAEL
You starve yourself all day, living on coffee and cottage cheese so that you can gorge yourself at one meal. Then you feel guilty and moan and groan about how fat you are and how ugly you are when the truth is you're no fatter or thinner than you ever are.

EMORY
Polly Paranoia.
    [*EMORY moves to the coffee table to take HANK's empty plate*]

79

HANK
Just great, Emory.

EMORY
Connie Casserole, no-trouble-at-all-oh-Mary, D.A.

MICHAEL
[*To HAROLD*]
...And this pathological lateness. It's downright *crazy*.

HAROLD
Turning.

MICHAEL
Standing before a bathroom mirror for hours and hours before you can walk out on the street. And looking no different after Christ knows how many applications of Christ knows how many ointments and salves and creams and masks.

HAROLD
I've got bad skin, what can I tell you.

MICHAEL
Who wouldn't after they deliberately take a pair of tweezers and *deliberately* mutilate their pores—no wonder you've got holes in your face after the hack job you've done on yourself year in and year out!

HAROLD
[*Coolly but definitely*]
You hateful sow.

MICHAEL
Yes, you've got scars on your face—but they're not that bad and if you'd leave yourself alone you wouldn't have any more than you've already award-ed yourself.

HAROLD
You'd really like me to compliment you now for being so honest, wouldn't you? For being my best friend who will tell me what even my best friends won't tell me. Swine.

MICHAEL
And the pills!
[*Announcement to group*]
Harold has been gathering, saving, and storing up barbiturates for the last year like a goddamn squirrel. Hundreds of Nembutals, hundreds of Seconals. All in preparation for and anticipation of the long winter of his death.
[*Silence*]
But I tell you right now, Hallie. When the time comes, you'll never have the guts. It's not always like it happens in plays, not all faggots bump themselves off at the end of the story.

HAROLD
What you say may be true. Time will undoubtedly tell. But, in the meantime, you've left out one detail—the cosmetics and astringents are *paid* for, the bathroom is *paid* for, the tweezers are *paid* for, and the pills *are paid for!*
[*EMORY darts in and over to the light switch, plunges the room into darkness except for the light from the tapers on the buffet table, and begins to sing "Happy Birthday." Immediately BERNARD pushes the swinging door open and COWBOY enters carrying a cake ablaze with candles. Everyone has now joined in with "Happy birthday, dear Harold, happy birthday to you." This is followed by a round of applause. MICHAEL turns, goes to the bar, makes another drink*]

EMORY
Blow out your candles, Mary, and make a wish!

MICHAEL
[*To himself*]
Blow out your candles, *Laura*.
[*COWBOY has brought cake over in front of HAROLD. He thinks a minute, blows out the candles. More applause*]

EMORY
Awwww, she's thirty-two years young!

HAROLD
[*Groans, holds his head*]
Ohh, my God!
[*BERNARD has brought in cake plates and forks. The room remains lit only by candlelight from the buffet table. COWBOY returns the cake to the table and BERNARD begins to cut it and put the pieces on the plates*]

HANK
Now you have to open your gifts.

HAROLD
Do I have to open them here?

EMORY
Of course you've got to open them here.
[*Hands* HAROLD *a gift.* HAROLD *begins to rip the paper off*]

HAROLD
Where's the card?

EMORY
Here.

HAROLD
Oh. From Larry.
[*Finishes tearing off the paper*]
It's *heaven!* Oh, I just love it, Larry.
[HAROLD *holds up a graphic design—a large-scale deed to Boardwalk, like those used in a Monopoly game*]

COWBOY
What is it?

HAROLD
It's the deed to Boardwalk.

EMORY
Oh, gay pop art!

DONALD
[*To* LARRY]
It's sensational. Did you do it?

LARRY
Yes.

HAROLD
Oh, it's super, Larry. It goes up the minute I get home.
[HAROLD *gives* LARRY *a peck on the cheek*]

COWBOY
[*To* HAROLD]
I don't get it—you cruise Atlantic City or something?

MICHAEL
Will somebody get him out of here!

82

[*HAROLD has torn open another gift, takes the card from inside*]

HAROLD
Oh, what a nifty sweater! Thank you, Hank.

HANK
You can take it back and pick out another one if you want to.

HAROLD
I think this one is just nifty.
        [*DONALD goes to the bar, makes himself a brandy and soda*]

BERNARD
Who wants cake?

EMORY
Everybody?

DONALD
None for me.

MICHAEL
I'd just like to sleep on mine, thank you.
        [*HANK comes over to the table. BERNARD gives him a plate of cake, passes
        another one to COWBOY and a third to LARRY. HAROLD has torn the paper off
        another gift. Suddenly laughs aloud*]

HAROLD
Oh, Bernard! How divine! Look, everybody! Bejeweled knee pads!
        [*Holds up a pair of basketball knee pads with sequin initials*]

BERNARD
Monogrammed!

EMORY
Bernard, you're a camp!

MICHAEL
Y'all heard of Gloria DeHaven and Billy de Wolfe, well, dis here is
Rosemary De Camp!

BERNARD
Who?

EMORY
I never miss a Rosemary De Camp picture.

HANK
I've never heard of her.

COWBOY
Me neither.

HANK
Not all of us spent their childhood in a movie house, Michael. Some of us played baseball.

DONALD
And mowed the lawn.

EMORY
Well, *I* know who Rosemary De Camp is.

MICHAEL
You would. It's a cinch you wouldn't recognize a baseball or a lawnmower.
[*HAROLD has unwrapped his last gift. He is silent. Pause*]

HAROLD
Thank you, Michael.

MICHAEL
What?
[*Turns to see the gift*]
Oh.
[*A beat*]
You're welcome.
[*MICHAEL finishes off his drink, returns to the bar*]

LARRY
What is it, Harold?
[*A beat*]

HAROLD
It's a photograph of him in a silver frame. And there's an inscription engraved and the date.

BERNARD
What's it say?

HAROLD
Just...something personal.
[*MICHAEL spins round from the bar*]

MICHAEL
Hey, Bernard, what do you say we have a little music to liven things up!

BERNARD
OK.

EMORY
Yeah, I feel like dancing.

MICHAEL
How about something good and ethnic, Emory—one of your specialties, like a military toe tap with sparklers.

EMORY
I don't do that at birthdays—only on the Fourth of July.
> [BERNARD *puts on a romantic record.* EMORY *goes to* BERNARD. *They start to dance slowly*]

LARRY
Come on, Michael.

MICHAEL
I only lead.

LARRY
I can follow.
> [*They start to dance*]

HAROLD
Come on, Tex, you're on.
> [COWBOY *gets to his feet but is a washout as a dancing partner.* HAROLD *gives up, takes out another cigarette, strikes a match. As he does, he catches sight of someone over by the stairs, walks over to* ALAN. *Blows out match*]

Wanna dance?

EMORY
> [*Sees* ALAN]

Uh-oh. Yvonne the Terrible is back.

MICHAEL
Oh, hello, Alan. Feel better? This is where you came in, isn't it?
> [ALAN *starts to cross directly to the door.* MICHAEL *breaks away*]

Excuse me, Larry...
> [ALAN *has reached the door and has started to open it as* MICHAEL *intercepts, slams the door with one hand, and leans against it, crossing his legs*]

As they say in the Deep South, don't rush off in the heat of the day.

HAROLD

Revolution complete.
> [MICHAEL *slowly takes* ALAN *by the arm, walks him slowly back into the room*]

MICHAEL

...You missed the cake—and you missed the opening of the gifts—but you're still in luck. You're just in time for a party game.
> [*They have reached the phonograph.* MICHAEL *rejects the record. The music stops, the dancing stops.* MICHAEL *releases* ALAN, *claps his hands*]

...Hey, everybody! Game time!
> [ALAN *starts to move.* MICHAEL *catches him gently by the sleeve*]

HAROLD

Why don't you just let him go, Michael?

MICHAEL

He can go if he wants to—but not before we play a little game.

EMORY

What's it going to be—movie-star gin?

MICHAEL

That's too faggy for Alan to play—he wouldn't be any good at it.

BERNARD

What about Likes and Dislikes?
> [MICHAEL *lets go of* ALAN, *takes a pencil and pad from the desk*]

MICHAEL

It's too much trouble to find enough pencils, and besides, Emory always puts down the same thing. He dislikes artificial fruit and flowers and coffee grinders made into lamps—and he likes Mabel Mercer, poodles, and *All About Eve*—the screenplay of which he will then recite *verbatim*.

EMORY

I put down other things sometimes.

MICHAEL

Like a tan out of season?

EMORY
I just always put down little "Chi-Chi" because I adore her so much.

MICHAEL
If one is of the masculine gender, a poodle is the *insignia* of one's deviation.

BERNARD
You know why old ladies like poodles—because they go down on them.

EMORY
They do not!

LARRY
We could play B for Botticelli.

MICHAEL
We *could* play *Spin* the Botticelli, but we're not going to.
     [*A beat*]

HAROLD
What would you like to play, Michael—the Truth Game?
     [*MICHAEL chuckles to himself*]

MICHAEL
Cute, Hallie.

HAROLD
Or do you want to play Murder? You all remember that one, don't you?

MICHAEL
     [*To HAROLD*]
Very, very cute.

DONALD
As I recall, they're quite similar. The rules are the same in both—you kill somebody.

MICHAEL
In affairs of the heart, there are no rules. Isn't that right, Harold?

HAROLD
That's what I always say.

MICHAEL
Well, that's the name of the game. The Affairs of the Heart.

COWBOY
I've never heard of that one.

MICHAEL
Of course you've never heard of it—I just made it up, baby doll. Affairs of the Heart is a combination of both the Truth Game and Murder—with a new twist.

HAROLD
I can hardly wait to find out what that is.

ALAN
Mickey, I'm leaving.
        [*Starts to move*]

MICHAEL
        [*Firmly, flatly*]
Stay where you are.

HAROLD
Michael, let him go.

MICHAEL
He really doesn't *want* to. If he did, he'd have left a long time ago—or he wouldn't have come here in the first place.

ALAN
        [*Holding his forehead*]
...Mickey, I don't *feel* well!

MICHAEL
        [*Low tone, but distinctly articulate*]
My name is Michael. I am called Michael. You must never call anyone called Michael Mickey. Those of us who are named Michael are very nervous about it. If you don't believe it—try it.

ALAN
I'm sorry. I can't think.

MICHAEL
You can think. What you can't do—is leave. It's like watching an accident on the highway—you can't look at it and you can't look away.

ALAN
I...feel...weak...

MICHAEL
You are weak. Much weaker than I think you realize.
[*Takes* ALAN *by the arm, leads him to a chair. Slowly, deliberately, pushes him down into it*]
Now! Who's going to play with Alan and me? Everyone?

HAROLD
I have no intention of playing.

DONALD
Nor do I.

MICHAEL
Well, not everyone is a participant in *life*. There are always those who stand on the sidelines and watch.

LARRY
What's the game?

MICHAEL
Simply this: We all have to call on the telephone the *one person* we truly believe we have loved.

HANK
I'm not playing.

LARRY
Oh, yes, you are.

HANK
You'd like for me to play, wouldn't you?

LARRY
You bet I would. I'd like to know who you'd call after all the fancy speeches I've heard lately. Who would you call? Would you call me?

MICHAEL
[*To* BERNARD]
Sounds like there's, how you say, trouble in paradise.

HAROLD
If there isn't, I think you'll be able to stir up some.

HANK
And who would *you* call? Don't think I think for one minute it would be me.
Or that one call would do it. You'd have to make several, wouldn't you?
About three long-distance and God only knows how many locals.

COWBOY
I'm glad I don't have to pay the bill.

MICHAEL
Quiet!

HAROLD
      [*Loud whisper to* COWBOY]
Oh, don't worry, Michael won't pay it either.

MICHAEL
Now, here's how it works.

LARRY
I thought you said there were no rules.

MICHAEL
That's right. In Affairs of the Heart, there are no rules. This is the goddamn
point system!
      [*No response from anyone. A beat*]
If you make the call, you get one point. If the person you are calling
answers, you get two more points. If somebody else answers, you get only
one. If there's no answer at all, you're screwed.

DONALD
You're screwed if you make the call.

HAROLD
You're a *fool*—if you screw yourself.

MICHAEL
...When you get the person whom you are calling on the line—if you tell
them who you are, you get two points. And then—if you tell them that you
love them—you get a bonus of five more points!

HAROLD
Hateful.

MICHAEL
Therefore you can get as many as ten points and as few as one.

HAROLD
You can get as few as none—if you know how to work it.

MICHAEL
The one with the highest score wins.

ALAN
Hank. Let's get out of here.

EMORY
Well, now. Did you hear that!

MICHAEL
Just the two of you together. The pals...the guys...the buddy-buddies...the he-men.

EMORY
I think Larry might have something to say about that.

BERNARD
Emory.

MICHAEL
The duenna speaks.
    [*Crosses to take the telephone from the desk, brings it to the group*]
So who's playing? Not including Cowboy, who, as a gift, is neuter. And, of course, le voyeur.
    [*A beat*]
Emory? Bernard?

BERNARD
I don't think I want to play.

MICHAEL
Why, Bernard! Where's your fun-loving spirit?

BERNARD
I don't think this game is fun.

HAROLD
It's absolutely hateful.

ALAN
Hank, leave with me.

HANK
You don't understand, Alan. I can't. You can...but I can't.

ALAN
Why, Hank? Why can't you?

LARRY
[*To HANK*]
If he doesn't understand, why don't you explain it to him?

MICHAEL
I'll explain it.

HAROLD
I had a feeling you might.

MICHAEL
Although I doubt that it'll make any difference. That type refuses to understand that which they do not wish to accept. They reject certain facts. And Alan is decidedly from The Ostrich School of Reality.
[*A beat*]
Alan...Larry and Hank are lovers. Not just roommates, *bed*mates. *Lovers.*

ALAN
Michael!

MICHAEL
No man's still got a *roommate* when he's over thirty years old. If they're not lovers, they're sisters.

LARRY
Hank is the one who's over thirty.

MICHAEL
Well, you're pushing it!

ALAN
...Hank?
[*A beat*]

HANK
Yes, Alan. Larry is my lover.

ALAN
But...but...you're married.

[*MICHAEL, LARRY, EMORY, and COWBOY are sent into instant gales of laughter*]

HAROLD
I think you said the wrong thing.

MICHAEL
Don't you love that quaint little idea—if a man is married, then he is auto-
matically heterosexual.
[*A beat*]
Alan—Hank swings both ways—with a definite preference.
[*A beat*]
Now. Who makes the first call? Emory?

EMORY
You go, Bernard.

BERNARD
I don't want to.

EMORY
I don't want to either. I don't want to at all.

DONALD
[*To himself*]
There are no accidents.

MICHAEL
Then, may I say, on your way home I hope you *will* yourself over an
embankment.

EMORY
[*To BERNARD*]
Go on. Call up Peter Dahlbeck. That's who you'd like to call, isn't it?

MICHAEL
Who is Peter Dahlbeck?

EMORY
The boy in Detroit whose family Bernard's mother has been a laundress for
since he was a pickaninny.

BERNARD
I worked for them too—after school and every summer.

EMORY
It's always been a large order of Hero Worship.

BERNARD
I think I've loved him all my life. But he never knew I was alive. Besides, he's straight.

COWBOY
So nothing ever happened between you?

EMORY
Oh, they finally made it—in the pool house one night after a drunken swimming party.

LARRY
With the right wine and the right music there're damn few that aren't curious.

MICHAEL
Sounds like there's a lot of Lady Chatterley in Mr. Dahlbeck, wouldn't you say, Donald?

DONALD
I've never been an O'Hara fan myself.

BERNARD
...And afterwards we went swimming in the nude in the dark with only the moon reflecting on the water.

DONALD
Nor Thomas Merton.

BERNARD
It was beautiful.

MICHAEL
How romantic. And then the next morning you took him his coffee and Alka-Seltzer on a tray.

BERNARD
It was in the afternoon. I remember I was worried sick all morning about having to face him. But he pretended like nothing at all had happened.

MICHAEL
Christ, he must have been so drunk he didn't remember a thing.

BERNARD
Yeah. I was sure relieved.

MICHAEL
Odd how that works. And now, for ten points, get that liar on the phone.
[*A beat.* BERNARD *picks up the phone, dials*]

LARRY
You *know* the number?

BERNARD
Sure. He's back in Grosse Pointe, living at home. He just got separated from his third wife.
[*All watch* BERNARD *as he puts the receiver to his ear, waits. A beat. He hangs up quickly*]

EMORY
D.A. or B.Y.?

MICHAEL
He didn't even give it time to find out.
[*Coaxing*]
Go ahead, Bernard. Pick up the phone and dial. You'll think of something. You know you want to call him. You know that, don't you? Well, go ahead. Your curiosity has got the best of you now. So...go on, call him.
[*A beat.* BERNARD *picks up the receiver, dials again. Lets it ring this time*]

HAROLD
Hateful.

COWBOY
What's D.A. or B.Y.?

EMORY
That's operator lingo. It means—"Doesn't Answer" or "Busy."

BERNARD
...Hello?

MICHAEL
One point.
[*Efficiently takes note on the pad*]

BERNARD
Who's speaking? Oh...Mrs. Dahlbeck.

MICHAEL
[*Taking note*]
One point.

BERNARD
...It's Bernard—Francine's boy.

EMORY
Son, not *boy*.

BERNARD
...How are you? Good. Good. Oh, just fine, thank you. Mrs. Dahlbeck...is...
Peter...at home? Oh. Oh, I see.

MICHAEL
[*Shakes his head*]
Shhhhiiii...

BERNARD
...Oh, no. No, it's nothing important. I just wanted to...to tell him...that...to
tell him I...I...

MICHAEL
[*Prompting flatly*]
I love him. That I've always loved him.

BERNARD
...that I was sorry to hear about him and his wife.

MICHAEL
No points!

BERNARD
...My mother wrote me. Yes. It is. It really is. Well. Would you just tell him I
called and said...that I was...just...very, very sorry to hear and I...hope...
they can get everything straightened out. Yes. Yes. Well, good night. Good-
bye.
[*Hangs up slowly.* MICHAEL *draws a definite line across his pad, makes a definite period*]

MICHAEL
Two points total. Terrible. Next!
[MICHAEL *whisks the phone out of* BERNARD's *hands, gives it to* EMORY]

EMORY
Are you all right, Bernard?

BERNARD
[*Almost to himself*]
Why did I call? Why did I do that?

LARRY
[*To BERNARD*]
Where was he?

BERNARD
Out on a date.

MICHAEL
Come on, Emory. Punch in.
[*EMORY picks up the phone, dials information. A beat*]

EMORY
Could I have the number, please—in the Bronx—for a Delbert Botts.

LARRY
A Delbert Botts! How many can there be!

BERNARD
Oh, I wish I hadn't called now.

EMORY
...No, the residence number, please.
[*Waves his hand at MICHAEL, signaling for the pencil. MICHAEL hands it to him. He writes on the white plastic phone case*]
...Thank you.
[*A beat. And he indignantly slams down the receiver*]
I do wish information would stop calling me "Ma'am"!

MICHAEL
By all means, scribble all over the telephone.
[*Snatches the pencil from EMORY's hands*]

EMORY
It comes off with a little spit.

MICHAEL
Like a lot of things.

LARRY
Who the hell is Delbert Botts?

EMORY
The one person I have always loved.
[*To MICHAEL*]
That's who you said call, isn't it?

MICHAEL
That's right, Emory board.

LARRY
How could you love anybody with a name like that?

MICHAEL
Yes, Emory, you couldn't love anybody with a name like that. It wouldn't look good on a place card. Isn't that right, Alan?
[*MICHAEL slaps ALAN on the shoulder. ALAN is silent. MICHAEL snickers*]

EMORY
I admit his name is not so good—but he is absolutely beautiful. At least, he was when I was in high school. Of course, I haven't seen him since and he was about seven years older than I even then.

MICHAEL
Christ, you better call him quick before he dies.

EMORY
I've loved him ever since the first day I laid eyes on him, which was when I was in the fifth grade and he was a senior. Then, he went away to college and by the time he got out *I* was in high school, and he had become a dentist.

MICHAEL
[*With incredulous disgust*]
A dentist!

EMORY
Yes. Delbert Botts, D.D.S. And he opened his office in a bank building.

HAROLD
And you went and had every tooth in your head pulled out, right?

EMORY
No. I just had my teeth cleaned, that's all.
[*DONALD turns from the bar with two drinks in his hands*]

BERNARD
[*To himself*]
Oh, I shouldn't have called.

MICHAEL
Will you shut up, Bernard! And take your boring, sleep-making icks somewhere else. *Go!*

[*MICHAEL extends a pointed finger toward the steps. BERNARD takes the wine bottle and his glass and moves toward the stairs, pouring himself another drink on the way*]

EMORY

I remember I looked right into his eyes the whole time and I kept wanting to bite his fingers.

HAROLD

Well, it's absolutely mind-boggling.

MICHAEL

Phyllis Phallic.

HAROLD

It absolutely boggles the mind.
[*DONALD brings one of the drinks to ALAN. ALAN takes it, drinks it down*]

MICHAEL
[*Referring to DONALD*]

Sara Samaritan.

EMORY

...I told him I was having my teeth cleaned for the Junior-Senior Prom, for which I was in charge of decorations. I told him it was a celestial theme and I was cutting stars out of tinfoil and making clouds out of chicken wire and angel's-hair.
[*A beat*]
He couldn't have been less impressed.

COWBOY

I got angel's-hair down my shirt once at Christmastime. Gosh, did it itch!

EMORY

...I told him I was going to burn incense in pots so that white fog would hover over the dance floor and it would look like heaven—just like I'd seen it in a Rita Hayworth movie. I can't remember the title.

MICHAEL

The picture was called *Down to Earth*. Any *kid* knows that.

COWBOY

...And it made little tiny cuts in the creases of my fingers. Man, did they sting! It would be terrible if you got that stuff in your...
[*MICHAEL circles slowly toward him*]
I'll be quiet.

EMORY
He was engaged to this stupid-ass girl named Loraine whose mother was truly Supercunt.

MICHAEL
Don't digress.

EMORY
Well, anyway, I was a wreck. I mean a total mess. I couldn't eat, sleep, stand up, sit down, *nothing*. I could hardly cut out silver stars or finish the clouds for the prom. So I called him on the telephone and asked if I could see him alone.

HAROLD
Clearly not the coolest of moves.
      [*DONALD looks at* ALAN. ALAN *looks away*]

EMORY
He said OK and told me to come by his house. I was so nervous my hands were shaking and my voice was unsteady. I couldn't look at him this time—I just stared straight in space and blurted out why I'd come. I told him…I wanted him to be my friend. I said that I had never had a friend who I could talk to and tell everything and trust. I asked him if he would be my friend.

COWBOY
You poor bastard.

MICHAEL
SHHHHHH!

BERNARD
What'd he say?

EMORY
He said he would be glad to be my friend. And anytime I ever wanted to see him or call him—to just call him and he'd see me. And he shook my trembling wet hand and I left on a cloud.

MICHAEL
One of the ones you made yourself.

EMORY
And the next day I went and bought him a gold-plated cigarette lighter and had his initials monogrammed on it and wrote a card that said "From your friend, Emory."

HAROLD
Seventeen years old and already big with the gifts.

COWBOY
Yeah. And cards too.

EMORY
...And then the night of the prom I found out.

BERNARD
Found out what?

EMORY
I heard two girls I knew giggling together. They were standing behind some goddamn corrugated cardboard Greek columns I had borrowed from a department store and had draped with yards and yards of goddamn cheese-cloth. Oh, Mary, it takes a fairy to make something pretty.

MICHAEL
Don't digress.

EMORY
This girl who was telling the story said she had heard it from her mother—and her mother had heard it from Loraine's mother.
[*To MICHAEL*]
You see, Loraine and her mother were not beside the point.
[*Back to the group*]
Obviously, Del had told Loraine about my calling and about the gift.
[*A beat*]
Pretty soon everybody at the dance had heard about it and they were laughing and making jokes. Everybody knew I had a crush on Doctor Delbert Botts and that I had asked him to be my friend.
[*A beat*]
What they didn't know was that I *loved* him. And that I would go on loving him years after they had all forgotten my funny secret.
[*Pause*]

HAROLD
Well, I for one need an insulin injection.

MICHAEL
Call him.

BERNARD
Don't, Emory.

101

MICHAEL
Since when are you telling him what to do!

EMORY
[*To* BERNARD]
What do I care—I'm pissed! I'll do anything. Three times.

BERNARD
Don't. *Please!*

MICHAEL
I said call him.

BERNARD
Don't! You'll be sorry. Take my word for it.

EMORY
What have I got to lose?

BERNARD
Your dignity. That's what you've got to lose.

MICHAEL
Well, *that's* a knee-slapper! I love *your* telling *him* about dignity when you
allow him to degrade you constantly by Uncle Tom-ing you to death.

BERNARD
He can do it, Michael. *I* can do it. But *you can't* do it.

MICHAEL
Isn't that discrimination?

BERNARD
I don't like it from him and I don't like it from me—but I do it to myself and
I let him do it. I let him do it because it's the only thing that, to him, makes
him my equal. We both got the short end of the stick—but I got a hell of a
lot more than he did and he knows it. I let him Uncle Tom me just so he can
tell himself he's not a complete loser.

MICHAEL
How very considerate.

BERNARD
It's his defense. You have your defense, Michael. But it's indescribable.
[*EMORY quietly licks his finger and begins to rub the number off the telephone case*]

MICHAEL
[*To* BERNARD]
Y'all want to hear a little polite parlor jest from the liberal Deep South? Do you know why *Nigras* have such big lips? Because they're always going "P-p-p-p-a-a-a-h!"
[*The labial noise is exasperating with lazy disgust as he shuffles about the room*]

DONALD
Christ, Michael!

MICHAEL
[*Unsuccessfully tries to tear the phone away from* EMORY]
I can do without your goddamn spit all over my telephone, you nellie coward.

EMORY
I may be nellie, but I'm no coward.
[*Starts to dial*]
Bernard, forgive me. I'm sorry. I won't ever say those things to you again.
[MICHAEL *watches triumphant.* BERNARD *pours another glass of wine. A beat*]
B.Y.

MICHAEL
It's busy?

EMORY
[*Nods*]
Loraine is probably talking to her mother. Oh, yes. Delbert married Loraine.

MICHAEL
I'm sorry, you'll have to forfeit your turn. We can't wait.
[*Takes the phone, hands it to* LARRY, *who starts to dial*]

HAROLD
[*To* LARRY]
Well, you're not wasting any time.

HANK
Who are you calling?

LARRY
Charlie.
[EMORY *gets up, jerks the phone out of* LARRY's *hands*]

EMORY
I refuse to forfeit my turn! It's *my turn*, and I'm taking it!

MICHAEL
That's the spirit, Emory! *Hit that iceberg—don't miss it! Hit it! Goddamnit!* I
want a smash of a finale!

EMORY
Oh, God, I'm drunk.

MICHAEL
A falling-down-drunk-nellie-queen.

HAROLD
Well, that's the pot calling the kettle beige!

MICHAEL
      [*Snapping. To* HAROLD]
I am not drunk! You cannot tell that I am drunk! Donald! I'm not drunk! Am I!

DONALD
I'm drunk.

EMORY
So am I. I am a *major drunk*.

MICHAEL
      [*To* EMORY]
Shut up and dial!

EMORY
      [*Dialing*]
I am a major drunk of this or any other season.

DONALD
      [*To* MICHAEL]
Don't you mean shut up and deal?

EMORY
…It's ringing. It is no longer B.Y. Hello?

MICHAEL
      [*Taking note*]
One point.

EMORY
…Who's speaking? Who?… Doctor Delbert Botts?

MICHAEL
Two points.

EMORY
Oh, Del, is this really you? Oh, nobody. You don't know me. You wouldn't remember me. I'm...just a friend. A falling-down drunken friend. Hello? Hello? Hello?
[*Lowers the receiver*]
He hung up.
[EMORY *hangs up the telephone*]

MICHAEL
Three points total. You're winning.

EMORY
He said I must have the wrong party.
[BERNARD *gets up, goes into the kitchen*]

HAROLD
He's right. We have the wrong party. We should be somewhere else.

EMORY
It's your party, Hallie. Aren't you having a good time?

HAROLD
Simply fabulous. And what about you? Are you having a good time, Emory? Are you having as good a time as you thought you would?
[LARRY *takes the phone*]

MICHAEL
If you're bored, Harold, we could sing "Happy Birthday" again—to the tune of "Havah Nageelah."
[HAROLD *takes out another cigarette*]

HAROLD
Not for all the tea in Mexico.
[*Lights up*]

HANK
My turn now.

LARRY
It's my turn to call Charlie.

HANK
No. Let me.

LARRY
Are *you* going to call Charlie?

MICHAEL
The score is three to two. Emory's favor.

ALAN
Don't, Hank. Don't you see—Bernard was right.

HANK
            [*Firmly, to* ALAN]
I want to.
            [*A beat. Holds out his hand for the phone*]
Larry?
            [*A beat*]

LARRY
            [*Gives him the phone*]
Be my eager guest.

COWBOY
            [*To* LARRY]
Is he going to call Charlie for you?
            [LARRY *breaks into laughter.* HANK *starts to dial*]

LARRY
Charlie is all the people I cheat on Hank with.

DONALD
With whom I cheat on Hank.

MICHAEL
The butcher, the baker, the candlestick maker.

LARRY
Right! I love 'em all. And what he refuses to understand—is that I've got to
have 'em all. I am *not* the marrying kind, and I never will be.

HAROLD
Gypsy feet.

LARRY
Who are you calling?

MICHAEL
Jealous?

LARRY
Curious as hell!

MICHAEL
And a little jealous too.

LARRY
Who are you calling?

MICHAEL
Did it ever occur to you that Hank might be doing the same thing behind your back that you do behind his?

LARRY
I wish to Christ he would. It'd make life a hell of a lot easier. Who are you calling?

HAROLD
Whoever it is, they're not sitting on top of the telephone.

HANK
Hello?

COWBOY
They must have been in the tub.

MICHAEL
[*Snaps at* COWBOY]
Eighty-six!
[COWBOY *goes over to a far corner, sits down.* BERNARD *enters, uncorking another bottle of wine. Taking note*]
One point.

HANK
...I'd like to leave a message.

MICHAEL
Not in. One point.

HANK
Would you say that Hank called. Yes, it is. Oh, good evening, how are you?

LARRY
Who the hell *is* that?

HANK
...Yes, that's right—the message is for my roommate, Larry. Just say that I called and...

LARRY
It's our answering service!

HANK
...and said...I love you.

MICHAEL
Five points! You said it! You get five goddamn points for saying it!

ALAN
Hank! Hank!... Are you crazy?

HANK
...No. You didn't hear me incorrectly. That's what I said. The message is for Larry and it's from me, Hank, and it is just as I said: *I...love...you.* Thanks.
    [*Hangs up*]

MICHAEL
Seven points total! Hank, you're ahead, baby. You're way, way ahead of everybody!

ALAN
Why?... Oh, Hank, why? Why did you do that?

HANK
Because I do love him. And I don't care who knows it.

ALAN
Don't say that.

HANK
Why not? It's the truth.

ALAN
I can't believe you.

HANK
[*Directly to* ALAN]
I left my wife and family for Larry.

ALAN
I'm really not interested in hearing about it.

MICHAEL
Sure you are. Go ahead, Hankola, tell him all about it.

ALAN
No! I don't want to hear it. It's disgusting!
[*A beat*]

HANK
Some men do it for another woman.

ALAN
Well, I could understand *that*. That's *normal*.

HANK
It just doesn't always work out that way, Alan. No matter how you might want it to. And God knows, nobody ever wanted it more than I did. I really and truly felt that I was in love with my wife when I married her. It wasn't altogether my trying to prove something to myself. I did love her and she loved me. But...there was always that something there...

DONALD
You mean your attraction to your own sex.

HANK
Yes.

ALAN
Always?

HANK
I don't know. I suppose so.

EMORY
I've known what I was since I was four years old.

MICHAEL
Everybody's always known it about *you*, Emory.

DONALD
I've always known it about myself too.

HANK
I don't know when it was that I started admitting it to myself. For so long I either labeled it something else or denied it completely.

MICHAEL
Christ-was-I-drunk-last-night.

HANK
And then there came a time when I just couldn't lie to myself anymore… I thought about it but I never did anything about it. I think the first time was during my wife's last pregnancy. We lived near New Haven—in the country. She and the kids still live there. Well, anyway, there was a teachers' meeting here in New York. She didn't feel up to the trip and I came alone. And that day on the train I began to think about it and think about it and think about it. I thought of nothing else the whole trip. And within fifteen minutes after I had arrived I had picked up a guy in the men's room of Grand Central Station.

ALAN
[*Quietly*]
Jesus.

HANK
I'd never done anything like that in my life before and I was scared to death. But he turned out to be a nice fellow. I've never seen him again and it's funny I can't even remember his name anymore.
[*A beat*]
Anyway. After that, it got easier.

HAROLD
Practice makes perfect.

HANK
And then…sometime later…not very long after, Larry was in New Haven and we met at a party my wife and I had gone in town for.

EMORY
And your real troubles began.

HANK
That was two years ago.

LARRY

Why am I always the goddamn villain in the piece! If I'm not thought of as a happy-home wrecker, I'm an impossible son of a bitch to live with!

HAROLD

Guilt turns to hostility. Isn't that right, Michael?

MICHAEL

Go stick your tweezers in your cheek.

LARRY

I'm fed up to the teeth with everybody feeling so goddamn sorry for poor shat-upon Hank.

EMORY

Aw, Larry, everybody knows you're Frieda Fickle.

LARRY

I've never made any promises and I never intend to. It's my right to lead my sex life without answering to *anybody*—Hank included! And if those terms are not acceptable, then we must not live together. Numerous relations is a part of the way I am!

EMORY

You don't have to be gay to be a wanton.

LARRY

By the way I am, I don't mean being gay—I mean my sexual appetite. And I don't think of myself as a wanton. Emory, you are the most promiscuous person I know.

EMORY

I am not promiscuous at all!

MICHAEL

Not by choice. By design. Why would anybody want to go to bed with a flaming little sissy like you?

BERNARD

Michael!

MICHAEL

[*To EMORY*]

Who'd make a pass at you—I'll tell you who—nobody. Except maybe some fugitive from the Braille Institute.

BERNARD
[*To* EMORY]
Why do you let him talk to you that way?

HAROLD
Physical beauty is not everything.

MICHAEL
Thank you, Quasimodo.

LARRY
What do you think it's like living with the goddamn gestapo! I can't breathe without getting the third degree!

MICHAEL
Larry, it's your turn to call.

LARRY
I can't take all that let's-be-faithful-and-never-look-at-another-person routine. It just doesn't work. If you want to promise that, fine. Then do it and stick to it. But if you *have* to promise it—as far as I'm concerned—nothing finishes a relationship faster.

HAROLD
Give me Librium or give me Meth.

BERNARD
[*Intoxicated now*]
Yeah, freedom, baby! Freedom!

LARRY
You gotta have it! It can't work any other way. And the ones who swear their undying fidelity are lying. Most of them, anyway—ninety percent of them. They cheat on each other constantly and lie through their teeth. I'm sorry, I can't be like that and it drives Hank up the wall.

HANK
There is that ten percent.

LARRY
The only way it stands a chance is with some sort of an understanding.

HANK
I've tried to go along with that.

112

LARRY
Aw, *come on!*

HANK
I agreed to an agreement.

LARRY
Your agreement.

MICHAEL
What agreement?

LARRY
A ménage.

HAROLD
The lover's agreement.

LARRY
Look, I know a lot of people think it's the answer. They don't consider it cheating. But it's not my style.

HANK
Well, *I* certainly didn't want it.

LARRY
Then who suggested it?

HANK
It was a compromise.

LARRY
Exactly.

HANK
And you agreed.

LARRY
I didn't agree to anything. You agreed to your own proposal and *informed me* that I agreed.

COWBOY
I don't understand. What's a me...menaa...

MICHAEL
A ménage à trois, baby. Two's company—three's a ménage.

COWBOY
Oh.

HANK
It works for some.

LARRY
Well, I'm not one for group therapy. I'm sorry, I can't relate to anyone or anything that way. I'm old-fashioned—I like 'em all, but I like 'em one at a time!

MICHAEL
[*To LARRY*]
Did you like Donald as a single side attraction?
[*Pause*]

LARRY
Yes. I did.

DONALD
So did I, Larry.

LARRY
[*To DONALD, referring to MICHAEL*]
Did you tell him?

DONALD
No.

MICHAEL
It was perfectly obvious from the moment you walked in. What was the song and dance about having seen each other but never having met?

DONALD
It was true. We saw each other in the baths and went to bed together but we never spoke a word and never knew each other's name.

EMORY
You had better luck than I do. If I don't get arrested, my trick announces upon departure that he's been exposed to hepatitis!

MICHAEL
In spring a young man's fancy turns to a fancy young man.

LARRY
    [*To* HANK]
Don't look at me like that. You've been playing footsie with the Blue Book
all night.

DONALD
I think he only wanted to show you what's good for the gander is good for
the gander.

HANK
That's right.

LARRY
    [*To* HANK]
I suppose you'd like the three of us to have a go at it.

HANK
At least it'd be together.

LARRY
That point eludes me.

HANK
What kind of an understanding do you *want!*

LARRY
Respect—for each other's freedom. With no need to lie or pretend. In my
own way, Hank, I love you, but you have to understand that even though I
do want to go on living with you, sometimes there may be others. I don't
want to flaunt it in your face. If it happens, I know I'll never mention it. But
if you ask me, I'll tell you. I don't want to hurt you but I won't lie to you if
you want to know anything about me.

BERNARD
He gets points.

MICHAEL
What?

BERNARD
He said it. He said "I love you" to Hank. He gets the bonus.

MICHAEL
He didn't call him.

DONALD
He called him. He just didn't use the telephone.

115

MICHAEL
Then he doesn't get any points.

BERNARD
He gets five points!

MICHAEL
He didn't use the telephone. He doesn't get a goddamn thing!
[*LARRY goes to the phone, picks up the receiver, looks at the number of the second line, dials. A beat. The phone rings*]

LARRY
It's for you, Hank. Why don't you take it upstairs?
[*The phone continues to ring. HANK gets up, goes up the stairs to the bedroom. Pause. He presses the second-line button, picks up the receiver. Everyone downstairs is silent*]

HANK
Hello?

BERNARD
One point.

LARRY
Hello, Hank.

BERNARD
Two points.

LARRY
...This is Larry.

BERNARD
Two more points!

LARRY
...For what it's worth, I love you.

BERNARD
Five points bonus!

HANK
I'll...I'll try.

LARRY
I will too.
> [*Hangs up.* HANK *hangs up*]

BERNARD
That's ten points total!

EMORY
Larry's the winner!

HAROLD
Well, that wasn't as much fun as I thought it would be.

MICHAEL
THE GAME ISN'T OVER YET!
> [HANK *moves toward the bed into darkness*]
Your turn, Alan.
> [MICHAEL *gets the phone, slams it down in front of* ALAN]
PICK UP THE PHONE, BUSTER!

EMORY
Michael, don't!

MICHAEL
STAY OUT OF THIS!

EMORY
You don't have to, Alan. You don't have to.

ALAN
Emory...I'm sorry for what I did before.
> [*A beat*]

EMORY
...Oh, forget it.

MICHAEL
Forgive us our trespasses. Christ, now you're both joined at the goddamn
hip! You can decorate his home, Emory—and he can get you out of jail the
next time you're arrested on a morals charge.
> [*A beat*]
Who are you going to call, Alan?
> [*No response*]
Can't remember anyone? Well, maybe you need a minute to think. Is that it?
> [*No response*]

HAROLD
I believe this will be the final round.

COWBOY
Michael, aren't you going to call anyone?

HAROLD
How could he? He's never loved anyone.

MICHAEL
[*Sings the classic vaudeville walk-off to* HAROLD]
"No matter how you figger,
It's tough to be a nigger,
[*Indicates* BERNARD]
But it's tougher
To be a Jeeeew-ooouu-oo!"

DONALD
My God, Michael, you're a charming host.

HAROLD
Michael doesn't have charm, Donald. Michael has counter-charm.
[*LARRY crosses to the stairs*]

MICHAEL
Going somewhere?
[*LARRY stops, turns to* MICHAEL]

LARRY
Yes. Excuse me.
[*Turns, goes up the stairs*]

MICHAEL
You're going to miss the end of the game.

LARRY
[*Pauses on stairs*]
You can tell me how it comes out.

MICHAEL
I never reveal an ending. And no one will be reseated during the climactic revelation.

LARRY
With any luck, I won't be back until it's all over.
[*Turns, continues up the stairs into the dark*]

MICHAEL
[*Into ALAN's ear*]
What do you suppose is going on up there? Hmmm, Alan? What do you imagine Larry and Hank are doing? Hmmmmm? Shooting marbles?

EMORY
Whatever they're doing, they're not hurting anyone.

HAROLD
And they're minding their own business.

MICHAEL
And you mind yours, Harold. I'm warning you!
[*A beat*]

HAROLD
[*Coolly*]
Are you now? Are you warning *me? Me?* I'm Harold. I'm the one person you don't warn, Michael. Because you and I are a match. And we tread very softly with each other because we both play each other's game too well. Oh, I know this game you're playing. I know it very well. And I play it very well. You play it very well too. But you know what, I'm the only one that's better at it than you are. I can beat you at it. So don't push me. I'm warning *you*.
[*A beat. MICHAEL starts to laugh*]

MICHAEL
You're funny, Hallie. A laff riot. Isn't he funny, Alan? Or, as you might say, isn't he amusing? He's an amusing faggot, isn't he? Or, as you might say, freak. That's what you called Emory, wasn't it? A freak? A pansy? My, what an antiquated vocabulary you have. I'm surprised you didn't say sodomite or pederast.
[*A beat*]
You'd better let me bring you up to date. Now it's not so new, but it might be new to you—
[*A beat*]
Have you heard the term "closet queen"? Do you know what that means? Do you know what it means to be "in the closet"?

EMORY
Don't, Michael. It won't help anything to explain what it means.

119

MICHAEL
He already knows. He knows very, very well what a closet queen is. Don't you, Alan?
    [*Pause*]

ALAN
Michael, if you are insinuating that I am homosexual, I can only say that you are mistaken.

MICHAEL
Am I?
    [*A beat*]
What about Justin Stuart?

ALAN
…What about…Justin Stuart?

MICHAEL
You were in love with him, that's what about him.
    [*A beat*]
And *that* is who you are going to call.

ALAN
Justin and I were very good friends. That is all. Unfortunately, we had a parting of the ways and that was the end of the friendship. We have not spoken for years. I most certainly will not call him now.

MICHAEL
According to Justin, the friendship was quite passionate.

ALAN
What do you mean?

MICHAEL
I mean that you slept with him in college. Several times.

ALAN
That is not true!

MICHAEL
Several times. One time, it's youth. Twice, a phase maybe. Several times, *you like it!*

ALAN
IT'S NOT TRUE!

MICHAEL
Yes, it is. Because Justin Stuart *is* homosexual. He comes to New York on
occasion. He calls me. I've taken him to parties. Larry "had" him once. *I*
have slept with Justin Stuart. And he has told me all about *you*.

ALAN
Then he told you a lie.
  [*A beat*]

MICHAEL
You were obsessed with Justin. That's all you talked about, morning, noon,
and night. You started doing it about Hank upstairs tonight. What an attractive fellow he is and all that transparent crap.

ALAN
He *is* an attractive fellow. What's wrong with saying so?

MICHAEL
Would you like to join him and Larry right now?

ALAN
I said he was attractive. That's all.

MICHAEL
How many times do you have to say it? How many times did you have to
say it about Justin: what a good tennis player he was; what a good dancer
he was; what a good body he had; what good taste he had; how bright he
was—how *amusing* he was—how the girls were all mad for him—what
close friends you were.

ALAN
We...we...were...very close...very good...friends. *That's all.*

MICHAEL
It was *obvious*—and when you did it around Fran it was downright embarrassing. Even she must have had her doubts about you.

ALAN
Justin...lied. If he told you that, he lied. It is a lie. A vicious lie. He'd say
anything about me now to get even. He could never get over the fact that *I*
dropped *him*. But I had to. I had to because...he told me...he told me about
himself...he told me that he wanted to be my lover. And I...I...told
him...he made me sick...I told him I pitied him.
  [*A beat*]

121

MICHAEL

You ended the friendship, Alan, because you couldn't face the truth about yourself. You could go along, sleeping with Justin, as long as he lied to himself and you lied to yourself and you both dated girls and labeled yourselves men and called yourselves just fond friends. But Justin finally had to be honest about the truth, and you couldn't take it. You couldn't take it and so you destroyed the friendship and your friend along with it.

[*MICHAEL goes to the desk and gets address book*]

ALAN

No!

MICHAEL

Justin could never understand what he'd done wrong to make you cut him off. He blamed himself.

ALAN

No!

MICHAEL

He did until he eventually found out who he was and what he was.

ALAN

No!

MICHAEL

But to this day he still remembers the treatment—the scars he got from you.

[*Puts address book in front of ALAN on coffee table*]

ALAN

NO!

MICHAEL

Pick up this phone and call Justin. Call him and apologize and tell him what you should have told him twelve years ago.

[*Picks up the phone, shoves it at ALAN*]

ALAN

NO! HE LIED! NOT A WORD IS TRUE!

MICHAEL
CALL HIM!
[*ALAN won't take the phone*]
All right then, *I'll dial!*

122

HAROLD
You're so helpful.
> [*MICHAEL starts to dial*]

ALAN
Give it to me.
> [*MICHAEL hands* ALAN *the receiver.* ALAN *takes it, hangs up for a moment, lifts it again, starts to dial. Everyone watches silently.* ALAN *finishes dialing, lifts the receiver to his ear*]

...Hello?

MICHAEL
One point.

ALAN
...It's...it's Alan.

MICHAEL
Two points.

ALAN
...Yes, yes, it's *me*.

MICHAEL
Is it Justin?

ALAN
...You sound surprised.

MICHAEL
I should hope to think so—after twelve years! Two more points.

ALAN
I...I'm in New York. Yes. I...I won't explain now... I...I just called to tell you...

MICHAEL
THAT I LOVE YOU, GODDAMNIT! I LOVE YOU!

ALAN
I love you.

MICHAEL
You get the goddamn bonus. TEN POINTS TOTAL! JACKPOT!

ALAN
I love you and I beg you to forgive me.

MICHAEL
Give me that!
[*Snatches the phone from* ALAN]
Justin! Did you hear what that son of a bitch said!
[*A beat.* MICHAEL *is speechless for a moment*]
…Fran?
[*A beat*]
Well, of course I expected it to be you!…
[*A beat*]
How are you? Me too. Yes, yes…he told me everything. Oh, don't thank *me*.
Please… Please…
[*A beat*]
I'll…I'll put him back on.
[*A beat*]
My love to the kids…

ALAN
…Darling? I'll take the first plane I can get. Yes. I'm sorry too. I love you
very much.
[*Hangs up, stands, crosses to the door, stops. Turns around, surveys the
group*]
Thank you, Michael.
[*Opens the door and exits. Silence.* MICHAEL *slowly sinks down on the couch,
covering his face. Pause*]

COWBOY
Who won?

DONALD
It was a tie.
[HAROLD *crosses to* MICHAEL]

HAROLD
[*Calmly, coldly, clinically*]
Now it is my turn. And ready or not, Michael, here goes.
[*A beat*]
You are a sad and pathetic man. You're a homosexual and you don't want to
be. But there is nothing you can do to change it. Not all your prayers to your
God, not all the analysis you can buy in all the years you've got left to live.
You may very well one day be able to know a heterosexual life if you want it
desperately enough—if you pursue it with the fervor with which you annihi-

late—but you will always be homosexual as well. Always, Michael. Always.
Until the day you die.
[*Turns, gathers his gifts, goes to* EMORY. EMORY *stands up unsteadily*]
Oh, friends, thanks for the nifty party and the super gift.
[*Looks toward* COWBOY]
It's just what I needed.
[EMORY *smiles.* HAROLD *gives him a hug, spots* BERNARD *sitting on the floor, head bowed*]
…Bernard, thank you.
[*No response. To* EMORY]
Will you get him home?

EMORY
Don't worry about her. I'll take care of everything.
[HAROLD *turns to* DONALD, *who is at the bar making himself another drink*]

HAROLD
Donald, good to see you.

DONALD
Good night, Harold. See you again sometime.

HAROLD
Yeah. How about a year from Shavuoth?
[HAROLD *goes to* COWBOY]
Come on, Tex. Let's go to my place.
[COWBOY *gets up, comes to him*]
Are you good in bed?

COWBOY
Well…I'm not like the average hustler you'd meet. I try to show a little
affection—it keeps me from feeling like such a whore.
[*A beat.* HAROLD *turns.* COWBOY *opens the door for them. They start out.*
HAROLD *pauses*]

HAROLD
Oh, Michael…thanks for the laughs. Call you tomorrow.
[*No response. A beat.* HAROLD *and* COWBOY *exit*]

EMORY
Come on, Bernard. Time to go home.
[EMORY, *frail as he is, manages to pull* BERNARD'S *arm around his neck, gets
him on his feet*]
Oh, Mary, you're a heavy mother.

BERNARD
[*Practically inaudible mumble*]
Why did I call? Why?

EMORY
Thank you, Michael. Good night, Donald.

DONALD
Good-bye, Emory.

BERNARD
Why...

EMORY
It's all right, Bernard. Everything's all right. I'm going to make you some coffee and everything's going to be all right.
[*EMORY virtually carries BERNARD out. DONALD closes the door. Silence. MICHAEL slowly slips from the couch onto the floor. A beat. Then slowly he begins a low moan that increases in volume—almost like a siren. Suddenly he slams his open hands to his ears*]

MICHAEL
[*In desperate panic*]
Donald! Donald! DONALD! DONALD!
[*DONALD puts down his drink, rushes to MICHAEL. MICHAEL is now white with fear, and tears are bursting from his eyes. He begins to gasp his words*]
Oh, no! No! What have I done! Oh, my God, what have I done!
[*MICHAEL writhing. DONALD holds him, cradles him in his arms*]

DONALD
Michael! Michael!

MICHAEL
[*Weeping*]
Oh, no! NO! It's beginning! The liquor is starting to wear off and the anxiety is beginning! Oh, NO! No! I feel it! I know it's going to happen. Donald!! Donald! Don't leave me! Please! Please! Oh, my God, what have I done! Oh, Jesus, the guilt! I can't handle it anymore. I won't make it!

DONALD
[*Physically subduing him*]
Michael! Michael! Stop it! Stop it! I'll give you a Valium—I've got some in my pocket!

MICHAEL
[*Hysterical*]
No! No! Pills and alcohol—I'll die!

DONALD
I'm not going to give you the whole bottle! Come on, let go of me!

MICHAEL
[*Clutching him*]
NO!

DONALD
Let go of me long enough for me to get my hand in my pocket!

MICHAEL
Don't leave!
[*MICHAEL quiets down a bit, lets go of DONALD enough for him to take a small plastic bottle from his pocket and open it to give MICHAEL a tranquilizer*]

DONALD
Here.

MICHAEL
[*Sobbing*]
I don't have any water to swallow it with!

DONALD
Well, if you'll wait one goddamn minute, I'll get you some!
[*MICHAEL lets go of him. He goes to the bar, gets a glass of water and returns*]
Your water, your Majesty.
[*A beat*]
Michael, stop that goddamn crying and take this pill!
[*MICHAEL straightens up, puts the pill into his mouth amid choking sobs, takes the water, drinks, returns the glass to DONALD*]

MICHAEL
I'm like Ole Man River—tired of livin' and scared o' dyin'.
[*DONALD puts the glass on the bar, comes back to the couch, sits down. MICHAEL collapses into his arms, sobbing. Pause*]

DONALD
Shhhhh. Shhhhhh. Michael. Shhhhh. Michael. Michael.
[*DONALD rocks him back and forth. He quiets. Pause*]

MICHAEL
...If we...if we could just...not hate ourselves so much. That's it, you know. If we could just *learn* not to hate ourselves quite so very much.

DONALD
Yes, I know. I know.
[*A beat*]
Inconceivable as it may be, you used to be worse than you are now.
[*A beat*]
Maybe with a lot more work you can help yourself some more—if you try.
[*MICHAEL straightens up, dries his eyes on his sleeve*]

MICHAEL
Who was it that used to always say, "You show me a happy homosexual, and I'll show you a gay corpse"?

DONALD
I don't know. Who was it who always used to say that?

MICHAEL
And how dare you come on with that holier-than-thou attitude with me! "A lot more work," "if I try," indeed! You've got a long row to hoe before you're perfect, you know.

DONALD
I never said I didn't.

MICHAEL
And while we're on the subject—I think your analyst is a quack.
[*MICHAEL is sniffling. DONALD hands him a handkerchief. He takes it and blows his nose*]

DONALD
Earlier you said he was a prick.

MICHAEL
That's right. He's a prick quack. Or a quack prick, whichever you prefer.
[*DONALD gets up from the couch, goes for his drink*]

DONALD
[*Heaving a sigh*]
Harold was right. You'll never change.

MICHAEL
Come back, Donald. Come back, Shane.

DONALD
I'll come back when you have another anxiety attack.

MICHAEL
I need you. Just like Mickey Mouse needs Minnie Mouse—just like Donald Duck needs Minnie Duck. Mickey needs Donnie.

DONALD
My name is Donald. I am called Donald. You must never call anyone called Donald Donnie...

MICHAEL
[Grabs his head, moans]
Ohhhhh...icks! Icks! Terrible icks! Tomorrow is going to be an ick-packed day. It's going to be a bad day at Black Rock. A day of nerves, nerves, and more nerves!
[MICHAEL gets up from the couch, surveys the wreckage of the dishes and gift wrappings]
Do you suppose there's any possibility of just burning this room?
[A beat]

DONALD
Why do you think he stayed, Michael? Why do you think he took all of that from you?

MICHAEL
There are no accidents. He was begging to get killed. He was dying for somebody to let him have it and he got what he wanted.

DONALD
He could have been telling the truth—Justin could have lied.

MICHAEL
Who knows? What time is it?

DONALD
It seems like it's day after tomorrow.
[MICHAEL goes to the kitchen door, pokes his head in. Comes back into the room carrying a raincoat]

MICHAEL
It's early.
[Goes to a closet door, takes out a blazer, puts it on]

DONALD
What does life *hold?* Where're you going?

MICHAEL
The bedroom is ocupado, and I don't want to go to sleep anyway until I try to walk off the booze. If I went to sleep like this, when I wake up they'd have to put me in a padded cell—not that that's where I don't belong.
    [*A beat*]
And...and...there's a midnight mass at St. Malachy's that all the show people go to. I think I'll walk over there and catch it.

DONALD
    [*Raises his glass*]
Well, pray for me.

MICHAEL
    [*Indicates bedroom*]
Maybe they'll be gone by the time I get back.

DONALD
Well, *I* will be—just as soon as I knock off that bottle of brandy.

MICHAEL
Will I see you next Saturday?

DONALD
Unless you have other plans.

MICHAEL
No.
    [*Turns to go*]

DONALD
Michael?

MICHAEL
    [*Stops, turns back*]
What?

DONALD
Did he ever tell you why he was crying on the phone—what it was he *had* to tell you?

130

MICHAEL
No. It must have been that he'd left Fran. Or maybe it was something else
and he changed his mind.

DONALD
Maybe so.
　　[*A beat*]
I wonder why he left her.
　　[*A pause*]

MICHAEL
...As my father said to me when he died in my arms, "I don't understand
any of it. I never did."
　　[*A beat.* DONALD *goes to his stack of books, selects one, and sits in a chair*]
Turn out the lights when you leave, will you?
　　[DONALD *nods.* MICHAEL *looks at him for a long silent moment.* DONALD
　　turns his attention to his book, starts to read. MICHAEL *opens the door and
　　exits*]

C U R T A I N

A BREEZE
FROM THE GULF

FOR MY MOTHER AND MY FATHER

A Breeze From the Gulf was first produced on the New York
stage by Charles Hollerith Jr. and Barnard S. Straus at the
Eastside Playhouse on October 15, 1973. The scenery was
designed by Douglas W. Schmidt, the lighting by Ken
Billington, and the costumes by Stanley Simmons. The
play was directed by John Going.

The original cast was:

LORAINE	*Ruth Ford*
TEDDY	*Scott McKay*
MICHAEL	*Robert Drivas*

The play is in two acts representing the passage of ten years—1950 to 1960.

The scenery should consist simply of levels and stairs of varied and interesting heights, with only the most basic and essential set and hand props employed to identify a playing area as a particular room or place or as an exterior locale.

Much of the action takes place in the Connelly home, the basic level representing the living room, another the kitchen, three others three bedrooms in which there are only three simple beds. Whenever the action occurs away from the Connelly home—on the beach, in an institution, in a hospital, in a coastline bar, a "screen drop" consisting of three separate panels flies in to mask the three permanent beds.

MICHAEL is to be portrayed by an actor of mature comprehension, yet one who physically belongs to that vague period between puberty and manhood. Within the convention of the play he must communicate an age range from fifteen to twenty-five years old. Because of the convention of the play, because he "remembers" the other two characters, he is outside of time, even though he appears in the scenes. Therefore, with the exception of an ordinary bathrobe, I would like him costumed in a dark blue suit, a dark blue necktie, and a beige raincoat throughout. Of course, he doesn't wear all the garments at the same time *all* of the time. Sometimes he wears only his undershorts, and other times he may wear the suit trousers and his shirt with the sleeves rolled up and the collar open. It depends on the age he is playing and the context of the scene.

LORAINE and TEDDY, the other two characters, change both costumes and makeup in accordance with the requirements and chronology of the material.

Although this play takes place in the state of Mississippi, I do not want it to drip with magnolias. Hence, only LORAINE speaks with a Southern accent. MICHAEL is basically a stranger in a foreign country from the very beginning, and TEDDY's speeches and the jargon employed will, hopefully, take care of his origins and current environment.

Characters:

LORAINE	The mother
TEDDY	The father
MICHAEL	The son

137

Act 1

SCENE 1

As the houselights dim, MICHAEL's silhouette appears, slowly tracing a path from bed to bed, from level to level, finally emerging through the panels of the screen drop, to be picked up by a spotlight as he comes down to the stage apron.

LORAINE
[Offstage]
MIIICHAEL! OHHHH, MIIIIICHAELLLLLLLL!
[A light comes up on LORAINE, standing on the opposite side of the stage, calling...out front]
MIIICHAEL! Come on inside, honey, and look at the house.— Oh, Michael!

MICHAEL
[After a pause, out front]
Yeeeeessuuuuummmmmmm.
[MICHAEL removes his suit jacket and his necktie, unbuttons his shirt collar, pulls the shirttail out, starts to roll up his sleeves and kick off his loafers]

LORAINE
[Turns to face him]
Come on inside and see the front room.
[MICHAEL turns slowly to face her but doesn't leave his position]
Stop that runnin'! Just slow up!

MICHAEL
[Still standing in place]
Yessum.

LORAINE
[Exasperated]
Ohh, Michael, how many times do I have to tell you, don't run!
[MICHAEL now begins to move, walking slowly toward LORAINE as she speaks]
I sound like a broken record. Don't run, don't run, don't run, don't run...

MICHAEL
I know better than to run.

LORAINE
You're just wringin' wet with perspiration! You're gonna have the croup
tonight just as sure as shootin'!

MICHAEL
P-U! It stinks in here.

LORAINE
No wonder—there hasn't been a breath of fresh air in here in twenty years.
Did you notice the roof? Don't you just love it—terra-cotta tile.

MICHAEL
And there's a triple-car garage!

LORAINE
They must have had automobiles to let! Oh, boy, oh, boy, I sure hope your
daddy's gettin' warm after all the buildin' up I've been doin'. After all the
times I've been drivin' by this place watchin' and watchin' that old "for
sale" sign. I've just gotta think of a way to convince him.

MICHAEL
Maybe if we say an "Our Father" real hard, it'll help.

LORAINE
Well, you pray and I'll think.

MICHAEL
No. You have to pray too or else it won't work.

LORAINE
[*Sighs*]
Well, anything's worth a try.
[*Looks heavenward*]
Please, dear God. For God's sake, don't trouble the water when I'm just
gettin' a bite.
[*TEDDY raps "shave-and-a-haircut-two-bits" and enters, dressed in a suit
and tie and wearing a hat*]

MICHAEL
Daddy!

TEDDY
[*To MICHAEL*]
Hello, Joe, whadda-ya know!

MICHAEL
Just got back from the picture show!

LORAINE
[*Ignoring TEDDY*]
Where's the real-estate man?

TEDDY
[*Removing his hat*]
Good afternoon. How are you today, you yummy tootsie-wootsie.

LORAINE
[*To MICHAEL*]
I'm married to a clown.
[*To TEDDY*]
Teddy, be serious. Where's the real-estate man?

TEDDY
He's not coming.

LORAINE
Not comin'! I don't believe it!

TEDDY
Would I shit a blind girl?

LORAINE
Honey, don't talk that way in front of your son. Lord only knows what
language he'll grow up to use.

TEDDY
[*To MICHAEL*]
Oh, I beg your pardon.

LORAINE
What went wrong?

TEDDY
It's already been sold.
[*Silence. A pause. Then he pulls a set of keys from his pocket and jingles them*]
Santy Claus!

LORAINE
—Oh, honey! I don't believe it! Oh, my stars!
[*And she rushes to him and throws her arms around his neck*]

MICHAEL
Oh-boy-oh-boy-oh-boy!

LORAINE
[*Hugging TEDDY ecstatically*]
You devil you!

TEDDY
I just hope it makes you happy.

LORAINE
Happy! I've never been so happy in all my life!

MICHAEL
Me too! Me too! Me too! Me too!
[*He rushes to embrace the two of them as they embrace each other*]

LORAINE
[*To TEDDY*]
You're happy too, aren't you?

TEDDY
[*Breaks away gently*]
You know me, Mama. I don't really care. To me, it's an awful lot of show. But
if it's what you and Michael want, that's all that matters.

LORAINE
[*Sincerely*]
Oh, honey, thank you.
[*She kisses him, turns to MICHAEL*]
You know, I just knew we were goin' to get this place. I knew it from the
moment I asked the man why the livin'-room floor sagged in the middle and he
said it was from so much dancin' at so many parties! He said one night at a party
everybody was high as Georgia pines doin' the Charleston when suddenly the
whole thing dropped four inches and they had to go into the basement and prop
it up. But once they did, everybody picked up where they left off and never
skipped a beat! Well. I knew I liked this house and this house liked me.

TEDDY
Are you planning on doing some entertaining?

LORAINE
Of course I'm not. You know I've never been one for socializin'. Thank God,
we don't have any friends so we won't *have* to entertain. But that's what this
house was built for. This livin' room is more like a ballroom. Imagine!
Eleven doors in four walls!

MICHAEL
And some of them seem to go nowhere.

LORAINE
But you'll notice most of them go to the porches all around. People must
have just danced out through one and had a cigarette and danced right back
in through another! I suppose we can seal up some of the dead ends—like
that botched-up affair that covers the old built-in bar.

MICHAEL
[*Disappointed*]
Awww, the bar is my favorite!

LORAINE
I wonder who you get that from.

TEDDY
Tear it out! I don't care. I'll have my toddies in the kitchen anyway.

MICHAEL
[*At the bar*]
It's even got a built-in radio!

LORAINE
I'm just gonna stucco over that whole space.

MICHAEL
And it still works! Listen!
[*"The Very Thought of You" starts to play. TEDDY starts to sing
along...TEDDY grabs LORAINE and starts to dance*]

TEDDY
"...the little ordinary things that everyone ought to do. I see your face in
every flower, your eyes in skies..."

MICHAEL
[*Interrupts their dance*]
What do you suppose this is?
[*TEDDY gives up—walks away*]

LORAINE
Oh! It's an ice shaver!

TEDDY
In case your ice has got five o'clock shadow at three a.m.

MICHAEL
[*Singing*]
Shave-and-a-haircut-two-bits!

LORAINE
[*To MICHAEL*]
It's to shave ice for frozen daiquiris and silver fizzes.

MICHAEL
First time I've ever seen one.

LORAINE
The first time I ever saw one was in the bar of the Edgewater Gulf Hotel in Biloxi. Remember, Daddy? Or was it the bar in the Palmettos? Well, it was on the coast somewhere. Sure never saw one till I saw you.

MICHAEL
Ouuuu! There's a dead mouse in the sink.

TEDDY
He's probably just passed out. Run a little water on him—maybe he'll come to.

LORAINE
Don't touch him! He's probably riddled with disease. That's where that ghastly odor is comin' from.

MICHAEL
[*To TEDDY*]
I'm afraid he's a goner.

TEDDY
Cirrhosis strikes again!

LORAINE
Open a door! Let's open all the doors! Let's let the sunset in!
[*She and MICHAEL open what would be all the doors to the porches, and the light changes*]

MICHAEL
Open sesame.

TEDDY
Now we got two nigger maids: Willy Mae and sesame.

LORAINE
Isn't it glorious! I know just how I'm gonna fix it up. I'm gonna paint everything green.

TEDDY
Well, I love green.

LORAINE
I don't mean Kelly green—a rich green, a luscious forest green with brilliant white enamel woodwork.
[*To MICHAEL*]
And I'm gonna do our bedroom in wallpaper of giant cabbage roses. I can see it now.

TEDDY
I can see you're gonna put me back in the poorhouse.

MICHAEL
Don't I get to have a bedroom of my own now?

LORAINE
Whatever for?

MICHAEL
Mama, I'm fifteen years old—it's beginning to make me nervous.

LORAINE
[*Reflectively*]
You know, although I'm a Southerner, I'm glad we didn't try and buy any of those antebellum or mainline magnolia homes. I think you really have to be aristocracy to live in them. Of course, I can put up a good front right along with the best of 'em if I have to—but I don't think I have to here. I feel like this house has just been sittin' here waitin' here for me.

MICHAEL
Daddy, are you considered a rebel, being born in St. Louis?

LORAINE
No, honey. Missouri's not in the South! Missouri's not even in the North. Missouri's nowhere.

TEDDY
[*To MICHAEL*]
In answer to your question, I am from what is known by most intelligent people as the Midwest. Your mother never heard of it.

LORAINE

You know, your daddy and I were always livin' in the spirit of this place even
if we *were broke* and livin' out of suitcases and taxicabs.

TEDDY
[*To MICHAEL*]
You were too little to remember it, but once we drove past the hotel where
you were born and I said, "Look, baby, that's where Jesus brought you."
And you looked up at me and said, "Did he bring me in a taxi?"

LORAINE
[*In her own world*]
I'm so beside myself with joy, I feel like doin' a dance!
[*LORAINE takes MICHAEL and starts to dance*]

TEDDY
Well, let's do one.
[*Pushes MICHAEL away*]
Turn up the music, son.
[*MICHAEL turns up the volume on the radio. "Deep Purple" is playing.
TEDDY joins LORAINE in the middle of the floor, puts his left hand up to her
right one, and wraps his right arm around her spine to rest his palm on her
behind. She reaches back, slaps his hand, pushes it up to the small of her
back*]

LORAINE
Come on, Daddy. Don't act dirty.

TEDDY
Oh, excuse me. I thought I was dancing with the aristocracy.

LORAINE
You've had a drink, haven't you?

TEDDY
Just a little toddy to be somebody.

LORAINE
I know it's the truth. You can't fool me.

TEDDY
I'm not trying to.

LORAINE
Well, let's not argue about it now. I'm too happy. I don't know why, but I feel
like, at long last, we've come home!

TEDDY
Heaven is *my* home.

LORAINE
Well, I don't know about you, but *I* am *in* heaven!
[*She exits*]

TEDDY
[*Surveys the house, slaps and rubs his hands together in a gesture of luck as if he has a pair of dice; rolls them as he speaks out front*]
Oh, Lawdy, Lawdy! I wonder what the po' folks are doin' tonight!
[MICHAEL *continues to dance as the light fades, but a spot stays on him. Music fades; he stops, a pause, puts hands in his pockets, reflects for a moment…*]

SCENE 2

A*n automobile horn toots "shave-and-a-haircut-two-bits."*

MICHAEL
[*Out front, singsongs*]
Daddy's home!
[*A light comes up on* TEDDY *in the kitchen area holding a brown paper bag behind his back*]

TEDDY
[*To* MICHAEL]
Santy Claus!

MICHAEL
I've been waiting up for you— Did you bring a sack?

TEDDY
[*Flatly*]
Aren't you even gonna say hello?

MICHAEL
Hello-did-you-bring-a-sack?

TEDDY
Where's that blond woman I live with?

MICHAEL
Upstairs lying down. What'd you bring?

LORAINE
[*Offstage*]
Yoo-hoo!

TEDDY
Who you yoo-hooin'?

LORAINE
[*Entering*]
I'm yoo-hooing you! Aren't you gonna say hello to *me*?

TEDDY
Hello, you.
[*He attempts to kiss her, she turns away.* MICHAEL *sees the paper bag*]

147

MICHAEL
[*Elated*]
You brought one!

TEDDY
[*To LORAINE*]
What's the matter—my breath bad?

LORAINE
No, indeed. You smell sweet—like always. You always smell just like orange juice.

TEDDY
That's just my natural fragrance. You sure look pretty tonight.

LORAINE
Why, thank you.

MICHAEL
What'd you bring?

LORAINE
[*To MICHAEL*]
Oh, honey, let the man get in the door!

MICHAEL
I want to know what's in the sack tonight!

TEDDY
Some real good ham—sliced thin as a whistle. Some Wisconsin cheese and some Swiss. You want some?

MICHAEL
Uh-uh.

TEDDY
Say, no sir, don't gimme any of that uh-uh business.

MICHAEL
No sir.

LORAINE
He couldn't eat another thing—we just got in a while ago. We went to Ambrosiani's and he had spaghetti.

MICHAEL
Smell *my* breath.

LORAINE
I had saltimbocca alla Romana.

TEDDY
Oh.

LORAINE
I told you I was gonna take him there this Saturday.

TEDDY
I forgot.
[*To* MICHAEL]
—And I brought you some new movie magazines.

MICHAEL
Oh, boy!
[*TEDDY takes the magazines out of the bag, hands them to* MICHAEL, *puts the bag on the kitchen table*]

LORAINE
[*To* MICHAEL]
Let me see! Let me see who's on the covers!—Oh, I can't stand *her.*
[*Flips to another magazine*]
Oh, I love *him.*
[*Flips to another*]
Oh, I can't stand *her.*

TEDDY
The score is two to one. The girls lose.
[*Meanwhile,* TEDDY *has proceeded to empty his pockets of their contents— money, glasses, pill bottles, leaflets, keys, and, lastly, his rosary, with which he reverently makes the sign of the cross and then places it with the other things on the table*]

LORAINE
[*Picking up a leaflet*]
What's this?

TEDDY
A pamphlet on the Immaculate Conception.

149

LORAINE
Oh.

TEDDY
I know—you can't stand *her*.

LORAINE
Honey!

TEDDY
[*Goes to LORAINE*]
How do you feel?

LORAINE
[*Pulling away*]
Pretty good. I've had a little old naggin' headache all day—but other than
that I'm OK.
[*Moving toward the kitchen counter*]
Think I'll just take another one of my pills.
[*She gets a glass of water and a bottle of pills and takes one*]
You look tired.

TEDDY
It's not that I'm so tired, it's just that my damn ankles have begun to swell
up so much.
[*He loosens his tie; places his jacket on the back of a chair*]

LORAINE
It's from standin' on your feet long hours. How are things at the place?

TEDDY
Hand over fist. I only hope the good Lord will let it hold out till I get the
building paid for and the last note on this house. Then we'll really be in
clover.
[*He has taken a bottle of gin out of the paper bag. LORAINE reacts unfavor-
ably as he picks up a glass and pours himself a drink*]

LORAINE
[*Picking up the empty sack with disdain, throwing it away. Moving off*]
They say it may snow.

MICHAEL
Just think! Wouldn't it be wonderful if we had snow for Christmas this year!

TEDDY
Well, if my in-laws show up, I can guarantee a little frost.

LORAINE
[*Bristling*]
Well, they'll be here!

TEDDY
In-laws and outlaws!

LORAINE
If you had any family left, I'm sure they'd be right here on top of us too!

MICHAEL
Daddy, does it snow a lot in St. Louis?

TEDDY
All the time. Why, I can remember when I was your age, my Aunt Maureen
having to break the ice in the water pitcher before she could wash her face.
She always made me stay in the bed till she got up and lit the stove and
heated the water for me.

MICHAEL
[*Lamely*]
Where was your...Uncle Brian?

LORAINE
Out drunk somewhere, no doubt.

TEDDY
Probably.

MICHAEL
[*Rather distantly*]
I remember it was cold the night you threw Uncle Brian out of our old
house.

LORAINE
That was too good for him—that dirty old s.o.b.—I went by the funeral parlor today to see Dr. Valkenberg and his Mexican matador. What a scandal
that's been. It has just rocked this town. They found strychnine in the bottle
of wine they were drinkin'—so it was murder as well as suicide.

TEDDY
That's too fancy for me.

LORAINE
You should have seen them. They looked just like wax. I declare, they were the most gorgeous corpses I've ever seen!

TEDDY
Sounds creepy to me.

LORAINE
I always liked Dr. Valkenberg. I was always sorry he wasn't a gynecologist so I could have tried him out. He was so nice to me when I was out to the hospital to have my partial hysterectomy. But you know and I know I could never leave Dr. LaSalle. He's just like a father to me.

TEDDY
I was thinking this year we might go to the Sugar Bowl game for Christmas.

MICHAEL
You mean go to New Orleans?

TEDDY
How would you like that, Mama?

LORAINE
You know me! I just love to travel! Boy, howdy! If I had my way, I'd keep one foot in the middle of the big road.

TEDDY
Well, I think we ought to try and plan on it. We could go to the track, have some good food, maybe take in a stage show, and see the game on New Year's Day.

LORAINE
[To MICHAEL]
I know you'll adore the clubhouse at the race track. It's not just like bein' *at* a movie, it's like bein' *in* a movie!

TEDDY
[To MICHAEL]
I can't see it myself. Stuck off to one side with those stuckups, when you can have box seats right down on the finish line!

LORAINE
[Remembering. Deflated]
Oh.— What'll I do about Hattiebeth?

TEDDY
All you have to do is write to her and politely inform her and her husband
that we have other plans this Christmas.

LORAINE
I hope she won't get her nose out of joint.

TEDDY
Why are you bothered about what those heathens think!

LORAINE
[*Bluntly*]
Listen, Teddy, regardless of what you think of my sister and her husband,
they have been damned nice to us.

TEDDY
I never did like that goddamn baby carriage!

MICHAEL
What baby carriage?

LORAINE
Your baby carriage! If it hadn't been for Aunt Hattiebeth and the Captain,
we'd have been pushin' you in a wheelbarrow!

TEDDY
[*Unlacing his shoes*]
And, Jesus, I'll never hear the end of it.

MICHAEL
Don't fight. Please.

TEDDY
We're not fighting.

LORAINE
Do you have to undress in the kitchen and empty your pockets out all over
creation!
[*Gathering up the articles on the table*]
Michael, take your daddy's things up to his room.

TEDDY
Can't I even relax in my own kitchen?

LORAINE
No.

TEDDY
Why not?

LORAINE
Because if your ankles are swollen, what you need is to elevate them. What
you need is to lie down. So, come on, I'll turn down your bed.
[*She takes his coat and his hat and exits*]

TEDDY
What I need is my head examined for putting up with this. I wonder what a
psychiatrist would say.

LORAINE
[*Going up the stairs*]
That you're crazy in the head.
[*MICHAEL has put TEDDY's things in TEDDY's bedroom. LORAINE enters, puts
his coat and hat down, and starts to turn down the bed with MICHAEL's
help.*]

TEDDY
[*Picking up his shoes and his drink and heading for the stairs*]
Did I tell you the joke about the cripple who went to the psychiatrist?—
Well, this one cripple was telling this other one that he'd been to a psychia-
trist to see if the reason he couldn't walk was because it was all in his head.
[*He stops on a step; has a sip of his drink*]
So the other one said, "So, what happened?" And the first cripple said,
"Well, the psychiatrist said there's only one way to find out—throw away
your crutches and take a step!"
[*He resumes ascending the stairs*]
So the other one said, "So then what happened?" And the first cripple said,
"Well, then I threw away my right crutch." And the other one said, "So then
what happened?" And the cripple said, "And then I threw away my left
crutch." And the other one said, "And then what happened?"
[*He appears in the bedroom*]
And the first cripple said, "And then I fell on my fucking face!"
[*MICHAEL starts to giggle. LORAINE starts to snicker, then laughs out loud as TEDDY
starts to laugh, sets his glass down, and pushes LORAINE over onto the bed with
him. MICHAEL collapses from the other side and the three of them lie in a heap,
roaring with laughter. Finally, LORAINE sits up, wiping tears from her face*]

LORAINE
[*Still through a few guffaws*]
...Oh!...that is the funniest thing I ever heard—my headache is just killin' me!
[*Her laughter dies away; she kisses TEDDY*]
Good night, honey.

[*She gets up and goes to her room and lies in a seductive pose on her bed, allowing the slit of her negligee to part and reveal her legs*]

MICHAEL
[*Crawls up and kisses TEDDY*]
Good night, Daddy.
[*MICHAEL goes to his bedroom, removes his shirt and pants, and gets into bed as TEDDY calls to him*]

TEDDY
Good night, son. Are you going to Holy Communion in the morning?

MICHAEL
Yes, sir.

TEDDY
Well, remember, don't have anything to eat or drink afterward until you swallow a few sips of water—in case any of the sacred host remains in your mouth. You hear?

MICHAEL
Yes, sir.

LORAINE
[*From her bed*]
Good night, darlin'.

MICHAEL
[*From his bed*]
Good night, Mama.

LORAINE
I love you.

MICHAEL
I love you too.

TEDDY
[*From his bed*]
I love you three.
[*And he takes the pamphlet and glasses out of his coat pocket, puts the glasses on, starts to read and sip his drink as the lights dim out on him and LORAINE while a spot holds on MICHAEL. Pause. The sound of the Gulf surf comes up. MICHAEL gets out of bed, picks up a beach towel, and comes center as the screen drop flies in...*]

155

SCENE 3

A *light picks up* TEDDY *in beach clothes and dark glasses. He has a pair of binoculars on a strap around his neck.*

TEDDY
[*Looking off through the binoculars*]
Get set. Here she comes.

MICHAEL
I'm ready. Are you ready?

TEDDY
Yeah, yeah, now remember, don't say a word and for Jesus' sake, don't laugh.

MICHAEL
I won't laugh. Don't *you* laugh.

TEDDY
Don't worry about me.

LORAINE
Teddy?

TEDDY
Now, hurry up! Here she comes.
[*MICHAEL puts an arm around* TEDDY's *neck and hops into his arms. Once* TEDDY *is holding him,* MICHAEL *releases his grip and bends backward, letting his head and arms dangle as his feet do*]

LORAINE
[*Offstage*]
What's goin' on? What're y'all doin'? Teddy?
[*TEDDY has a glazed expression and moves forward a step at a time. MICHAEL allows his head to wobble as* LORAINE *darts onstage wearing beach clothes and carrying a Kodak*]
Teddy, what happened? What's wrong? ANSWER ME!
[*Simultaneously on cue,* MICHAEL *flips up and...*]

TEDDY AND MICHAEL
BOO!!!

LORAINE
[*Recoils with fright, then recovers*]

...You bastards!
[*TEDDY and* MICHAEL *fall to the ground, laughing*]
...I've told you not to do that to me!

MICHAEL
Oh, Mama, not again!

TEDDY
[*To* MICHAEL, *with his arm around him*]
You see! What'd I tell you—she fell for it again! What a sucker you are,
Loraine!

LORAINE
[*Furious*]
Because I'm always terrified somethin' has really happened to my child!

MICHAEL
I'm not a child anymore.

LORAINE
I don't care if you're seventy! You'll always be my baby!

TEDDY
[*Shaking his head, patting* MICHAEL]
She fell for it again! I don't believe it!
[*LORAINE picks up the towel, which has fallen on the ground, and goes to put
it around* MICHAEL's *shoulders. He does not see her at first, is startled by her
proximity, and flinches*]

LORAINE
Watcha flinchin' for? You thought I was gonna pop you one, didn't you?
'Cause you know you need it. Here.
[*Pulling* MICHAEL *away from* TEDDY]
Put this towel around your shoulders. You're gonna get blistered and make
yourself sick.

MICHAEL
[*Dully*]
Let's go for a walk.

TEDDY
Good deal. Let's walk a ways so Mama can cool off. She's mighty hot under
the collar.

LORAINE
I rue the day you ever floated down the Mississippi! I should have taken one look at you and run for dear life in the other direction!
      [*Pause. They stroll*]

TEDDY
Look, Loraine!

LORAINE
What?

TEDDY
That big open space over yonder.

LORAINE
That empty lot across the highway?

TEDDY
Yeah.

LORAINE
Well, I see it. What about it?
      [*Gasps*]
Oh, my goodness! Oh, my goodness gracious!

TEDDY
Ain't that somethin'!

MICHAEL
What?

LORAINE
That's where the Palmettos was! Have you ever! What happened, Teddy? Did a hurricane get it?

TEDDY
I don't know. Maybe they tore it down.

LORAINE
Gone! Oh, that just gets away with me so!

TEDDY
I'm just as glad it's gone.

LORAINE
Oh, Daddy, how can you say that?

TEDDY
I'm glad those days are over and done with.

MICHAEL
What was it like?

LORAINE
Well, from the outside it appeared to be one of the most swell-elegant private residences along this entire coastline. But inside it was the swankiest casino on the Gulf of Mexico. Your daddy and I worked there years ago. My God, Teddy, what do you suppose ever became of Clayton?

TEDDY
Who knows?

MICHAEL
Who?

LORAINE
Clayton Reed. The Reed brothers. There were three of them—Clayton and Ramsey and Bubber Reed. And they were all the best-lookin' things you ever laid eyes on. And rich as Croesus!

TEDDY
I always thought maybe you took a shine to Clayton.

LORAINE
I did no such thing! Clayton was my favorite and that's all there was to it!
    [*To MICHAEL*]
They were born gamblers—had it in their blood just like your daddy. That's why they got along so well.

TEDDY
We got along because they trusted me. Clayton knew if they were gonna be successful crooks, they needed an honest crook to help 'em.

LORAINE
The story was that they had won the Palmettos in a poker game, but no one knew for sure. Daddy and I had just been married and I wasn't dry behind the ears. I used to hang around the bar late at night, playin' the slot machines, waitin' for Daddy to get off—when one night Clayton came up to me and said, "Lollie, you sure are a pretty thing. How'd you like to make a little somethin' on the side?" And I said, "Doin' what, I'd like to know." And he told me. And the next day he took me in this limousine to the best shop in Biloxi and bought me a lime-green evenin' dress. I'll never forget it

159

as long as I live. He did all the talkin'—said, "We'd like to be shown the finest dinner dresses you have." And with that they brought out the most gorgeous clothes I've ever seen in my life. One after another—satin and beaded and spangles, and I was just ga-ga! But Clayton didn't react to a single thing until they showed us this one made of lime-green crepe de chine with no trim on it at all. And then he said, "Lollie, why don't you try on that one?" And I did. It had kind of a flared skirt and long, full, full puff sleeves that hung down and were gathered up by a band at the wrists. And it was high in the front and had no back at all. And I floated out of the dressin' room like green smoke. And Clayton said, "We'll take it!" I asked him why he had chosen that particular one. He said, "Because it was the simplest and the most dignified—and because of those big, beautiful sleeves. I hope you like it." And I said, "I think it was my favorite all along and I just never knew it till you told me."

MICHAEL
Was that your job?

LORAINE
I was the shill. Clayton said people would watch my good looks rather than the dice and so they gave me money to play with and I stood on the left side of Daddy, who was ridin' the stick. On a big bet I would place a chip on the field, and my big, beautiful sleeve would spread on the board and cover Daddy's hand as he switched dice. God! We had nerve in those days! I did that time and time again and never batted a beaded eyelash, and now it scares me just to think of it.

TEDDY
Oh, yeah, I think you were stuck on Clayton all right.

LORAINE
Oh, honey, he didn't mean a thing to me. I liked him like a father. He was so reserved and genteel.

MICHAEL
What ever became of him?

LORAINE
Well, Clayton just played out and picked up and moved on. No one has seen nor heard of him since. That's one thing in this life—we never know what will happen to us.

TEDDY
[Looking through the binoculars]
Look at what's become of that big old place over there.

LORAINE
I can see a cross above the porch, but what does the sign say?

TEDDY
Retreat House.

LORAINE
Is that like a monastery?

TEDDY
Yeah. But more. Michael, tell your mama what a retreat house is.

MICHAEL
It's a place where you can sort of be a monk for a day. Or two days or a week, depending on how long the retreat lasts. For ladies I guess it's like temporarily taking the veil. You read and meditate and listen to talks and keep a vow of silence. I don't think you'd like it.

LORAINE
Do you have to abstain from alcohol?

TEDDY
I would never drink while making a retreat.

LORAINE
Then I'm all for your makin' one.

TEDDY
It would defeat the point. I'd take a pledge—I'd promise God that I wouldn't drink.

MICHAEL
For how long?

TEDDY
Well, certainly during the time of the retreat—but maybe longer.

LORAINE
That's too good to be true.

TEDDY
You don't think I could do it, do you?

LORAINE
Oh, honey, I know you could do it. When you make up your mind to do
somethin', you do it. You've got a will of iron. I only wish a little of that
could rub off on me.

MICHAEL
Will you, Daddy?

TEDDY
We'll see. We'll see.
  [*Looking back at the house through the binoculars*]
Sure is a snazzy layout—don't you think?

LORAINE
Uh-huh.

TEDDY
I think it's a dilly!

LORAINE
  [*Looking in the opposite direction*]
I just can't get over it bein' gone. Poor Clayton...
  [*Lights fade on* LORAINE *and* TEDDY. *The spot stays on* MICHAEL, *looking
  back and forth from* TEDDY *to* LORAINE, *from* LORAINE *to* TEDDY, *almost as if
  he were watching a tennis match, as sound of surf comes up...*]

SCENE 4

*M*ICHAEL *slowly crosses to the proscenium, where he exchanges the beach towel for two white turkish ones. He throws one over his shoulder and wraps the other around his waist and then removes his boxer shorts. Over the above action* LORAINE *can be heard.*

> LORAINE
> [*Offstage*]
>
Michael! Ohh, Michael!

> MICHAEL
> [*Out front*]
>
Yessum!

> LORAINE
> [*Offstage*]
>
What's takin' you so long up there?

> MICHAEL
> [*Out front*]
>
I'm taking a bath.

> LORAINE
> [*Offstage*]
>
Your supper's ready.

> MICHAEL
>
What'd Willy leave on the stove?

> LORAINE
> [*Offstage*]
>
Nothin' but goodwill. *I* am the chef tonight!

> MICHAEL
> [*Incredulous but delighted*]
>
You cooked?— What'd you fix?

> LORAINE
> [*Offstage*]
>
It's *suppose* to be a surprise! Now stop that dawdlin' and come on! You could have taken ten baths as long as you've been up there. And with as much water as you always put in that tub!

MICHAEL
You need a lot of water to take a bubble bath.

LORAINE
[*Offstage*]
Bubble bath! Honestly, Michael, you should have been a girl.
[*LORAINE enters to catch MICHAEL in a pose—perhaps wrapping his head in
a towel as if it were a nun's wimple, dipping his fingers into the washbasin as
if it were a holy-water font, making a pious sign of the cross before his
mirror*]

MICHAEL
[*With a start*]
Ohhh!

LORAINE
[*Surprised as well*]
What's the matter?!

MICHAEL
You scared me!

LORAINE
Whatcha scared of—your shadow?

MICHAEL
You might as well *be* my shadow. Why don't you knock?

LORAINE
Why do I have to knock? I'm your mother. Now, let me see behind your
ears.

MICHAEL
Don't pull 'em!

LORAINE
I'm not gonna pull 'em.

MICHAEL
You do sometimes.

LORAINE
Only when you need it.
[*She pushes him by the shoulders to sit down and investigates his ears. He
grimaces*]
Just look!—there's a blackhead! Now, let me get it!

MICHAEL
NO!

LORAINE
[*Firmly*]
Michael, stop squirmin' and sit still. I'm not gonna have you with filthy ears!

MICHAEL
Well, do it fast!

LORAINE
I'm not gonna hurt you.

MICHAEL
You always say that.

LORAINE
[*Commanding*]
Hush!
[*She bends his head to one side and commences her excavation. He begins a low moan...*]

MICHAEL
Ooowwwwwww!

LORAINE
Whatcha yellin' about—it's all over!

MICHAEL
[*Rubbing his ear*]
You lied, you hurt!

LORAINE
Look at it! Big as a tick! Believe you me, you didn't have dirt in your ears as long as I bathed you in the tub with me.

MICHAEL
Well, don't get any ideas—we won't fit anymore!

LORAINE
Oh, my nails are just horrible!— Now let me see your little thing.

MICHAEL
No!

LORAINE
Come on, Michael, let me look at your talliwacker.

165

MICHAEL
No! I don't have any blackheads there.

LORAINE
Stop stallin' and let me look!

MICHAEL
Mama!

LORAINE
Michael. *You hear me.*

MICHAEL
[*Defeated*]
Ohhh, *all right!*
[*And he snaps his towel open upstage. She has a look and a poke*]

LORAINE
…Well…OK.
[*He glumly closes his towel*]
Now, that wasn't so bad, was it?
[*Observing* MICHAEL, *who is still drying himself*]
Now, put on your robe this instant—I don't want you catchin' cold. And
hurry up about it!
[*She exits and quickly goes downstairs. He pulls on his robe, steps into his
slippers, and follows her down to the kitchen*]

MICHAEL
[*En route*]
Can I listen to *Lux Presents Hollywood* tonight?

LORAINE
Not until you do your lessons.
[*He enters the kitchen*]
Go sit down and put your napkin in your lap.

MICHAEL
What's the menu on this special occasion?

LORAINE
[*Serving him*]
Peas and okra—stop playin' with the silver—fried corn, smothered steak,
sliced tomatoes! How's that suit your apparatus?
[*He smiles broadly for the first time*]
What're you grinnin' at? Huh? Sweet thing. Who do you love?

[*She bends and kisses him. He giggles*]
Silly willy!
[*She goes for a bowl, returns holding it with pads*]
Watch out for this one—hot, hot, hot. Stop singin' at the table! Honestly,
Michael, everyone always tells me what lovely table manners you have, but
God knows, one would never know it when you're at home!

MICHAEL
[*Through a mouthful of food*]
Mama, please...

LORAINE
And don't talk with your mouth full. How is it?

MICHAEL
[*Through clenched teeth*]
Mmmmmmmmmmmmmmm.

LORAINE
I think I'll tidy up here. I just can't stand things out of place.

MICHAEL
Aren't you gonna eat any supper?

LORAINE
Oh, honey, I couldn't eat a mouthful right now. I just can't cook food and
smell it and have any appetite left. By the time you've finished foolin' with
it, it makes you sick at your stomach to look at it— Why aren't you eatin'
your good supper?

MICHAEL
I'm full.

LORAINE
[*Incredulous*]
Whaaat? Michael, all I ever hear is "Why don't we ever have meals like
other people?" And when I *do* cook, you won't eat.

MICHAEL
Why don't we ever eat together?

LORAINE
Well, you know why...your daddy's at work. He has to work to keep this
terra-cotta tile roof over our heads. And I... Well, I just told you, I'd be sick
if I tried to eat right now.
[*Pause. She sees the look on his face*]

Ohhh, I know what you mean. But I gave up a long time ago, tryin' to get this family together for a meal. And if we ever do, you know how it ends up.

MICHAEL
Excuse me.
 [*Pointedly polite, he gets up from the table and goes upstairs*]

LORAINE
Where're you goin'?
 [*Blankly staring at the food*]
Looks like I cooked it just so I could throw it out.— What're you doin' up there?

MICHAEL
Turning on the radio. The program goes on in a minute.

LORAINE
 [*Clearing away the table*]
You haven't done your lessons yet. You heard what I told you!

MICHAEL
I don't have any homework. The sisters never give any the first week.

LORAINE
Well, the summer is over. We are not on the coast now. You know what that means. You know your daddy's rules—no picture shows except only on Friday and Saturday, and no radio until after you do your lessons.

MICHAEL
What time is he coming home?

LORAINE
How would I know?

MICHAEL
 [*Finding the radio station*]
Hurry up! It's just about to start!

LORAINE
 [*Excited*]
I'm comin'! I'm comin'! Get out my negligee and the nail-polish remover and my emery boards.
 [*There are muffled sounds from the radio as he adjusts it. Then he retrieves the manicure articles. She continues talking as if he were still in the room, during which she opens a bottle of beer*]

I think I'll just work on myself tonight. Give myself a manicure, shampoo my hair. Roll it, set it, pluck my eyebrows, and try to get myself lookin' like a halfway-decent human bein' for Mass Sunday. What story's on tonight?

MICHAEL
Rebecca—hurry up!
[*She starts up the stairs with the beer and two glasses*]

LORAINE
Oh, that was a grand picture—Laurence Olivier and Jo Ann Fontaine.

MICHAEL
Joan Fontaine.

LORAINE
She's Olivia de Havilland's sister. They were born in China, you know.

RADIO VOICE
[*Following fanfare*]
Lux Presents Hollywood!

LORAINE
[*Enters bedroom*]
Boy! Put your feet under that cover!
[*He does. She hands him a glass and pours hers full; he unzips her dress for her*]
You're just bound and determined to get the croup, aren't you?
[*She slips out of her housedress and into her negligee as MICHAEL stares at her, filing his nails*]

MICHAEL
I don't have croup anymore. I have asthma.

LORAINE
Well, asthma then.

MICHAEL
[*Extending his glass*]
Just a tap, thank you.

LORAINE
[*Pouring MICHAEL beer. Studying her glass of beer*]
I don't really like beer. Beer just goes through me like Sherman went through Georgia.
[*And she has a big swallow*]

MICHAEL
Shhhhh!!!

RADIO VOICE
And now, Daphne du Maurier's *Rebecca*.

LORAINE
[*Sits on bed, hugs* MICHAEL]
Are you warm enough?

MICHAEL
[*Smiles*]
Um-hum. Warm as toast.

LORAINE
It's still the best bed in the world.
[*She snuggles closer as the lights dim, leaving only* MICHAEL *in a spot. The* RADIO VOICE *begins. A pause, and he gets out of bed and moves to his own room as the narration finishes*]

RADIO VOICE
"Last night I dreamt I went to Manderley again. It seemed to me I stood by the iron gate leading to the drive, but the way was barred to me by a padlock and chain. I called to the lodge keeper but, peering closer through the rusted spokes of the gate, I saw that the lodge was uninhabited."

SCENE 5

Lights come up full on TEDDY *in the kitchen and* LORAINE *in her bed.*
MICHAEL *is visible in his room, eavesdropping as he dresses.*

TEDDY
Get your ass down here now and answer me.
[*Pouring a drink*]

LORAINE
Please, Teddy, I've got cramps pretty severe and I'm on edge and I want to
stay on the bed.

TEDDY
You've always got cramps or a headache or you're down in your back or some
damn thing when I want you to account for something.

LORAINE
[*Taking pills from a bottle by her bed*]
Look, I'm nervous as hell and I don't feel like arguin'.

TEDDY
Are you nervous because you've got something to hide?

LORAINE
I most certainly am not! I'm late and I'm afraid when I do start I'll start
floodin' again! And if that keeps up, I'll have to have another operation.

TEDDY
Yeah, so LaSalle can have another Cadillac.

LORAINE
I wouldn't be alive today without that man.

TEDDY
Alive so you can live it up on the sly.

LORAINE
Leave me alone, please.

TEDDY
I said, Get your ass down here.
[LORAINE *gets out of her bed and slowly comes downstairs*]

171

LORAINE
Anyone else drinks on the job, you fire them.

TEDDY
It's my place of business—I can do as I damn well please—and while I'm
workin' at night, you go out! And you take Michael with you and pick up
your friends.

LORAINE
I do not. I don't have any friends to speak of. I don't want any friends.

TEDDY
Well, then, where are you while I'm at work?

LORAINE
Right here in this house! Alone with my child. Night after night, except on
the weekends when Michael and I go for rides—or window shoppin'! I'd
take an oath.

TEDDY
You act like I never take you anywhere.

LORAINE
    [Getting a glass of water and taking a pill]
I didn't say that, Teddy.

TEDDY
We go to the coast.

LORAINE
Yes, and I love it when we do...

TEDDY
I took you to the World Series last year, didn't I?

LORAINE
The less said about that, the better.

TEDDY
You're just guilty about the way you acted.

LORAINE
The way *I* acted!

TEDDY
The same damn way you've always acted in front of other men.

LORAINE
That's not fair to say that of me! Because it's not true!
[*MICHAEL has come into view a few speeches back, edging his way down the stairs, listening to this exchange. He is now wearing his shirt and trousers*]

MICHAEL
[*Entering*]
What are you two arguing about?

LORAINE
Go back upstairs, honey.

MICHAEL
I can hear you upstairs.

TEDDY
Do what your mother said!

LORAINE
I can't help it if men look at me!

TEDDY
You don't have to look back! You don't have to *smile* back!

LORAINE
If they smile at me, I do. I'm flattered.

TEDDY
You're just like your sister!

LORAINE
No, I'm not!

MICHAEL
Please. Please, don't fight.

LORAINE
I have never been man-crazy in my life!

TEDDY
It's no news to anybody that I'm not keen on my brother-in-law—in fact, I despise his guts. But sometimes I feel sorry for the poor son of a bitch because you pair of heathens make such a sucker out of him.

LORAINE
He's not all that easy to live with—fogy as hell.

TEDDY
She put her ass in a butter tub is what she did. If we don't go to the Sugar Bowl, I am not having those barbarians in this house at Christmastime!

LORAINE
Well, they're comin'! It's already been settled.

TEDDY
If I so much as see that goddamn black Buick in the driveway, I'm gonna get the pistol out of the safe and blow their fucking heathen heads off!

LORAINE
You'll have to kill me first!

TEDDY
With pleasure! You'll be target practice!

MICHAEL
Daddy!

LORAINE
It won't be the first time. There's already one bullet hole in my bedroom to prove what a mean and crazy bastard you are!

MICHAEL
Mama!

TEDDY
I will not subject myself to that bitch taking over around here. I will not sit still and watch you slobber all over the old man.

MICHAEL
I like Aunt Hattiebeth.

TEDDY
Oh, sure. Oh, sure.

MICHAEL
And I like going to visit them during vacation.

TEDDY
Because they let you run hog-wild! Feed you chocolate candy till you start gasping for breath or puke all over the place. Not to mention letting you

hang around roadhouse honky-tonks all night playing the jukebox while
they tank up!

LORAINE
Look who's talkin'!

TEDDY
I don't want him with people who have no concern for his spiritual welfare.

LORAINE
Hattiebeth always makes him go to Mass on Sunday when he's up there
visitin'— He is the one who doesn't want to go and who talks her into lettin'
him skip it!

TEDDY
You'd let him stay in bed too if I didn't stand over you like some wild-animal
trainer in the circus! You only agreed to be married by a priest to shut me
up. You don't believe in anything!

LORAINE
What do you know about what I think or feel? Just because I'm not a fanatic
like you!—in the front pew every time the bell rings! One thing I'll say for
my sister and brother-in-law, at least *my* relatives never molested your son!

TEDDY
[*Lunges at her*]
Don't you dare throw that in my face!

MICHAEL
[*Running between them*]
NO! No! Keep away from her!

TEDDY
[*Trying to push him aside*]
Get out of the way!

LORAINE
Go ahead, beat me to a pulp! Set some good example!

MICHAEL
Mama, please...

TEDDY
[*To LORAINE*]
You shut up!

175

MICHAEL
Both of you, please! Stop it!

LORAINE
[*To* MICHAEL *as* TEDDY *goes to retrieve a bottle and a glass and pours himself a drink*]
You asked me about those photographs taken at the Stork Club and at Leon and Eddie's—why I had taken a razor blade and cut out my face. Well, I'll tell you. Because my eyes were so blacked and my cheeks so swollen you wouldn't have known it was your mother!

TEDDY
[*Taking a gulp of his drink*]
You slut.

LORAINE
You got me mixed up with some of your friends.

TEDDY
You shut up!

LORAINE
Don't you accuse me of anything after the mornings you've stumbled in dead drunk after having holed up with God knows who—so soused you didn't even know you were wearin' a pair of satin bedroom mules!
[TEDDY *throws the drink in her face*]

MICHAEL
DADDY!
[*And* MICHAEL *rushes to* LORAINE]

LORAINE
It's all right. It's all right.

MICHAEL
Oh, Mama, Mama...here...sit down. Sit down and let me dry your face.
[*He grabs a dishcloth and starts to gently blot her tears and the drink from her face*]
...Don't cry. Mama, shhh, don't...don't cry.
[TEDDY *silently watches for a second, then turns, weaves unsteadily away and out of sight*]

LORAINE
Oh, *I'm* all right. He didn't hurt *you*, did he?

MICHAEL
No.

LORAINE
[*Drying her eyes, getting up*]
Well, come on, we're gonna pack our things and get out of here.

MICHAEL
We are?

LORAINE
I'm just afraid of him when he's like this.

MICHAEL
—I was hoping you'd say we'd leave! This time, let's never come back.

LORAINE
What do you mean?

MICHAEL
If you got a divorce, then we'd never have to come back! Then we could
move away together somewhere. To a city— Say yes. Oh, please, say yes.

LORAINE
Oh, Michael. I don't know about any of that right now. I just want to get
away from here before he has any more and starts in on me again.

MICHAEL
Then where will we go? To Aunt Hattie's?

LORAINE
No. I don't want to go there. A little of her goes a long ways. I don't feel well
and I've got to take a little somethin' for it and be quiet for a while.

MICHAEL
I wish I could drive. I wish I could drive us far, far away.

LORAINE
We'll go out on the edge of town and find some little motor court for the
night. And tomorrow or the next day he'll be himself again and then we can
come back.

MICHAEL
But I don't want for us to come back.
        [*Pause*]

LORAINE
[*Quite calmly and directly*]
Michael—he's your father. And you know I've always tried to teach you to love him, no matter what he's done. He means well. And he tries. I will just have to try a little harder too. But I want you to respect him—I mean that. Because, after all, he is your father.
[*MICHAEL is silent*]
Now, come and help me pack.
[*Lights fade, leaving only* MICHAEL *illuminated by the follow spot. He slowly crosses to the proscenium to retrieve his raincoat, a Kotex box wrapped in plain brown paper, and a pharmacy bag. Throughout this action* LORAINE *can be heard emitting a faint moan…*]

SCENE 6

Lights come up on LORAINE *in bed.*

LORAINE
Darlin', is that you?

MICHAEL
    [Entering]
Yes, ma'am.

LORAINE
Did you bring the Demerol?

MICHAEL
Yes, ma'am.

LORAINE
...and the Kotex?

MICHAEL
Yes.

LORAINE
Did you have enough money?

MICHAEL
I charged it. How do you feel?

LORAINE
    [Anxiously taking the bag from him, removing a pharmacy bottle]
I'll be OK just as soon as this medicine takes effect.
    *[*MICHAEL *gets a spoon from the bed table, kneels on the mattress beside her]*
Oh, honey, don't shake the bed! Just the slightest touch is like a knife goin'
through my brain.

MICHAEL
    [Taking the bottle from her, rising]
I'm sorry.

LORAINE
Don't spill it! Don't spill it!
    *[*MICHAEL *carefully pours out a spoonful; she opens her mouth and he gives it*
    to her]
I thank you.

[*He replaces the cap on the bottle and moves toward the bathroom*]
And, baby, pick up your feet. Please, tiptoe. Tiptoe.

MICHAEL
I'm sorry. I'll put this in the medicine cabinet.

LORAINE
No.— Just leave it here by my bed.
[*He returns the bottle and spoon to her bedside table*]
Have you got many lessons?

MICHAEL
I did them at recess.

LORAINE
—Whatcha starin' at?

MICHAEL
I think I'll go out in the yard for a while.
[*He tiptoes into TEDDY's room to get the binoculars*]

LORAINE
Well, be sure and button up. And don't run.

MICHAEL
I never run. The boys down the street are playing basketball and I just want to watch them through the binoculars.

LORAINE
Willy left your supper on the stove whenever you're hungry.

MICHAEL
I'm not hungry.

LORAINE
You didn't buy any chocolate at the drugstore and spoil your appetite, did you?

MICHAEL
You know I'd get asthma if I did that.

LORAINE
—Thank you for stoppin' by Dr. LaSalle's to pick up the prescription.

MICHAEL
You're welcome.
> [*Over this action, there is a distant, prolonged train whistle*]

LORAINE
Listen at that train. It makes me want to travel. I wonder where it's headed.

MICHAEL
No telling.
> [*He tiptoes out— She continues the weak, rhythmic moan. He comes down the stairs and walks slowly out to the apron of the stage. Kneeling, clasping his hands together and looking up*]

Dear God, I want to make a deal with you. Please don't punish my mama for my sins. I'm sorry for offending you—and I promise you that if you let her get well, I won't commit any more acts of self-abuse. No matter how strong the temptation. So please, let me have wet dreams and I'll keep my end of the bargain if you'll keep yours.
> [*And then he takes a Tootsie Roll out of his raincoat pocket, tears off the wrapper, and starts to eat it as he raises the binoculars to his eyes. The light on LORAINE fades out, but the spot holds on MICHAEL…*]

SCENE 7

Thunder. TEDDY *lights a candle to reveal basement stairs. Sound of rain is heard.* MICHAEL *runs to* TEDDY's *protective arms and they huddle tightly every time there is a roll of thunder.*

TEDDY
...And stay away from water and never turn on a light switch with a wet hand.

MICHAEL
Yes, sir.
> [*Pause. A thunderclap. It subsides.* MICHAEL *is now seated a step or two below so that* TEDDY's *knees form a kind of armchair*]
I wish we could fix it up down here.

TEDDY
You and your mama can think of more ways to spend money.

MICHAEL
To have a place where I could bring some people and we could dance. It's comfortable and cozy down here.

TEDDY
That's because it is what it is—a cozy cellar. If you fix it all up, it would be like the rest of the house. A little more concentration in the area of your studies and a little less time spent on becoming the local Fred Astaire might not be a bad idea.

MICHAEL
You're not gonna yell at me anymore, are you?

TEDDY
I'm through yelling. I'm now going to give you a quiet ultimatum. If you don't bring your marks up by next term, every privilege gets taken away. If you only knew how many people in this world don't have the opportunity...

MICHAEL
I know. I know all about it.

TEDDY
Well, if you know so much, why the hell don't you do something about it!

MICHAEL
Don't yell at me. That doesn't do any good. It just makes it worse—like the time I misspelled the word on the card of your Christmas present. All it did was make me sick.

TEDDY
I'll never get over that. How could anybody spell a simple word like "from" with an e! "To Daddy, *frome* your son!"
    [*He pronounces the word "frommy." There is a clap of thunder. MICHAEL makes a dive back into TEDDY's arms. TEDDY holds on to him and ducks his head. Then, after it has passed, slowly looks up*]
…Mainly you shouldn't be around trees. When it rains a lot of people run and stand under a tree. Well, there's nowhere more dangerous to be when lightning strikes. So remember—stay away from trees.

MICHAEL
Yes, sir.
    [*MICHAEL gets up again, takes a few steps in a different direction. He stops, picks up an old, partially deflated basketball, tries to bounce it. Dust billows out as it plops to the floor and softly rolls away*]

TEDDY
I was sure happy when you asked me to buy that. Of course I never disapproved of your having dolls. But I can't deny, when you asked for a basketball I was really thrilled. Not to mention that I nearly fell over in the toy store.

MICHAEL
I wanted to learn how to catch. I hate it when people throw things at me and expect me to catch them—like boots and key rings…and basketballs.

TEDDY
I can't understand it. You've got good coordination and timing—you can dance. You should be able to find some rewarding athletic outlet. I don't mean football, of course. But…*possibly*…basketball. Tennis surely. Or golf—which has always looked boring as hell to me, but you might like it.

MICHAEL
I'd get asthma if I tried any of those things. You know that!

TEDDY
Maybe you'd overcome it by doing them.

MICHAEL

Maybe if we lived up north I could learn to ski. Skiing requires coordination and timing but there's no exertion required. All you have to do is stand there and slide down the hill.

TEDDY

I'm sure there must be more to it than that. If there isn't, that sounds boring as hell too.

[*Another roll of thunder.* MICHAEL *runs back to* TEDDY *and they huddle together until it dies away. A door opens at the top of the stairs, spilling a shaft of light on* TEDDY *and* MICHAEL *as* LORAINE *is revealed, wearing a negligee. She never comes down the steps toward them but remains above them throughout her appearance*]

MICHAEL

[*Holding up his arms defensively toward her*]

Shut the door!

LORAINE

[*Amused*]

Well, if you two aren't a couple of screwballs!

TEDDY

Ohhhh, Jesus.

LORAINE

I felt like I needed a good laugh so I thought I'd come down and take a look at you two chicken-hearted coo-coos.

MICHAEL

Shut the door because of the draft!

LORAINE

I always know where to find y'all when it's rainin'.

MICHAEL

Drafts attract lightning!

LORAINE

Now who told you that, as if I don't know.

TEDDY

I didn't tell him that. He told *me!*

LORAINE

What are y'all talkin' about?

184

MICHAEL
Nothing.

LORAINE
Are you talkin' about me?

TEDDY
No, we're not talking about you!

LORAINE
Well, what *are* you talkin' about?

TEDDY
We were talking about your son's rotten, stinking grades.

LORAINE
Y'all are not fightin', are you?

TEDDY
Not yet.

LORAINE
[*To* MICHAEL]
What's the matter, honey? Did you get a bad report card?

MICHAEL
Well...not as good as they have been.

TEDDY
It was a thoroughly disgusting stinkeroo.

LORAINE
What could be causin' this?

MICHAEL
I don't know.

LORAINE
I used to be able to help you with your lessons when you were smaller. I used to drill you and drill you on your catechism. You didn't fail your cate-chism, did you?

MICHAEL
It's called religion now. I failed math.

LORAINE
Arithmetic?

TEDDY
He better not have failed religion or you really would hear some yelling around here.

LORAINE
[*All clear to her now*]
Oh, well. I never could help you on arithmetic. Although I did drill you on the multiplication table.

MICHAEL
I still don't know the twelves.

LORAINE
Well, honey, who does?

TEDDY
You taught him to count on his fingers, which is positively the wrong way to even begin to go about it!

LORAINE
Well, you're *teachin'* him to be afraid of lightnin'! Which is positively crack-pot!

MICHAEL
Will you please shut the door.

TEDDY
On your way *out!*

LORAINE
Lightnin' can't hurt you, honey. Why, I used to love to play in the rain when I was a child—couldn't wait for it to pour down so I could get wringin' wet!—or make paper boats and watch 'em go sailin' down the gutter and get swallowed up by the sewer! Of course, once Eldred Barlow was swingin' on a limb when lightnin' struck the tree, and he was split in half and burned to a crisp.

TEDDY
What did I tell you about trees?

LORAINE
But that was a freak accident! Freak accidents happen all the time—not just when it's rainin'. You ought to just gimme your hand right this very minute and let's march outside together and just stand there and say, *I am not afraid!*

MICHAEL
No!

TEDDY
Defy the elements! That's the rule of thumb you apply to everything!
[*Thunder and lightning.* MICHAEL *and* TEDDY *huddle*]

LORAINE
Rain is so relaxin'. I love to sleep in rainy weather. I think I'll get back on the bed right now and try and relax a bit. Excuse me.
[*And she moves out of sight, leaving the door ajar. Pause*]

TEDDY
I don't suppose she's told you, but I'm going to have to take her to Memphis to a hospital.

MICHAEL
Why Memphis?

TEDDY
It's a private place. It's been highly recommended by Dr. LaSalle.

MICHAEL
Why doesn't Dr. LaSalle treat her like he always has?

TEDDY
That old French-fried fart says it's beyond him now. Too many pills and shots for migraines and female trouble and nerves. She's hooked. And I'm going to have to take her to this hospital to get her off and back to where she can manage without being dependent on anything. Willy Mae can take care of you.
[LORAINE *is up in her bedroom by now and has begun to sing "Red River Valley"*]

MICHAEL
[*Hearing her*]
She didn't shut the door.

TEDDY
The rain has stopped anyway. We can go out now.

[*LORAINE continues to sing as* MICHAEL *blows out the candle. Light fades from the scene but he alone remains encircled in the spotlight. He picks up his raincoat and removes a letter in an envelope from his pocket*...]

SCENE 8

MICHAEL
[*Out front*]
Peabody Hotel, Memphis, Tennessee, Dear Son...
[*A spot comes up on* TEDDY *on opposite side of stage*]

TEDDY
[*Out front*]
Got a kick out of your note and I don't mean to be critical but you spelled
"towel" with two *l*'s and "pursue" p-*e*-r-s-u-e. Now, two misspelled words on
one penny postcard is a bit strong to my way of thinking, so I would appreciate it if you would get the dictionary and check these out.

Mama is doing fine. All our fears seem to have been utterly unfounded. I
always suspected she might be a bit of a schizo, but the doctors say she is as
sane as sane can be. They also say that she is uncooperative as hell, but this
is my side of it.

I think you would like the Peabody. It has a very swanky dining room—
maître d' and all—and right in the middle of the lobby there's a fountain
with a lily pond around it and real live ducks quacking and paddling about.
It's all a little rich for my blood, but Mama wanted to stay here and I wanted
to do everything in my power to smooth things over and keep peace before I
had to admit her to the hospital. Memphis, however, is one of the deadliest
holes I've ever been caught with my pants down in. I just can't understand
it for a river town. Absolutely no action. You practically have to go to the
Arkansas side to poop, and once you go, there's nothing but a couple of
buckets of blood laughingly called nightclubs, and one or two package
stores. Man, I've really got the Beale Street Blues. So, as soon as I have
another consultation with the head of the joint to find out how long she's
going to have to stay to get straight, and pay the bill, I'm going to catch the
Panama and leave this burg in the shade.

MICHAEL
[*Out front*]
I.L.U.B.I.T.W.

TEDDY
[*Out front*]
I love you best in the world.
[*Light fades on* TEDDY. *Spot holds on* MICHAEL *as he puts on his raincoat
and...*]

189

SCENE 9

Marian Anderson begins to belt out "Ave Maria" at an earsplitting volume. Lights come up to reveal TEDDY, prone on the kitchen floor, passed out amid scattered phonograph records, snoring. MICHAEL crosses to look at TEDDY a moment, walks around him to turn off the portable phonograph, pick up and look at an empty gin bottle. He raps "shave-and-a-haircut" on the top of the cabinet, waits for a moment...

MICHAEL
Hello?— Anybody home?
    [*Another snore from TEDDY*]
Oh. Out for the evening, as it were.
    [*Pause*]
Here, catch.
    [*And he tosses a set of keys on the floor*]
Thank you kindly for the use of your new car. It's a dilly!
    [*He heads for the stairs, starts to ascend them, stops, looks back, turns, walks
    back to stand over TEDDY. MICHAEL takes off his raincoat and spreads it over
    him and goes up the stairs to his room to undress as TEDDY continues to
    snore, then gets up, gets his bearings, and heads for MICHAEL's room. TEDDY
    enters the room to find MICHAEL asleep. He sits on the edge of the bed and
    picks up MICHAEL's hand. Pause*]
Daddy!

TEDDY
    [*Hushed*]
Yeah, it's only me. Shhhh...

MICHAEL
You scared me!

TEDDY
Oh. Sorry. Shhh...

MICHAEL
Why are you shushing? There's no one to wake up but me.

TEDDY
Oh. Forgot. Sorry. Can't seem to keep track of when the madame is "at home" or the madame is "at sea."

MICHAEL
What are you doing up?

TEDDY
Just holding your hand. Just listening to you breathe.

MICHAEL
I have to get up at five fifteen— I have to serve six o'clock mass.

TEDDY
Oh, I'm so sorry I woke you up. Go back to sleep.

MICHAEL
OK. Good night.
    [*He takes his hand from* TEDDY's, *turns away*]

TEDDY
I'm sure proud of you. Serving Mass has always been a secret yen of mine.
Maybe we could go by the church some time when it's empty and you could
give me a few tips.

MICHAEL
It's a deal. Some time, but not now.
    [*He turns over again*]

TEDDY
What's that nice odor?— Kinda like lemons.

MICHAEL
It's some aftershave I bought.

TEDDY
    [*Reaching to touch him*]
I can't believe you have to shave already—your face is still so smooth.

MICHAEL
That's because I shave. Twice a week.

TEDDY
    [*Laughs*]
I smell like oranges and you smell like lemons. All we need is a couple of
bells and we'd hit the jackpot!

MICHAEL
[*Laughs, then stops*]
By the way, I didn't pay for it, I charged it.

TEDDY
[*Stops laughing*]
Michael, you know I don't like that.

MICHAEL
I know, but I needed it and I had spent my allowance.

TEDDY
Son, you have to watch running up debts that you cannot pay. Your word *must* be your bond. *No compromising.*

MICHAEL
Yes, sir.

TEDDY
[*Going right on*]
It's not that I don't want you to have luxuries. And the money's not important to me—it's the *principle.*

MICHAEL
Yes, sir. I know.

TEDDY
Jesus once said, when someone criticized Mary Magdalene for using the perfume on his feet instead of giving the price of same to the poor—"The poor you will always have with you." So, he meant some things to be used for adornment. But he didn't say anything about charging them.

MICHAEL
Yes, sir. I won't do it again.

TEDDY
Mary Magdalene, by the way, is one of my favorite saints. And one of Jesus' too. This is one of the most consoling lessons in the life of Christ—to love deeply the acknowledged sinner.

MICHAEL
Five fifteen is going to come awfully early.
[*Pause*]

TEDDY
Would it make you happy if I went on the wagon?

MICHAEL
[*Sitting up*]
What did you say?

TEDDY
I don't mean, take the plunge. I don't mean, swear before God in writing.
But I will give you my word that, for a while, I'll dry out. At least till Mama
gets home once again.

MICHAEL
[*Elated*]
Ohhhh, Daddy!
[*He throws his arms around* TEDDY *and hugs him*]

TEDDY
Now, you better get to sleep.
[TEDDY *lowers* MICHAEL *back onto his pillow and then kisses him on the fore-
head and tucks him in*]
Good night. I love you best in the world.

MICHAEL
I love you three.
[TEDDY *exits as lights dim to spot on* MICHAEL. *Pause.* MICHAEL *begins to get
out of bed and put on his pants and shirt as…*]

SCENE 10

A *light comes up on* LORAINE *in her room on the telephone.*

LORAINE
[*Desperately and irately*]
…What do you mean, Dr. Dillon is not in his office—not in his office to *me?*
Is that what you mean! This is the thirty-seven-thousandth time I've called
in the past two days, so you tell that bastard he'd better get on the line or
I'm gonna have the law on his tail for everything from sellin' morphine to
performin' abortions quicker'n he can say Booker T. Washington!
[*Pause*]
Hello?… Hello!
[*And she rapidly starts flashing the telephone bar as all the lights come up*]

MICHAEL
[*Entering her bedroom*]
Dr. Dillon won't help you anymore, Mama. He told you to stop calling him.

LORAINE
[*Putting down the phone*]
I wasn't callin' Dillon! I was tryin' to call your daddy.

MICHAEL
[*Hopelessly shaking his head*]
Oh, come on. You've been hiding from him all day yesterday and today—
pretending you're asleep when he leaves; pretending you're asleep when
he comes in.

LORAINE
He's not comin' in early tonight, is he?

MICHAEL
Let's hope the hell not.

LORAINE
You think he knows?

MICHAEL
He knows it's just a matter of time.

LORAINE
I'm not goin' back to Memphis again! I've been in and out of that place too
many times, and it just does no good! He's gonna have to try it *my way* for a
change.

MICHAEL
You know he'll never go for that.

LORAINE
Maybe if you tried to convince him.
    [*MICHAEL doesn't answer*]
Well, what am I gonna do?

MICHAEL
I've tried to offer a solution.

LORAINE
Oh, Michael, that's so far-fetched.

MICHAEL
You won't listen to me, just like he'll never listen to you. It's a vicious circle.

LORAINE
Everything's a circle and it's all vicious. First, I'm overdue and get one of
those unbearable migraines, or else start floodin', or both. And how long do
you think any human bein' could stand such pain without takin' something
to kill it? The last headache went on for eleven days before I finally gave
in—and then there's no turnin' back. And then, sooner or later, it runs out.
And here we are—right back where we were—not a c.c. of anything left, not
even a bottle of paregoric, and me goin' into withdrawal like greased lightnin'! I tell you, when the Lord put me together, I think it must have been
from the leftovers.

MICHAEL
    [*Quickly retrieves a slop jar from behind the bed*]
Are you going to be sick again?

LORAINE
No. But I better get back on the bed.
    [*MICHAEL helps her to lie down, covers her*]
Is it cold in here to you?

MICHAEL
No.

LORAINE
Oh.— How are things at St. Iggy's?

MICHAEL
Winding up slowly but surely. Boy, will I ever be glad to get away from that
bunch of meatheads.

LORAINE
I just can't feature your graduatin' and goin' off to college in the fall. Where
has the time gone?

MICHAEL
It's seemed like forever to me.

LORAINE
That's because you're young. I was the same way when I was your age. Only
I never finished high school. Hattiebeth did. But I never had the chance. I
went to work when I was in the tenth grade as a switchboard operator.

MICHAEL
Aunt Hattie was the favorite, wasn't she?

LORAINE
That's puttin' it mild. After my pa died, my ma took everything we had and
gave it to her. All I ever got was my ears boxed if I didn't chop enough wood
or pump enough water from the cistern, while Hattiebeth stayed dressed up
like a department-store dummy lookin' out the window at me work.

MICHAEL
Is that why you didn't go to Grandma's funeral?

LORAINE
I had a sick headache that day.— You know, I've often thought that might be
one of the reasons I have these headaches—'cause my ma made me see stars
so many times. I used to think it was from bleachin' my hair—that the per-
oxide seeped right straight through to my brain. And, of course, I never had
anything to take for them. I'd just crawl up to the edge of the back porch
and let my head hang over the side and vomit and vomit. Nobody ever bothered me. Nobody even knew I was there.
    [Pause]

MICHAEL
Are you all right?

LORAINE
Oh, darlin', I wish I could answer yes, but I'm beginnin' to shake to pieces.

MICHAEL
[*Insistent but encouraging*]
Mama, please, instead of thinking of ways of trying to get more stuff—and
since you don't want to have to go anyplace again—let's do it here; go
through it together. Right now, before Daddy gets home.

LORAINE
Oh, darlin'!

MICHAEL
How long does it take?

LORAINE
You don't understand what it's like.

MICHAEL
Yes, I do. It won't scare me.

LORAINE
No. It takes time. I'd lose control. You couldn't manage me.

MICHAEL
Please, Mama, trust me.

LORAINE
Oh, I do trust you. But it's dangerous. I won't be able to stand it. I can tell
that now. I'm chilled.

MICHAEL
I'll fill the tub up with hot, hot water—it'll relax you.
[*He dashes offstage into the bathroom*]

LORAINE
What if I went into convulsions and your daddy caught us!
[*The sound of running water begins.* MICHAEL *reappears...*]
...I can't. It's no use.

MICHAEL
Please. Please try. It'll be the answer to everything. You won't have to go
anywhere and Daddy will never have to know. I'm sure we can do it together. Now, come on!

LORAINE
No! No, darlin', don't try to pick me up. I'm too heavy for you.

MICHAEL
No, you're not.

LORAINE
You'll hurt yourself.

MICHAEL
No, I won't.
[*He pulls her to a sitting position on the bed*]

LORAINE
Oh, I'm cold. I'm so cold!

MICHAEL
The water will warm you up and relax you too. Come on!

LORAINE
[*With a touch of panic*]
Oh, Michael…honey…what am I gonna do?

MICHAEL
Please, Mama. Let me help you!

LORAINE
[*Unsteadily approaching him*]
OK—OK—whatever you say.

MICHAEL
Come on, now. Please, come on!

LORAINE
[*Near the bathroom entrance*]
…My nightgown.
[*She tries to pull the straps down over her arms*]
…I can't get it off.

MICHAEL
Never mind. Just get in the tub with it on. I'll find the scissors and cut it off
you after you relax. Now…please, please…

LORAINE
I'm comin'! I am.

[*MICHAEL helps her out. TEDDY enters the kitchen. He has a paper bag with him. He climbs the stairs to his room, retrieves a glass, removes a half-empty fifth of gin, and pours himself a drink. He is drunk but with a lucidity that alcohol produces when it removes inhibitions— He is in an articulate but violent rage. The following dialogue is offstage*]

MICHAEL'S VOICE
Now, be careful. Don't slip. Don't slip.
        [*There is the sound of mild splashing and stirring of water*]

LORAINE'S VOICE
...Ohhhh...Ohhhh...

MICHAEL'S VOICE
Does that feel good?

LORAINE'S VOICE
...Yes...Ohhh, yes...

MICHAEL'S VOICE
Is it too hot?

LORAINE'S VOICE
...Ohhhh! Michael!... I'm cold...I'm cold!

MICHAEL'S VOICE
I'll turn on the tap—let some more hot run...

LORAINE'S VOICE
No! It's too deep! I've got to get out! I've got to get out!

MICHAEL'S VOICE
Then grab me around the neck. That's right. Careful now...careful.
        [*TEDDY polishes off the drink, sets the bottle and glass down in his bedroom*]

LORAINE'S VOICE
I've got to get back on the bed!

MICHAEL'S VOICE
Hang on! Hang on!
        [*TEDDY enters LORAINE's bedroom just as MICHAEL appears, carrying LORAINE in his arms. The ends of her hair and her nightgown are thoroughly soaked, causing the fabric to become partially transparent and to stick to her skin and reveal her body. MICHAEL's shirt front and sleeves are wet*]

TEDDY
What the fuck do you think you're doing?

LORAINE
[*After a moment*]
Put me down, honey. I'm all right. I'm all right! Put me down and get my
bathrobe!
[*MICHAEL stands her up and rushes back into the bathroom*]
You've fallen off the wagon.

TEDDY
What did you fall off—a diving board?

LORAINE
No, dear. Just the deep end. I only fell off the deep end.
[*MICHAEL returns with a thick, full-length terry-cloth robe. He assists her to
put it on*]
Thank you, my angel.

TEDDY
A certain doctor came to see me today. It seems you owe him a bit of a bill.

LORAINE
Teddy, don't fuss at me now. Please.
[*She ties the robe, moves to sit on the bed*]

TEDDY
Michael, I want to talk to your mother in private.

MICHAEL
[*Flatly*]
I already know about Dr. Dillon. I picked up one of the prescriptions and
had it filled myself.

TEDDY
You *what?!*

MICHAEL
She needed it! She said it would be the last!

TEDDY
You fool! You punk!

LORAINE
Leave him alone, Teddy! I made him do it. So Dillon came by to collect in
person. Well, I guess everybody and his sister Sue knows now.

TEDDY
I guess they do—'cause there we sat in my place of business for all to see—
me and the biggest nigger doctor in town!

LORAINE
All right! So now you know. I get it when and where I can—behind your
back, under your nose! Now maybe you'll listen to reason and try it my way!

TEDDY
Reason! What you're talking about don't make good sense!

LORAINE
It makes as much sense to me as whiskey does to you. I got along just fine
until I couldn't get any more. If I stay in Memphis six weeks or six months, I
shall always be as I am now. I want and need a shot. Why not let's try it this
way for once. Let me have a shot every four hours and I'll never try any way
of gettin' any more. Let me live the rest of my life in as much peace as possible. I think this will be agreeable with Michael.
   [*TEDDY is silent. MICHAEL is silent. LORAINE turns to MICHAEL...*]
Tell him, Michael. Tell him it's all right with you.

MICHAEL
   [*Softly*]
It's...all right with me.

TEDDY
   [*Cynically*]
It's OK by you, is it?

MICHAEL
Maybe it would work.

LORAINE
   [*Trying to be firm but really being desperate*]
I would like to know one way or the other as I'll try and make other plans.

TEDDY
   [*Mockingly*]
Oh, I see.

MICHAEL
We've tried everything else, it seems.

TEDDY
[*Same attitude as before*]
I see. I see. I have to check with my adolescent son if it's OK to supply you with dope—oh, but it's all right because he gives me his approval. And my wife, the dopehead, lays it on the line that if I do not *approve*, she will make other plans.

LORAINE
Now, don't take it the wrong way. *Please.*

TEDDY
[*Heated*]
What's the right way to take it? And why should I take it at all!
[*To MICHAEL*]
I don't have to ask your permission for anything!
[*To LORAINE*]
And go ahead with your other plans. I'd like to know what they are. If you're gonna leave me—all right then, get out!
[*To MICHAEL*]
And you get out with her! You seem to prefer her company—to be in cahoots with her—so be it!
[*He goes back into his bedroom, takes the bottle of gin, starts to pour another one. MICHAEL quickly follows him but keeps his distance*]

MICHAEL
[*Mock disbelief*]
You're not gonna take another drink!

TEDDY
I am. I most certainly am. And I don't need nor want your permission.

LORAINE
Michael, come away. Leave him alone.
[*TEDDY pushes past MICHAEL, going back to LORAINE's bedroom to confront LORAINE directly*]

TEDDY
[*Deliberate innuendo*]
And not *everything* has been tried!

LORAINE
You wouldn't let them give me those treatments! You promised you'd never let them do that to me!

TEDDY
You promised every trip to Memphis would be the last one!

LORAINE
The last one *was* the last one, as far as I'm concerned! I'm never goin' back there again.

TEDDY
You better believe it, you're not! Because I'm not throwing good money after bad. I'll be damned if I let you break me when you have no intention of changing!

LORAINE
That's right! As long as it is there to take, *I am goin' to take it!*

TEDDY
[*Grabs hold of her*]
I am going to have you committed! I'm going to have the shit shocked out of that crazy brain of yours!

LORAINE
[*Rushing to* MICHAEL]
NO! Michael! Michael, take me away from here!

TEDDY
And it won't be in some fancy joint either! I am going to have you put away in the state institution!

MICHAEL
[*Lashing out*]
You shut up! Don't you say those things to her!

TEDDY
[*Boiling*]
You just shut up your mouth, you impudent little shitass!

MICHAEL
You're the one who's crazy!

LORAINE
Michael!

TEDDY
What did you say to me?

MICHAEL
I said, you're the one who's crazy, you goddamn drunk!
[*TEDDY lunges at* MICHAEL]

LORAINE
TEDDY!

MICHAEL
[*Pulling away from him; fiercely*]
Get your goddamn paws off me, you drunken son of a bitch!
[*TEDDY swings at MICHAEL, misses. But MICHAEL violently pushes him in the
same direction he has swung, which causes TEDDY to fall to his knees. The
moment he is down, MICHAEL rushes upon him, beating him with his fists*]

TEDDY
[*Bellowing drunkenly*]
Go on! Go on! Hit me! Hit me! HIT ME! HIT ME!
[*And he starts to laugh. Meanwhile, LORAINE runs between them, tries desper-
ately to pull MICHAEL off TEDDY*]

LORAINE
Michael, stop it! *Stop it! He's your father!* HE'S YOUR FATHER!
[*TEDDY stops laughing, grabs LORAINE by both her arms and hurls her aside
with such force that she is thrown to the floor. She screams. TEDDY now sub-
dues MICHAEL's arms, pulling himself to his feet at the same time. The moment
he is up, he knocks MICHAEL back onto the landing. LORAINE screams again*]
NO! NO! NOOOOOOOO!
[*TEDDY starts to come at MICHAEL again. MICHAEL backs into TEDDY's room,
grabs the gin bottle, and cracks it over his skull, smashing the bottle. TEDDY is
genuinely physically stunned by the impact—stops, staggers forward a step or
two, loses balance—one knee bends and he falls. MICHAEL is frozen with fear.
LORAINE is still crouched on the floor, whimpering. A moment...a tick of the
clock or a heartbeat when all are breathlessly still. Then TEDDY grabs his head
as blood begins to stream down over his face. LORAINE sees it and covers her
mouth to suppress a still-audible, monotonous moan. MICHAEL remains
immobile—transfixed. TEDDY removes his hand from his head, holds it before
him to see his bloody palm*]

TEDDY
[*Incredulously; glazed look at MICHAEL*]
...You!...You've hurt me.
[*He loses his equilibrium and falls forward to catch himself with his free
arm*]

MICHAEL
> [*With increasing volume*]

...Willy! *Willy Mae!* WILLY MAE!
> [*And he bolts down the stairs, yelling*]

CALL AN AMBULANCE! CALL AN AMBULANCE!
> [*He stops at the foot of the stairs, trembling visibly.* LORAINE *has gotten to her feet, staggered to her bed where she collapses, sobbing...* TEDDY *has now crawled to the top of the stairs,* MICHAEL *turns to see him*]

...Oh, God, oh, God, oh, God, oh, God, oh, God...
> [*And he starts to run—this direction, then that direction—then another, and another, until he bolts to the apron of the stage and doubles up on his knees, sobbing... Lifts his head heavenward and screams through clenched teeth*]

...Oh, God! Oh, God— Goddamn you, God. You broke your end of the bargain! *GODDAMN YOU!*

BLACKOUT

Act 2

SCENE 1

A *spot comes up on* MICHAEL, *lying in his bed. Then lights come up to reveal* LORAINE *in her room. A brief pause, and she crosses toward* MICHAEL'*s room. She is wearing a jersey negligee. The fabric clings to her curves and falls to the floor in soft, flowing folds; however, she is dissipated, slightly disheveled, and ill.*

LORAINE
Darlin'? Can I come in?

MICHAEL
[*Tonelessly*]
—Sure.

LORAINE
[*Entering*]
It's so dark in here—don't you want me to open the venetian blinds?

MICHAEL
No, ma'am.

LORAINE
...Or turn on a lamp?

MICHAEL
No, ma'am.

LORAINE
Or turn down the air conditioner—it's like the North Pole in here.

MICHAEL
No. I like to listen to the hum.

LORAINE
Well, it's gonna rain this afternoon and cool off. Have you got a headache?

MICHAEL
No.— How's yours?

LORAINE
Better. There's still a little throbbin' in one temple and I'm weak as a kitten
but I just need some rest.
[*Picking up a box of candy by his bed*]
Chocolate bonbons! Where'd they come from?

MICHAEL
I bought them. Would you like one?

LORAINE
No thank you.— Kinda heavy.— Maybe that's what got you feelin' bad.

MICHAEL
I eat chocolate all the time now.

LORAINE
No more asthma attacks?

MICHAEL
No.

LORAINE
Why, that's the best news I've had since Hector was a pup! You must have
outgrown it.

MICHAEL
I must have.

LORAINE
Well, don't eat too much of it or it'll make you sick anyway.

MICHAEL
I won't.
[*There is a roll of thunder*]

LORAINE
Ohhh! Just listen at that thunder!
[*Peeping out through the venetian blinds*]
We are goin' to have an electrical storm. It is just as hot and still as it can be.
Clouds have covered the sun and the trees, and the grass looks like green
neon.
[*Turns back to* MICHAEL, *crosses slowly toward his bed*]
...Is that why you're lyin' here in the dark, honey? Are you still scared of the
lightnin'?

MICHAEL
No.

LORAINE
[*Sits on bed, takes his hand*]
Why, your little hand is like ice! Michael, you've got me worried. All you've
done this entire week is mope. Seems like the only reason you came home
from college was to deliver your dirty laundry.

MICHAEL
[*Distantly*]
Has it only been a week?

LORAINE
You remind me of some of those vegetables I've been locked up with who
do nothin' but stare into space.

MICHAEL
I just don't feel like getting up, that's all.

LORAINE
[*Continuing to warm his hand*]
Do you miss Washington and your friends at school?

MICHAEL
Some of them.
[*Another roll of thunder. She embraces him*]

LORAINE
—I know what's wrong with you—you need a girl. Come on, now. Why don't
you get up and call up some of your old friends here? Maybe they'll take you
out to the country club for a swim. You like goin' out there, don't you?

MICHAEL
Not always as their guest.

LORAINE
Well, you know your daddy and I don't care a thing about that crowd of
social climbers. He would *never* join, but he has always said he'll pay for your
membership as soon as you're old enough to be accepted on your own.

MICHAEL
I wouldn't go near any swimming pool with it so threatening out.

LORAINE
—Well...why don't you give a party?

MICHAEL
When?

LORAINE
Tonight!

MICHAEL
A party—with you sick in bed?

LORAINE
Oh, honey, don't mind me—you're young! You've got to have your friends!
[*Pause*]

MICHAEL
Wouldn't all the noise...

LORAINE
I won't hear a thing way upstairs in my room.

MICHAEL
But what about Daddy?

LORAINE
Oh, you know he won't care—he wants you to enjoy your summer vacation.
Why don't you get on the phone right now and call everybody and say
you've just decided to have a bash!

MICHAEL
I'd have to have something to serve them when they showed up.

LORAINE
Tell Willy to boil a pot of shrimp and fry some chickens and make a great
big bowl of potato salad.

MICHAEL
Willy won't like the idea.

LORAINE
She ain't got nothin' to say about it. There's plenty of liquor in the house,
and if you run out, there's plenty more where that came from!
[*There is a flash of lightning, followed by a clap of thunder. MICHAEL flinches
visibly, buries his face in his pillow. She puts her arms around him*]

Don't be such a scaredy-cat. No matter what Daddy says, lightnin' won't hurt you. It's really pretty. Look at it sometimes.
> [*No response*]

Move over and let me lie down. My headache is just killin' me.
> [*He slides over a bit and she gets under the covers with him, holding him in her arms. As the light dims on them, light comes up on* TEDDY, *glass in hand, slowly climbing the back stairs to his room. He picks up a pamphlet, settles on bed to read it while sipping his drink. A spot comes up on* MICHAEL, *tying his tie. A piano is playing some Cole Porter in the background.* MICHAEL *goes to the door, raps "shave-and-a-haircut" on it, then quietly enters*]

MICHAEL
> [*Sotto voce*]

Daddy?

TEDDY
Hi. Whatcha doing up here?

MICHAEL
I'm just checking to see if you're home. I didn't hear you come in.

TEDDY
Been here about an hour. Took some of your ice from the kitchen and came up the back way. Didn't want to interrupt anything.

MICHAEL
You always say that. You wouldn't have interrupted anything. You should have come in for once and said hello to everyone.

TEDDY
Now, Michael, you know that's not my speed.

MICHAEL
Just to say hello?

TEDDY
Let's not argue about it, shall we?

MICHAEL
Why are we whispering?

TEDDY
Why did you tiptoe in? We're conditioned not to wake the sleeping beauty in the next room.

210

MICHAEL
If she can sleep through the music from downstairs, she's not going to hear us through a closed door.

TEDDY
I wouldn't take odds on it. Our whispers produce an effect on her eardrums not yet discovered by RCA Victor!

MICHAEL
What are you reading?

TEDDY
Some new religious literature I sent away for and the *What's On in Las Vegas* magazine.

MICHAEL
Well. What's on?
[*Sits on bed beside* TEDDY *and lights cigarette*]

TEDDY
I haven't gotten there yet. I'm still stumbling through the desert with Thomas Aquinas.

MICHAEL
Sure you won't stumble downstairs with me for just a second?

TEDDY
Honey, don't put me on the spot. I'm all for you and I want you to be right along with the next one—but all that to-do is just too strong for me. Let me enjoy my nip by myself.

MICHAEL
…Well…OK. Please don't drink too much.

TEDDY
Don't worry about me getting swacked; just watch out for yourself.

MICHAEL
Do I seem high to you?

TEDDY
No. But you seem mellow as hell.

MICHAEL
Well, let's not argue about that, shall we?

TEDDY
I have nothing against your choice of friends—I mean the fact that they are quite a bit older than you—that doesn't matter. I always ran with an older crowd—it's a great way to learn the score. But they are adults and they can really put the sauce away—so don't you feel like you have to match 'em or you'll wind up on your ass.
[*LORAINE sweeps in, dressed to the nines—hair, jewelry, the works*]

LORAINE
I thought I heard you two in here.

TEDDY
Well now, looka here. I'd say you're dressed up enough to go to a party.

LORAINE
How do I look?

MICHAEL
Like you've recovered.

TEDDY
I thought you weren't feeling well today.

LORAINE
You know me, I can put up a good front. I felt like it wasn't fair to our son not to have one of his parents put in an appearance.

TEDDY
[*To MICHAEL*]
She doesn't want them to think that we're myths!
[*To LORAINE*]
Where'd you get the snazzy outfit?

LORAINE
I bought it ages ago. But it's still in style—simple things always are!
[*To MICHAEL*]
Why aren't you downstairs? What were you two talkin' about?

MICHAEL
Nothing.

LORAINE
Were y'all talkin' about me?

TEDDY
No, God, no, we weren't talking about you.

LORAINE
[*To* MICHAEL]
Well, you ought not to be away from your guests so long.

TEDDY
Then I guess it's left up to you to rectify the situation.

LORAINE
I'm only goin' to stay for a second. Just long enough to let everybody know you do have a mother.

TEDDY
There'll be little doubt of that by the time you leave.

LORAINE
Fortunately I *have* been blessed with the gift of gab. But you can just about win anybody over if you are warm and charmin'.
[*To* MICHAEL]
Don't you be long. I don't want them to think *you're* rude.

MICHAEL
I'll be right down.

LORAINE
[*Takes* MICHAEL's *cigarette*]
Tell me who's here so I'll know what to expect.

MICHAEL
Oh, Mary Jo and Charleen and Jerome and the same old crew.

LORAINE
Charleen Cunningham! Why, she's got children as old as you!

MICHAEL
I don't like her children. I like her.

LORAINE
Well, wish me luck!
[*She exits the bedroom and sweeps down the stairs… Descending grandly*]
Why, Charleen, what a surprise to see you here! And Jerome! I haven't seen you since the Valkenberg-Ortega rites. Weren't they the most gorgeous corpses you've ever seen?
[*She exits as the lights dim, except for the spot which follows* MICHAEL *as he comes center. Pause. He goes to the proscenium…*]

SCENE 2

...to get his raincoat and a valise. Lights come up full on TEDDY *in the living room. He is wearing pajamas and a dressing gown.* MICHAEL *enters the scene.*

MICHAEL
I still don't understand why you haven't written a word since you were in Washington. What's going on? Have you been on a tear ever since you got back—you were well on your way when you left.

TEDDY
I hope you have the Christmas spirit.
[*MICHAEL sets down the valise, notices an oxygen tank on a dolly*]

MICHAEL
[*Removing his raincoat*]
What's the lowdown on this attractive accessory for the home?

TEDDY
In case of emergency. The living room is now my bedroom. Stairways are not advised.

MICHAEL
What happened?

TEDDY
I'd been back from seeing about you for almost three weeks when I just ran down. The doctor said that digitalis wouldn't get my ticker back on the track and that I'd better check into the hospital. The following morning I had a spell, which was later diagnosed as angina pectoris. After the storm and treatment I was released and have been here ever since.

MICHAEL
I knew something was up.

TEDDY
That has absolutely nothing whatsoever to do with why I have not answered your letters.

MICHAEL
[*Referring to the tank*]
I guess one is not supposed to smoke around this thing.

TEDDY

Not unless you'd like us to personally attend Jesus' birthday party. We can go in the next room.

MICHAEL

Never mind. Don't keep me in suspense any longer.

TEDDY

It was impossible for me to write because I was terribly upset by the disrespect shown me, particularly the night I took you and your friend to supper. It's taken time for me to think it out and try to understand why *I* am always to blame.

MICHAEL

Has it ever occurred to you that you might start by considering your behavior?

TEDDY

Believe it or not, I was trying my damnedest to be on my *good* behavior. When I found out that your impacted tooth was nothing and that you'd already recovered, I thought we might celebrate and shoot the works.

MICHAEL

Well, you shot a little wide of the mark. Your behavior, if there can be any doubt in your mind, was insulting and embarrassing to me and to my friend.

TEDDY

A great deal of it could have been avoided by a little tact on your part.

MICHAEL

Why should I have to account for *your* conduct! You *are* an adult, aren't you?

TEDDY

You're damn right, I am. And I am your father too!

MICHAEL

So that's it. What you want is for *me* to apologize to *you*.

TEDDY

No matter what you believe, I did not come to Washington to get drunk. I can do that here. I did pretty well until that night.

MICHAEL

Yeah, and then you got smashed and made up for lost time. Made an ass of yourself in the restaurant and fell asleep in the theater. Snored so loudly that you had to be dragged back to the Willard and undressed and dumped into bed like a heap of garbage.

TEDDY
And you told me that you *hated* me!

MICHAEL
I *did!* And I've got a witness!

TEDDY
And that your mother and I had no love for you.

MICHAEL
You've got a keen memory even when you're fried!

TEDDY
Not such a very long while back, here in this very house, I heard you say to your mother that you wished she were dead. And now, in a hotel room in Washington D.C., you tell me that you…hate me!

MICHAEL
Jeeezuz, we haven't been together five minutes and…

TEDDY
Who held you when you were a baby and had the croup and couldn't breathe? Your mama used to sit up all night in a rocker with you on a pillow. You might not believe it, but I did get up occasionally to check on you. And when you were still frail, Mama would drive to St. Ignatius' Academy and feed you hot soup on the backseat. Several of these times your father was present.

MICHAEL
What do you want, a medal for not letting me suffocate or starve?

TEDDY
I insisted on your being an altar boy throughout school…

MICHAEL
That you certainly did.

TEDDY
Besides which, you had all the material things of life: toys, clothes, money, warm home, the use of a car at an early age, and either one or two idiots worrying about the time of night, watching every passing vehicle to see if it would turn safely into the driveway.

MICHAEL
[*Boiling*]
I still say that if you really loved me so much, you wouldn't have tried to pay me
off so but would have tried to do something about your sorry state of affairs.

TEDDY
What your mother and I do to ourselves has got nothing to do with *you!*

MICHAEL
But it does! I am included whether you want me to be or not! All the three
of us do is torture each other. You call this a home? A home to come home
to? It's a nightmare!

TEDDY
I never wanted this place.

MICHAEL
I know! It was for *me*. Always for me.

TEDDY
Your mama wanted it too. And don't say you didn't.

MICHAEL
Of course I did. I was dumb enough to believe that if it looked legit from
the outside, it must be legit inside!— How many times do you think I've
watched that same street for hours wondering where the hell either of you
were, and when you *did* show up, wondering if you could make it by the
side of the house without taking off half the porch—which you have accomplished on occasion.

TEDDY
Since you were eleven years of age you seemed to have a contempt for me. I
figured it would wear off with the years. But I see you now resent me more
than ever. Certainly you know the only way to overcome this is to bring it
out in the open. According to what you say, the trouble with me seems to be
overdrinking. Is that really all?

MICHAEL
That's too cryptic for me. I'm afraid you'll have to bring that out in the
open!

TEDDY
I remember once I was ashamed of your Aunt Maureen and our home in
St. Louis because I ran with a better financial class of boys. We had neither
electricity nor bath facilities, and your Aunt Maureen was dressed about fifteen years behind the times, and it made me feel backward.

MICHAEL
I am not exactly reluctant to invite my so-called "social-climbing" friends
into this house. Everyone in this town knows exactly who we are—your
place of business is on display on the busiest corner of the main drag.

TEDDY
Everyone in this town is a cornball and you know it.

MICHAEL
It is you who signs hotel registers with your occupation as "merchant."

TEDDY
It's a good word to cover a lot of things! Besides, that is what I am. A tobacco
merchant. But I am not unaware for one minute that Connelly's Smoke
House has nothin' to do with sausages. It's a pool hall. And there are punch
boards and tips on the games and dominoes and a bar that serves liquor in a
dry state and a lunch counter with one of the best short-order cooks this side
of the penitentiary. But beyond that, it is a sports center, a fine one, like it
says on the stationery, "Where All Good Fellows Meet." And you never
need be ashamed of the Connelly background—my grandmother was a nun!

MICHAEL
What do you mean she was a nun?

TEDDY
A novice, that is, and she hightailed it over the wall to marry a brick contrac-
tor who was working in the convent. He was one of the best, mind you, laid
every brick street in St. Louis.

MICHAEL
Among other things.

TEDDY
That friend of yours who was the witness to the debacle in the capital city—
he was a nice boy, but I daresay he'd seen a drunk before in his life. And if
he hadn't, it was an enlightening experience for him. What was his name?

MICHAEL
David Zimmerman.

TEDDY
Oh, yes. Well, maybe he never *had* seen one before. I understand there's not
a high rate of alcoholism at B'nai B'rith.
  [*He picks up a liquor bottle, looks at the bottle, shakes his head, looks back to*
  MICHAEL, *puts it down*]

I received a letter today from Mama telling me that she had convulsions and chewed up her tongue pretty bad.

MICHAEL
I don't care if she chewed it up, swallowed it, and digested it. At least I'd never have to listen to her again.

TEDDY
She had to have three blood transfusions—they had to cut into her arms to find the veins.

MICHAEL
I don't care if they had to amputate her arms—then *I'd* never have to get another letter from her.

TEDDY
[*Incensed*]
She said to tell you she received her birthday gift and was most pleased. And to tell you that she is not able to write you.

MICHAEL
Able to write you but not me.

TEDDY
I didn't think you wanted to hear from her!

MICHAEL
I don't want to hear that shit! That's all I've ever heard. Do you know how I dread getting a letter from her? I start shaking the moment I see the god-damn envelope. I break out in a cold sweat and get dizzy when I finally tear it open, and after I read it, I cry and throw up. If once, if only once, I could get a letter that wasn't a horror story! I am so goddamn sick of highballs and hypodermics, attempted suicides and oxygen tanks, remorse, self-delusions, broken promises, and, on top of it all, God, God, God. God, God!

TEDDY
Stop it! I can't take it!

MICHAEL
You can take it. If you can dish it out, you can take it. And if you can't, have a heart attack right here on the spot and let me watch. Yes, yes, yes, I said it before and I'll say it again, *I wish she were dead and I hate you and I hate her and I wish you were dead!*

219

TEDDY

GODDAMN YOU, YOU ARROGANT SNOB! I'm going to tell you the same as I told your mother the day you left home to go away to college. I said I had your entire education paid for and it was a tremendous pressure off of me and I was not going to be abused anymore by anybody!

MICHAEL

ALL RIGHT THEN, GODDAMNIT. ALL RIGHT, YOU WIN. I'M SORRY! If that's what you want to hear, then Christ Jesus all right, I'M SORRY! PLEASE FORGIVE ME! FORGIVE ME, FATHER. FORGIVE MY SINS. OK?— OK?
    [*Sighs*]
No. I mean it. I do. I am sorry. I am. I am. And I guess I *am* sorry that you aren't a doctor or a lawyer but a cigar-store Indian chief. And that she always behaved like Betty Grable and Lana Turner and never did what Claudette Colbert did or what Irene Dunne done.
    [*Quiet. Pause*]

TEDDY

I hope you will not continue to profane God's name. That's reducing your-self to my class.

MICHAEL

Do we *have* to drag God into this?

TEDDY

And I don't mean, by any measure, I expect you to be a goody-goody. I have no time for them.

MICHAEL

You don't have to worry about that with me.

TEDDY

We do not know who is right or wrong. God will judge us all— So I ask you...that as long as you live...don't ever try to get even with anyone.
    [*Lights dim on* TEDDY, *spot stays on* MICHAEL...]

SCENE 3

...as he moves and sits down.

MICHAEL
[*Out front*]
Dear David...I think the main reason you and I never write to each other is because we feel that if we write we have to write well. I say to hell with that—so for better or worse, here goes. I miss you, you dumb Jew! How I wish I'd accepted your parents' invitation for the holidays. Here it's strictly the same song, second verse. The past few New Years seem only to have introduced a new illness or another operation. Consequently we've been skipping the Sugar Bowl jaunt and deluding ourselves that it's so much nicer to plan a real Christmas at home with just the three of us. This usually consists of my extravagant overdecoration of the house, only to have Loraine spend the day in the local clinic singing "Red River Valley," for me to eat dinner at someone else's home, and for Teddy to wind up blotto on the kitchen linoleum with "Ave Maria." Oh, how I wish I were with you, blotto on your living room rug, singing "Rio Rita"!

But again this year she broke down like clockwork around the end of November, so Teddy has revived the New Orleans gambit in an attempt, I suppose, to take the curse off things. He and I are about to leave now. But first we have to go visit her on our way.

The scenario goes like this: After you turn off Highway 80, just outside of Jackson, there is a short drive on a country road before you reach Whitfield, Mississippi. And to anyone who's ever heard of it, that word in itself is synonymous with, and euphemistic for, insane asylum. Because, after all, that's what it is—primarily. But there are others who are not there on mental papers but who have been legally committed for alcoholism and narcotic addiction.

After you've ridden along the side road for a way, the first indication that you are nearing the place is the appearance of a long double row of tall shade trees on either side of the blacktop. It's one thing to me to drive beneath those welcoming trees in the summertime; whether it is taking her out there once again or passing back through them after a visit, either way, coming or going, in summer that phalanx of green means *freedom*.

But always at this time of the year—or rather, at this time of day on this very same day of the year, the bare branches against the December light are never a thrilling indication that, at last, at least for a while, it is almost over. On this day, there is always a sense of disappointment that already we have arrived...

[*A spot comes up on* TEDDY, *holding a tray on which there are several brown paper bags covering various pots and pans*]

221

TEDDY
[*Out front*]
Give her the signal on the horn.

MICHAEL
There's no need to—there she is waving through that upstairs window.
[*A spot comes up on* LORAINE, *waving*]

TEDDY
[*Out front*]
Give it to her anyway.

MICHAEL
[*Out front*]
Daddy, it's a hospital.

TEDDY
[*Out front*]
Shit, it's Christmas too.
[*Car horn sounds "shave-and-a-haircut-two-bits" as* MICHAEL *rises and goes to the proscenium to collect a gift-wrapped package*]

LORAINE
[*Out front*]
Hurry up there! Hurry up with the key to this ward! Woman, you are as slow as molasses in January!

MICHAEL
[*Out front*]
My God, you can hear her even through a steel door. I sure would hate to be cooped up with her with nothing stronger than vitamin B$_{12}$.

TEDDY
[*Out front*]
She was a wonderful mother to you when you were young. She helped you when you couldn't help yourself. She can't help herself now. Be kind to her.
[*All the lights come up*]

LORAINE
Hey there!

MICHAEL
Hi.

TEDDY
Santy Claus!

LORAINE
[*Rushing forward*]
Oh, my goodness gracious! You both look just beautiful!
[*They all embrace and kiss simultaneously*]
...Oh, look at that package! It's just wrapped grand!
[*To MICHAEL*]
Did you do that, darlin'?

MICHAEL
Not this year. I had it done at the Special Wrapping Desk at Julius
Garfinckel's.

TEDDY
[*Indicating the tray*]
And we got a sack!

LORAINE
Oh, and I bet I know what's in it.

TEDDY
Good old cornbread dressing that Willy Mae made. And giblet gravy.

MICHAEL
And turkey...

TEDDY
And sweet potatoes with marshmallows on the top that Hattiebeth sent.

LORAINE
Well, you know I've never been one for sweets. But it all sounds delicious.
Here, put these down a minute so I can get a good look at my husband and
my child.
[*To MICHAEL*]
I guess I should say my son—you're a grown man, aren't you? But you'll
always be my baby. I love your haircut—shaped so becomin'. And that's
a gorgeous suit. Is it new?

MICHAEL
Uh-huh. I got it at the Georgetown Shop. It's Ivy League.

TEDDY
[*To LORAINE*]
The Ivy League sounds like the Big League, don't it?

LORAINE
[*To* TEDDY, *flirty*]
You look pretty Big League to me yourself.

TEDDY
[*Tongue-in-cheek*]
I still smell like orange juice.

LORAINE
[*Kissing him, nuzzling his cheek*]
Mmmmmmmmmm. You sure do. And a little something else too.

TEDDY
[*Breaking away*]
Oh, Lordy, here we go.

LORAINE
[*Defensively*]
Now, did I say something? I'll change the subject.

TEDDY
[*Directly*]
I told you, Mama, I took a pledge till Christmas Day and I have honored that pledge.

LORAINE
I know you've been good. Your word is as good as gold. I didn't mean anything. You look wonderful. You do.

TEDDY
And so do you.

LORAINE
[*Flattered, fishing for a compliment*]
Do I?

TEDDY
[*Sincerely*]
You sure do. You look just as pretty as the first day I ever saw you.

LORAINE
Well, I tried. I was so excited about seein' the two of you—I've been up half
the night tryin' to decide what to wear—laid out my clothes a hundred
times. It seems like no matter what I do to *myself*, I take such good care of
my things—*they* just never wear out. I hope I don't look tired, do I? I'm not.
Just nervous as a cat with a crocheted tail. Guess you can tell that, though.

TEDDY
You seem fine.

MICHAEL
Yes. Just fine. You look marvelous.

LORAINE
It's just gonna take a little time, that's all.

MICHAEL
Sure.
     [*TEDDY is silent. LORAINE senses this*]

LORAINE
What Mass did you go to?

MICHAEL
Eleven.

LORAINE
Did you both go to Communion?

MICHAEL
     [*Flatly*]
Side by side.

LORAINE
Well, have you had anything to eat?

MICHAEL
I had a glass of water and then a piece of turkey.

TEDDY
I had a drink.— Just one. Just a little toddy to be somebody.

LORAINE
     [*Exasperated*]
Oh, I declare, you two! A piece of turkey and a toddy!

225

TEDDY
We're savin' space for all that good rich food in Noo Awlens.

LORAINE
And all the bourbon on Bourbon Street.

TEDDY
Now, Mama, don't razz me.

LORAINE
What y'all got planned?

TEDDY
Same thing as always.

MICHAEL
Drive down by way of the coast so Daddy can stop at the monastery and see some of those priests who conduct those retreats.

TEDDY
Just to say hello and slip 'em a fin.

LORAINE
You can't buy your way into heaven, you know.

TEDDY
Don't have to. Heaven is my home.

LORAINE
And I know *you* in our old stompin' ground.— You'll have to stop at the Edgewater or Paradise Point...

TEDDY
[*Pleasurably and acknowledgingly*]
...and have one good jolt and some great seafood.

LORAINE
Well, all I ask is, please be careful.

TEDDY
I'm not going to be driving, *he* is.

LORAINE
I know he'll be drivin'—but not all the drunks on the highway are behind the wheel. I mean, be careful about your health. If you don't know it by now,

226

you never will—that when you lose your health nothin' else is worth very much.

TEDDY
That's right. If I don't know it by now...

MICHAEL
Please, let's not have a fight right here.

TEDDY
Who's fighting?

MICHAEL
We are about to.

LORAINE
That's another thing—I don't want you two fightin' on this trip!

MICHAEL
We never fight when there's just two of us.— Well, not as much.
    [*To* LORAINE]
Just like you and I don't fight when there's just the two of us. And the two of you get along better without me.

TEDDY
I guess we don't work in threes as well as we do in twos.

LORAINE
Well, then, since *I* won't be there, try to have a good time.

TEDDY
We *always* have a good time.

MICHAEL
Better every year. Really.

TEDDY
Careful what you say—she might not be in here when you get home next Christmas.

LORAINE
Oh, I'm not jealous of you two! It's just that when you talk about nice places and lovely things, it sure makes me want to be out of here. I wonder just how long I really will be here.

TEDDY
Well, if you would cooperate with the doctors for a change, instead of *defying* them to help you...

LORAINE
I want to do everything in my power to do the right thing this time. Nobody believes me!

MICHAEL
Mama...

LORAINE
I'm really gonna be well and my old self again after this trip here. I *want* to be like I used to be—and I intend to be.— I just don't know what happened to me along the way.
      [*She looks to each of them for corroboration—both are silent*]
I get so put out with myself for thinkin' I'm not able to do somethin' better with my life. I simply *have* to find a remedy for my situation.

MICHAEL
Mama, don't cry...please.

LORAINE
Oh, hell, I'm not cryin'. You think I want to be here! You don't know what goes on—it gets pretty rough.

TEDDY
Aw, Christ Almighty, woman, if you start now, I'm gonna sing "Jingle Bells."

MICHAEL
Daddy!

TEDDY
I'm sorry.

LORAINE
No, I'm the one who's sorry.

TEDDY
Oh, come on, let *me* be sorry.

MICHAEL
Daddy, please...

LORAINE
It's just gonna take time—and plenty of it. But that's what I do have plenty of.
     [*Brightly*]
One thing for sure—it can't be for always.
     [*Neither answers for a moment*]

TEDDY
Here comes the nurse.

LORAINE
     [*Looks to MICHAEL*]
Already?

MICHAEL
Good-bye, Mama.

LORAINE
Good-bye, my angel. Drive careful and have fun and go back to school and
study real hard. Are you learnin' some French?

MICHAEL
I'm in third year.

LORAINE
That's good. Most everything I read has a lot of French words in it, which, of
course, leaves me blank.

TEDDY
Merry Christmas, Mama.

LORAINE
     [*Turns to TEDDY*]
Merry Christmas, Daddy.
     [*They kiss each other*]
It's a shame you have to be married to someone like me. I'll try some way to
make up for everything I've left out all these years.

MICHAEL
I love you.

LORAINE
I love you too.

TEDDY
I love you three.

[*LORAINE moves off as the lights dim to leave only the spot on* MICHAEL, *and the sound of the Gulf surf comes up...*]

SCENE 4

MICHAEL *joins* TEDDY *on a barstool. They both have drinks. In the background a saxophone, wailing some progressive jazz, replaces the sound of the surf.*

TEDDY
The thing I like about this bar—apart from the view and the salt-sea air—is that it never changes year after year. Been the same since the Depression. Makes me feel young.

MICHAEL
Well, they've stopped asking me for my draft card, so *I* feel older.

TEDDY
If *I* lived up in New York City, my hair'd turn white overnight!

MICHAEL
Heaven may be *your* home, but Manhattan is *mine.*

TEDDY
Well, as long as you're doing what makes you happy. And even though the magazines haven't yet bought any of your material, the reports seem to be universally positive.

MICHAEL
It's all Russian roulette, but I love it.

TEDDY
Now, tell me the truth, wasn't Father O'Reilly a honey?

MICHAEL
I liked him.

TEDDY
Only one who ever convinced me I could learn to serve mass at my age.

MICHAEL
I liked him—for a priest.

TEDDY
Oh, I know what must have been going through your mind when I up and write you and say I want you to take an Irish missionary out to a Broadway show and buy him a steak in Sardi's.

231

MICHAEL
As long as you sent the money, I was delighted.

TEDDY
Mama said when I got his thank-you note, I was grinning ear to ear. You played your hand and your heart perfectly.

MICHAEL
I had a wonderful time.

TEDDY
I'm sure you both had a wonderful time—real people! Keep like that and you'll find lots of happy moments regardless of your down-in-the-dumps periods. Don't lose faith in humanity because you run into a few dogs now and then.

MICHAEL
Yes, sir.

TEDDY
[*Takes a sip of his drink. Pause*]
You know that time with Uncle Brian...

MICHAEL
What about it?

TEDDY
I never have forgiven myself for leaving you alone in the house with him.

MICHAEL
You didn't know he'd do what he did.

TEDDY
I should have. He did the same thing to me. Worse, I think, 'cause I was older. He made me bend over. He didn't do that to you, did he?

MICHAEL
No.
[*Pause*]

TEDDY
How's David Zimmerman?

MICHAEL
Boring as hell, probably. He has a sense of humor like a cement matzoh.

TEDDY
You haven't fallen out, have you?

MICHAEL
No, I just smile and mentally do my laundry list while he bores on. I haven't seen him in a while. He's going to graduate school in Washington.

TEDDY
He knows his stuff, though. He's strictly on the ball.

MICHAEL
You liked his parents, didn't you?

TEDDY
I thought they were jam-up!

MICHAEL
I thought you'd like them.

TEDDY
Just don't quite understand why they would choose to send their boy to a Catholic university.

MICHAEL
They're very broad-minded.

TEDDY
Well, I have nothing but praise for them.

MICHAEL
In a crazy way, they remind me at times of you and Loraine.

TEDDY
Please don't compare me with them. They are extraordinary people in my book.

MICHAEL
I just meant...

TEDDY
First of all, the Zimmerman family is a family of love—mother, father, off-spring, and in-laws. Mama makes the home and runs the family—as it should be. Mr. Zimmerman has money and a fine legitimate racket. I don't know how long he has been making the dough, but it don't take long with wholesale maternity dresses.

MICHAEL
And the Connelly family?

TEDDY
Is a family of…

MICHAEL
Of?

TEDDY
Of mother, father, son, in-laws, and outlaws.

MICHAEL
And who runs the family?

TEDDY
Daddy grabs the reins and holds on and tries to run the family. But Daddy is
a thirty-year-old loser who has spent his life being smart-aleck, Casanova,
ne'er-do-well black sheep!

MICHAEL
How old are you?

TEDDY
I was thirty when you were born. The previous ten years of manhood practi-
cally a parasite. Quit school, ran away, lived in crap games and whorehouses.
Finally, *with* one *in* one. Daddy was a dude.

MICHAEL
[*Finally understanding, at last*]
—The satin bedroom slippers.

TEDDY
Got syphilis, got arrested, got wise. Daddy at this turn is not near as smart as
Papa Zimmerman. Daddy doesn't make much money—Daddy doesn't *make*
any money, and he meets sweet Loraine. And shows her the ropes and falls
in love. And marries her. And for a while life is duck soup. Win or lose. Then
the little man comes along and Daddy is really determined to grow up, go to
work, and be the breadwinner. But things don't happen overnight.
　　Daddy is weak as hell through this early period, but as usual, he has his
bottle to fall back on. Daddy and Mama don't seem to hit it off anymore
since he isn't successful at this time—he just don't seem to come up with
the bright ideas that the Cap'n does who, by now, is everybody's boy!

234

The little man is fondled and wooed and pampered by Mama and Aunt Hattiebeth and Uncle Bright Boy, the Cap'n—try to buck that combo with nothin' and then check your blood pressure. Daddy is all wrong—no good, nuts, fanatic, religious crank. Makes no difference, Daddy is determined to bring the little man up to amount to something. Daddy didn't do it right, but he didn't have Mama Zimmerman. Result: interference—no harmony. Outcome: I am still the big louse. Reward: THE KID MADE IT!

[*A moment*]

I feel the difference between the Zimmermans and the Connellys is this: Zimmermans—give proper love, you receive same. Connellys—if you can't figure out your child's resentment, then check up on Daddy and you'll find out that Daddy caused it somewhere along the line. I don't blame *you*—but I will blame you if you don't come through now. Not anytime soon—no rush—just try. I'm glad that you are patient and understanding with your friends. It's a mark of compassion—how I love that word. A great and happy virtue. One that if cultivated can be your source of future great joy; to give and to give in. Just remember, be good, be meek, be humble, but don't let no son of a bitch walk over you!

[*A moment*]

MICHAEL
Funny how warm the breeze is for this time of year.
[*Lights dim. Spot remains on* MICHAEL...]

SCENE 5

A *light comes up on* LORAINE.

LORAINE
[*Out front*]
My goodness, this is such a grand connection, you sound like you're across
the street!

MICHAEL
[*Out front; puzzled*]
Where are *you*?

LORAINE
I'm home again!
[*Sincerely*]
And for the first time in many, many times, Michael, I feel like I can make it
on my own and never have to take anything again.

MICHAEL
When were you released?

LORAINE
Last week. Hattiebeth came and picked me up.

MICHAEL
Why didn't Teddy come for you?
[*Pause*]

LORAINE
Well, that's really why I'm callin' you. He's in Good Samaritan Clinic.

MICHAEL
How bad off is he?
[*Pause*]

LORAINE
Could you manage to get away from your work for a day or two?

MICHAEL
I'm not working.

LORAINE
Do you have the money for plane fare, honey?

MICHAEL
I'll use a credit card. Now listen, Loraine, you hang on till I get there, you hear me?

LORAINE
Don't worry about me. I'm the rock of Gibraltar when the chips are down.
[*Pause. He and* LORAINE *join each other in the playing area*]
He's asleep now so let's not disturb him.

MICHAEL
How are you holding up?

LORAINE
You couldn't kill me with a meat cleaver. All I want is for *you* to get quieted down.

MICHAEL
I'm great. You know, just great. Really.

LORAINE
God, you sound like a Yankee! How do you like my hair?

MICHAEL
When can I talk to his doctor?

LORAINE
He's makin' rounds right now, so it won't be too long.

MICHAEL
Well, what's the story?

LORAINE
Well, his heart is enlarged 29 percent and his ankles are swollen up mighty bad—caused from his heart not bein' able to pump all of the water through his kidneys. So it settles in his ankles. It's called...edema. That's the way the nuns explain it to me, I think. They are so educated, and they seem to think everyone else is.

MICHAEL
What do you think?

LORAINE
I think it's a serious business. He goes off at times and has a wild look, and then again he'll talk perfect sense. But don't get me wrong, with time we'll get everything back in place and try again to make a happier life.

MICHAEL
Are you…are you taking anything?—for your nerves, I mean?

LORAINE
[*Looking him squarely in the eye*]
I haven't had as much as an aspirin tablet!

MICHAEL
[*Gently but wryly*]
You wouldn't tell me a tale, would you?

LORAINE
[*Defensively serious*]
I'd take an oath!
[*TEDDY moans, MICHAEL reacts, gets up, moves over to where the sickroom would be… LORAINE gets up; sotto voce*]
Tiptoe! Tiptoe!
[*Light comes up on another area to reveal TEDDY lying in a hospital bed*]

TEDDY
[*Weakly*]
…Mama…Mama?

LORAINE
I'm right here, darlin'. And guess who else is here.

MICHAEL
Daddy?

TEDDY
…Who is that?… Son? Son? Is that *you*?

MICHAEL
Yes, Daddy, it's me.
[*He goes to TEDDY, kisses him*]

TEDDY
Oh, Jesus-Mary-and-Joseph, I must really be in bad shape! Now, who called you? Who told you about all this mess?

LORAINE
[*Winks at MICHAEL*]
He just decided he wanted to come home.

TEDDY
That'll be the day.

MICHAEL
How do you feel?

TEDDY
Like cutting a rug.

LORAINE
I know it's the truth.

TEDDY
I'm OK—if I could just get my damn kidneys to act. I keep telling myself that if I think about having to have the good sisters catheterize me, I'll pee from now till doomsday. But it seems to have a reverse effect.

LORAINE
That's 'cause you'd like any woman foolin' with your talliwacker, even if she's married to God.
[MICHAEL laughs]

TEDDY
Don't make me laugh. Believe me, it's no picnic.
[To MICHAEL]
Always remember, don't kid around with your kidneys!

LORAINE
Oh, I think you're gettin' well. You're actin' mighty feisty!

TEDDY
You been getting my letters and clippings?

MICHAEL
Every one of them.

TEDDY
I particularly like that little poem I cut out of the *Clarion-Ledger.*— "Year after year I plainly see my son is growing more like me— And for his sake I'm just a bit regretful I'm like me so much."

LORAINE
Awwwww, Daddy!

MICHAEL
I love the letters the most.

LORAINE
What did he say? Things about me?

MICHAEL
Sometimes. But only good things.

TEDDY
I'm happy that you said you had a good time in Noo Awlens at the Sugar
Bowl—even though it did wind up in a free-for-all in Antoine's.

MICHAEL
Give and give in, isn't that it?—even via airmail.

TEDDY
I was a little concerned about how the tone of my last few sermons might
affect you.

MICHAEL
I know my spelling is a washout.

LORAINE
You get that from me. You get all the bad things from me. Of course, you get
your artistic nature from me—although Daddy does love pretty things.

TEDDY
I'm not beefing about your spelling at the moment; however, there is no
excuse for a college graduate to misspell "forty" f-o-u-r-t-y. And on a bank
check too—that's unpardonable! I am referring to the fact I felt you were
being complacent and getting in a rut.

MICHAEL
I'm sorry if I sounded down in the mouth. I'm really very optimistic about
my career—even though I can soon paper my apartment with editors' rejec-
tion slips.

TEDDY
I'm sure everything will work out on schedule. After all, you've only been
out of school a little over a year and a half. With your temperament—if you'd
gotten anywhere too quickly—your head might have swelled up
bigger than my bladder.
    [MICHAEL and LORAINE laugh]
Mama wants to come to New York as soon as the weather is nice.

240

LORAINE

That can wait till Daddy gets on his feet again and I get a little more time
behind *me*. But we do want to see your livin' quarters—we don't understand
what a cold-water flat is. What, no hot water—no heat?

MICHAEL

No, no, it has heat.

LORAINE

Can you cook in one?

MICHAEL

The kitchen's the biggest room. It even has a bathtub in it.

LORAINE

It just sounds godawful to me. Do you have a warm bed?

MICHAEL

Of course I have a warm bed.

LORAINE

Well, I just want to know what you have in the way of comfort. To think of
you in real need would kill *both* of us.

TEDDY

You get your tact from her too.

LORAINE

We'll just never get used to your bein' gone. If you're not sellin' your stories,
are you doin' anything else? I don't seem to know anything much about you
anymore.

TEDDY

Leave him alone, Mama. That's his business. He's a young man out in the
world on his own.
    [*To MICHAEL*]
And on that score I have this to say: If you commit a mortal sin, say an act
of contrition immediately and then go to confession as soon as possible.
Gamble if you must, but don't gamble with your soul. I know you already
know this—just a reminder. And now, I think I'd like to try to use the toilet.

LORAINE

Oh, good! Let me ring for the orderly.

TEDDY
No. I want Michael to help me.

> [*Pause. MICHAEL comes to the opposite side of the bed from LORAINE; TEDDY weakly extends an arm. MICHAEL takes it, begins to gently pull him from the pillow, slipping his other arm behind TEDDY's back. As TEDDY is raised and his feet swing out to dangle in space, LORAINE hurries closer to be of assistance. During this, TEDDY gives out with a faint gasp and all freeze silently once he is in a sitting position. He is pale as a dead man. Pause*]

Oh, Lord, I don't want any cheese—I just want to get my head out of the trap!

> [*There is a moment before both MICHAEL and LORAINE begin to assist him to stand. Then, as they simultaneously start to lift him, he hesitates and gently pushes LORAINE away*]

No, Mama. Michael can handle me.

> [*LORAINE helplessly backs away, then looks to MICHAEL and gives him a little sign, as if to say he has her permission to continue. MICHAEL kneels to put TEDDY's slippers on him*]

Now ain't this some fine come-off! I never thought I'd hear myself say this—but if somebody offered me cold beer right now, I'd have to turn 'em down.

LORAINE
Don't waste your breath, darlin'. Concentrate on what you're doin'.

TEDDY
Since Mama is looking so sharp, if the Yankees win again, I think we'll surely have to bring her to the World Series, but I see no real reason to wait till then. So as soon as you get back, I want you to get tickets to whatever shows you think we should see.

MICHAEL
Yes, sir.

TEDDY
There'll be no trouble selling mine in case at the last minute I can't go. But get those tickets *immediately* and I will reimburse you.

MICHAEL
Yes, sir.

LORAINE
It's too cold yet!

TEDDY
Well, Easter is next Sunday. Maybe the temperature will rise with the Lord.
[*MICHAEL helps TEDDY to stand and assists him to move slowly toward the area that would be the bathroom*]

LORAINE
I pray we don't have a dark and rainy day on Easter. All the little children will be disappointed they can't show off in their new spring clothes.

TEDDY
Old Bess Donahue is out here too—supposed to have died last Tuesday, but she's rallied some and they say, if she recovers, she'll be mental the rest of her life. Cirrhosis of the liver, et cetera...

LORAINE
Alcohol.

TEDDY
[*Barman's yell*]
Last call for alcohol!
[*He pauses*]

MICHAEL
You wanna stop for a minute?

TEDDY
Hell no! I can't wait to get there—when we do, I just want you to turn on the faucet and step away a bit so I won't feel self-conscious.

LORAINE
[*Alarmed*]
Who's gonna hold you up, honey?

TEDDY
I'm gonna hold myself up. I'm gonna hold on to the wall!
[*On his way again*]
Joe Ambrosiani has been serving six-o'clock mass with me every morning till I had to come out here...

LORAINE
On the Q.T., the food in that restaurant has gone down, down, down.

TEDDY
One morning he said to me, "Does Michael still go to church?" And I said,
"Sho', Joe! Did you ever meet a Connelly without the purpose to become
involved? Well, this is involvement in the world and concern for the individ-
ual *is* the church!"

LORAINE
Slow up, Teddy. You're just bound and determined to overdo it.

TEDDY
All I'm worried about is whether I can *do it* or not.

MICHAEL
We'll soon see.
   [*They have arrived at the entrance to the bathroom*]

TEDDY
Now stay out of here, Mama.

LORAINE
Hold on to him tight, Michael. He's so weak he couldn't swat a fly.

TEDDY
Now stand back—stand back for your life!
   [*MICHAEL has led TEDDY to a point where he faces upstage. MICHAEL secures
   him and steps away. LORAINE is a distance apart from them as if she is still
   in the other room. Pause. TEDDY, looking down, then with a horrible, fright-
   ened moan...*]
OHHHHHHHH!!!!
   [*MICHAEL dashes to him, looks down...*]

MICHAEL
OH, MY GOD, THERE'S BLOOD IN HIS URINE! MAMA! GET THE
DOCTOR!

TEDDY
OHHHHHHH, NO!— OHHHHHHH, *SHIT!*
   [*Loraine gasps but does not scream; lunges out into what would be the corri-
   dor, running...*]

LORAINE
   [*In a desperate, earsplitting whisper*]
Doctor! Doctor! Nurse!

MICHAEL
GET MY MOTHER OUT OF HERE, DON'T LET HER SEE!

244

LORAINE
[*Then, farther away, she increases the volume, exiting hysterically*]
SOMEBODY! HELP! GET A PRIEST! GET A PRIEST!
[*Simultaneous to this action,* TEDDY *collapses backward into* MICHAEL's
arms and MICHAEL *swiftly drags him back toward the bed, but* TEDDY *collapses to floor, center*]

TEDDY
[*Wildly in shock*]
Aunt Maureen? Don't leave me! I gotta get out of here! Who are *you?*

MICHAEL
Daddy, Daddy! This is Michael! I am Michael!

TEDDY
Michael? Son?

MICHAEL
Yes! Yes! Your son! Now, listen! I want you to say the act of contrition with
me. Do you understand?

TEDDY
Michael? Michael?

MICHAEL
Yes, yes, I'm here. Now, help me say the prayer. I need you to help me.
Come on, now!… "Oh, my God, I am heartily sorry…"
[*Mumbling in unison, audibly, inaudibly…*]

TEDDY
I…I…

MICHAEL
…for having offended Thee…

TEDDY
…offended…

MICHAEL
…and I detest all my sins…

TEDDY
…all my…sins…

MICHAEL
…because I dread the loss of heaven and the pains of hell.

245

TEDDY
...pains of hell...

MICHAEL
...but, most of all because they have offended Thee my God, who art all good and deserving of all my love.

TEDDY
...love.

MICHAEL
I firmly resolve...
    [He stops. Pause]

TEDDY
    [Looking up directly at MICHAEL*]*
I don't understand any of it. I never did.
    [He goes limp, and MICHAEL *sobs and cradles him in his arms and rocks him*
    back and forth... Slow dim to black]

SCENE 6

Spots come up simultaneously on MICHAEL *leaning against the proscenium with his back to the audience and* LORAINE *seated center.*

LORAINE
[*Out front*]
Dear Michael: Ohh! It's so good to be home again and out of Whitfield. I am gonna put a curl in my hair and work on my clothes and try to look like somebody again. Please take care of yourself, for you are all I have now and I love you more than anything else left in this world.
[*Light change*]
I am back in the A and N building after ten days in hydro, which I wouldn't describe even if the mail from here wasn't censored. But I am feelin' fine. I am also *cooperatin'*. I am gonna stay here this time until I know I can walk out of here and never come back.
[*Light change*]
As soon as I got back home, I decided to let Willy Mae go. I can do what little there is to do around here. I tried to call you but your answerin' service picked up. I know you don't like me to call if it's just for nothin', but it's been so long since I've seen you, I just wanted to hear your voice. I worry about you up there by yourself. You know that as long as I have a place to sleep, so do you.
[*Light change*]
I had a long talk with the doctor today and told him how I regret all the years of not lettin' him help me in some way to help myself. I am disgusted with myself for not tryin' to see things as they really are. I would certainly hate to ever let myself believe that your and my dreams were all in vain.
[*Light change*]
It's imperative that I sell the house. The upkeep here is just too much. I remember a little dollhouse on the coast that I always admired. Who knows, maybe it's just sittin' there waitin' for me. Please let me hear from you and please try not to disagree. This place is just too full of memories.
[*Light fades on* LORAINE *but holds on* MICHAEL]

247

SCENE 7

...MICHAEL reaches for his coat as lights come up. He walks into LORAINE's bedroom. She is in a negligee seen earlier, but now it is terribly faded and worn—not soiled or torn; it looks as if it had been washed and ironed too many times.

MICHAEL

I suppose you're gonna tell me you haven't had anything more than an aspirin tablet.

LORAINE
[*Heavily drugged*]
I suppose you're gonna start in on me again.

MICHAEL

I stopped by the garage where they towed the car to have a look at it. It's a miracle you got out of it alive. It's a total loss—you had let the insurance expire.

LORAINE
It's probably for the best.

MICHAEL

Oh, sure. Now we can't collect a cent, and we can't even sell it—except for scrap.

LORAINE
I mean, it's best I don't have a car. Good riddance, I say.

MICHAEL

It's a good thing you feel that way—especially since you have been booked and arrested and your driver's license revoked permanently.

LORAINE
And if I *wanted* to drive this minute, I'd damn well do it!

MICHAEL
It's a pity you've never felt that hell-bent about your rehabilitation.

LORAINE
What did you do with the paregoric? It's missin' from the medicine cabinet.

MICHAEL
Never you mind what I did with it.

LORAINE
All right then, don't tell me. I couldn't care less.

MICHAEL
You look like you need a dose of paregoric!

LORAINE
You didn't pour it out, did you?

MICHAEL
You're so full of goofballs right now, it's all you can do to speak.

LORAINE
And if I wanted a dose of somethin', I'd get it!

MICHAEL
What would you bargain with at the drugstore? Warmth and charmth?

LORAINE
I don't need any of your cocky college-degree remarks.

MICHAEL
When you are down to taking paregoric, it means one thing—you're broke.
And you can't afford anything better. And times have changed. The days of
bribing a black doctor are over.

LORAINE
Black, white, or polka-dotted, the day that money ceases to talk will be the
day Atlas drops the ball!

MICHAEL
I also found out a few other details which you forgot to fill me in on.

LORAINE
Go on, chew my head off.

MICHAEL
The lawyers informed me that you told the judge in court that you *deliberately* ran into those people in that pickup truck.

LORAINE
I *did!* They were takin' up all the highway. I kept honkin' the horn for them
to move over and let me pass—but they were deliberately drivin' slow and
right down the middle of the road just so I couldn't get by. So I fixed
them—I stepped on the gas and tore off the back end of that rattletrap!

MICHAEL
You could have killed them!

LORAINE
I was so mad I didn't care! Still don't.

MICHAEL
It's beyond me why those farmers haven't sued.

LORAINE
What the hell do those rednecks know!

MICHAEL
We could have lost this house—which is about all we've got left. And now there's nothing to do but sell it before we lose it, or you let it fall down around you.

LORAINE
And the quicker it's sold, the better.

MICHAEL
Well, it's not going to be grabbed up overnight. I only hope we can get a reasonable price for it.
    [*Directly and cutting*]
One that will allow me to reclaim some of our possessions!

LORAINE
I don't have the slightest idea what you're referrin' to.

MICHAEL
To this.
    [*He holds up a yellow receipt*]
It's a pawn ticket, in case your memory needs refreshing.

LORAINE
Where did you get that?

MICHAEL
I found it in your *empty* change purse. I went by the pawnshop to find out what you've hocked—and the only thing that surprised me is how little was there.

LORAINE
[*Pathetically concerned*]
Did that old man sell my silver? Time hasn't run out! He didn't go against
his word, did he?

MICHAEL
No. All the flatware is still there, and your tea set—and the candelabra...

LORAINE
[*Greatly relieved*]
Oh, thank the Lord!

MICHAEL
What I want to know is, *where is your jewelry!* Your solitaire and your sapphire
bracelet and the diamond wristwatch!

LORAINE
You know I never wear any of those unless I'm puttin' on the dog.

MICHAEL
And what is all this about a gun, and where the hell have you hidden it?

LORAINE
The only thing that's been hidden is the paregoric.

MICHAEL
The man said that along with the other stuff you also pawned a gun, but a
week or so later you came back and claimed it. *What* gun? And for *what*?

LORAINE
It's just that little pearl-handled pistol Daddy used to keep downtown in the
safe. I need it now—for protection!

MICHAEL
Protection from what?

LORAINE
Anybody and everybody—thieves—riffraff! I am a woman alone in a large
house!

MICHAEL
I'm asking you again, where is your jewelry? It's not at the pawnshop, it's
not on your hands, and it's not on a safety pin in your brassiere! I looked! All
that's between your tits is a St. Christopher medal.

LORAINE
All of it's in my jewelry box.

MICHAEL
Show it to me.

LORAINE
And that's in the safety-deposit vault at the bank.

MICHAEL
There's nothing in that tin can at the bank!
[*She is trapped and knows it*]

LORAINE
[*Defiant admission*]
They were stolen, goddamnit! And that's all there is to it! I was brutally
taken advantage of by someone I trusted. And I don't mean what you think!
He and I were friends and that's all. He was a very nice man. Cultivated.
Only he was a dope fiend from way back. And he told me he could get me
anything I wanted and that I wouldn't have to pay black-market prices. He
said he had some connections in Shreveport. And like a fool I believed
him.— Don't look at me that way. I can't be to blame every time the wind
changes!

MICHAEL
[*Quietly disgusted*]
Ohhhh, shit. I feel like beating your brains out just to see if they are really
there.

LORAINE
Don't say that, honey. It's already beat me so. But I am not gonna let this
throw me. For some reason, I can't help but think it's for the best.

MICHAEL
Is there anything to drink in the house?

LORAINE
I'm sorry, honey, you know I don't drink.
[*MICHAEL starts to laugh—a little hysterically—not much, just a little, and a
little sadly, and trails off, shaking his head, as LORAINE asks...*]
...What did you do with the paregoric?

MICHAEL
I poured it out.

LORAINE
Oh, no! You didn't!

MICHAEL
Of course I didn't. But if you think I'm gonna give it to you, you *are* nuts!

LORAINE
You give me that paregoric or else. I'm warnin' you!

MICHAEL
I'm not afraid of you anymore. The days of your digging your sharp red fingernails into my flesh and twisting my earlobes off are long gone!

LORAINE
I just wanted you to have some manners and trainin' and be a gentleman. You don't know what the meanin' of bein' whipped is! I was beaten all my life. And so I can tell you one thing, mister, I am not gonna take it from you now. I'll kill you first!

MICHAEL
Give me the gun, Loraine!

LORAINE
You give me the paregoric and I'll give you the gun.
    [*He starts toward her; she flinches*]
Don't you hit me!

MICHAEL
You know you need it. Where's that goddamn gun!?
    [*He pushes* LORAINE *aside, goes to the bureau, tears open a drawer, starts flinging the contents into the air—little glass cylinders clink together and fly out along with lingerie and scarves...*]

LORAINE
You stay out of there! Those are my personal belongin's!

MICHAEL
Christ! Every goddamn receptacle in this house has got needles and syringes tucked into it! I bet you've got hypos hidden in the inner springs!

LORAINE
NO!
    [*They both instantly look at the bed, then back to each other. Suddenly she makes a dash for the bed and scampers into it, up against the pillows and headboard*]

MICHAEL
[*Quickly coming toward her*]
Get out of that bed!

LORAINE
You keep away from this bed!

MICHAEL
Get off that bed or I'm gonna pull you off bodily!

LORAINE
You do and you'll regret it!

MICHAEL
[*Quickly moving closer*]
You heard me.

LORAINE
Don't you come another step!

MICHAEL
You think I'm talking to myself? Get away from those goddamn pillows!
[*He lunges at her*]

LORAINE
DON'T YOU TOUCH ME!
[*He starts to rip the pillows away; she recovers, fighting to prevent his getting the gun. The gun now flashes into view and they are both desperately struggling for it*]

MICHAEL
Give me that fucking gun!

LORAINE
Let go of me, YOU PRICK!

MICHAEL
LET GO!

LORAINE
NOOOOOOOO!!!
[*Screams*]
IT'S MINE! GIVE IT TO ME AND LET ME STICK IT IN MY
MOUTH AND PULL THE TRIGGER!!!

MICHAEL
[*Struggling with her*]
If only you had the guts, you cunt! If only you had the nerve to kill your worthless self on your own time! But you won't! AND I'M NOT GOING TO LET YOU DO IT ON MINE!
[*The gun goes off! She screams again and he finally manages to wrench it from her hands. She collapses back onto the remaining pillows, sobbing hysterically*]

LORAINE
I wish I was in hell with my back broke!

MICHAEL
[*Removing the bullets*]
You *are* in hell! And I am now going to escort you to Whitfield.

LORAINE
[*Springing upright*]
NO!! You wouldn't do that to me!

MICHAEL
[*Puts the bullets in his pocket, tosses the gun into the open bureau drawer*]
Oh, yes I would and *am*—just as soon as I pack a few of your precious garments, of which you take such remarkable care.

LORAINE
[*Forcefully; getting off the bed*]
Oh, no! Oh, no, Mister Big Shot! You're not gonna put me behind bars and walk off to New York City on *my* allowance.

MICHAEL
[*Gathering articles of clothing*]
You have no allowance! You have run through everything he left you and you're in debt over your head. And so am I. I haven't got a nickel to my name. I'm going back to New York the way I came—on my credit card—my *bad* credit card!

LORAINE
Your daddy would die.

MICHAEL
My daddy *is* dead.

LORAINE
Poor Daddy.
[*MICHAEL has now retrieved a small suitcase and is stuffing things into it*]

MICHAEL
Poor Daddy, my ass.

LORAINE
He was good!

MICHAEL
He was a maniac!

LORAINE
Don't you say a word against him!!!

MICHAEL
Don't you defend him to *me!* And damnit, put your clothes on!

LORAINE
You can't take me anywhere! You've gotta have the papers!

MICHAEL
I've *got* the papers! And I've got the fifty dollars—I borrowed it from Willy
Mae. And I've got a tankful of gasoline. And when I see those big green
trees on either side of the road, I'm gonna let out a yell that'll shake the
ghost of Teddy Connelly!
[*LORAINE is wide-eyed with fright. She runs in panic. MICHAEL races after her,
clutches her*]
You come back here! I'm through having you run out in the street half
naked. So help me God, if there is one—this is the last time I'm dragging
you to the goddamn loony bin!

LORAINE
[*Breaks*]
Please, Michael! For God's sake, show a little mercy.

MICHAEL
[*Releasing his grip hostilely*]
My mercy has run out. We are fresh out of mercy, and understanding and
patience, and forgiveness forever!

LORAINE
[*Terrified*]
They'll put me in hydro! You don't know what that means!

MICHAEL
I did not put you in this position.

LORAINE
[*Lashing out savagely*]
Well, your life is far from perfection!

MICHAEL
GET DRESSED! OR I AM GOING TO DRESS YOU!

LORAINE
[*Instantaneous switch to a soft, pleading tone*]
Please, Michael! I beg you.

MICHAEL
There's no use begging me!
[*LORAINE finally realizes that he is serious…*]

LORAINE
Then please…please have the charity to give me the paregoric. If you don't,
I'll go into convulsions before we get there.

MICHAEL
No! You're not getting it!

LORAINE
[*Desperately sincere*]
Believe me, baby. I'll be in acute withdrawal before we're even halfway
there. And God knows what I'll put you through. And…and…Michael…I'm
scared. This time… If I go into a coma—I'm scared I'll die.
[*Quiet. Pause. He goes, picks up LORAINE's Kodak, opens the back, and lets
five small bottles of paregoric fall out onto the mattress*]

MICHAEL
That's all there was left.
[*Before the words are out, she has pounced upon the bottles, tearing one after
another open, drinking them dry, and letting them fall to the floor until all
five empties lie scattered at her feet. Pause*]

LORAINE
I thank you.
[*She slowly gets up from the bed*]
What shall I wear?

MICHAEL
Whatever you'll be comfortable in.

LORAINE
I wanna *look* decent.
[*She starts to wander off to her clothes closet*]

MICHAEL
Mama...
[*She stops*]
...I apologize.

LORAINE
[*She retrieves a dress from the debris on the bed*]
I know you don't mean it, darlin'. I know you're sorry. And if you can believe
it, I am too. Here. Help me get this off.
[*He helps her out of her nightgown and into her dress*]
...Please believe me when I say I never meant to hurt you—of all people. Or
anyone, for that matter. And I *want* you to get as far away from all this as you
can. There's no need of you grievin' your life away over my shortcomings.
[*He turns away. She goes to the living-room area*]
You didn't mean what you said about Daddy, did you?

MICHAEL
Of course not.

LORAINE
I didn't think so. We all say things when we're aggravated we don't really
mean at all.
[*MICHAEL returns to stand before her with a pair of her shoes*]

MICHAEL
[*Extending them*]
Put on your traveling shoes, sweet Loraine.
[*She hesitates. He kneels and slips them on her feet*]

LORAINE
[*Looking around*]
Well. That's the second bullet in the wall. Whoever buys this place is gonna
think there was a firin' squad in that room.

MICHAEL
They'll just know we lived here.

LORAINE
I guess you're right. If I only had the ability to put into words what I would really love to say to you. It's times like this I realize how insecure and no good for nothin' I really am.

MICHAEL
Hush, Mama. I won't hear a word of that.

LORAINE
I know it may sound peculiar, but this living room has always been more like a ballroom, and if you squint your eyes, you would think it's the beach. Let's just sit here a moment with our eyes shut and pretend that a lovely breeze is blowin' in off the Gulf. If we think about it, that's where we spent our happiest moments. We had only moments of happiness—and they were always on the Gulf Coast—but they were enough to make up for a lifetime.
   [*Pause*]
Do you mind if I sing? It might lighten things.

MICHAEL
Be my guest. Sing to your heart's content.
   [*LORAINE starts to sing gently "Red River Valley" as the lights dim, till only a spot remains on MICHAEL…*]

LORAINE
Michael?— Michael?

MICHAEL
Yessum.

SPOT FADES TO BLACK

FOR REASONS THAT REMAIN UNCLEAR

For Millie and Toby Rowland
ON THE OCCASION OF THEIR FIFTIETH WEDDING ANNIVERSARY—
WITHOUT WHOSE INSTIGATION, ENCOURAGEMENT, AND LOVE…

For Reasons That Remain Unclear was first presented on November 9, 1993, at the Olney Theatre, Olney, Md., James A. Petosa and Bill Graham Jr., producing directors. The scenery was designed by James Wolk, the lighting was by Howard Werner, and the play was directed by John Going.

The original cast was:

PATRICK   *Philip Anglim*
CONRAD   *Ken Ruta*
WAITER   *Fred Iacova*

A*t rise, the stage is dark and uninhabited. Through a floor-length window center right, the intense violet light of a dying summer day—poised between late afternoon and early evening—slowly fades up to "half" to partially reveal a light wood-paneled bed/sitting room in the Hassler Hotel in Rome.*

Brocade portieres with sheer center curtains cover the tall glass doors which open onto a shallow balcony overlooking the Piazza Di Spagna. The exterior shutters are folded back, admitting the refracted iridescence. The glass doors are slightly open, and a gentle breeze stirs the gauzy fabric, casting soft patterns across the heavily shadowed interior.

Upstage left on a wide raised platform, there is a double bed with its covers and linen sheets neatly turned down. The headboard and dust ruffle are of the same brocade as the draperies. On either side of the bed, there are built-in night tables above which there are brass "extension" wall lamps in mirrored panels, presently not illuminated. On the stage-right table there is a bottle of mineral water and a tumbler on a tray. On the stage-left table there is a panel of service buttons.

Along the left wall is a chest of drawers with a Venetian-style mirror above it. On top of the chest, there is a handsome toiletry case and various smart toilet articles in evidence—cologne, talcum, a comb and brush. A door center left leads to a marble-walled bath. Luxurious towels, featuring the name and logo of the hotel, can be seen folded over a brass warming rack.

Downstage of the bathroom door, against the wall, there is a luggage stand with an expensive suitcase on it. Out from the wall, almost at the curtain line, there is a low drumlike upholstered dressing stool.

Within wood-paneled arches, supported by slender marble columns, in the up-center-right and stage-right walls of the sitting area, there are unlit Venetian-style glass sconces with half shades. Standing away from the walls, there is a brocade settee facing front, a brocade lounge chair angled stage right of it, and a low drinks/coffee table before them.

(All the wooden pieces of furniture are reproductions of traditional Italian designs of the eighteenth century. The upholstered ones are of the fascist period.)

A man's pale gray linen suit on a Hassler clothes hanger is neatly folded over the back of a chair. In a flat wicker basket on the seat of the settee, there are some stacks of colorful shirts and some white silk boxer-style undershorts which have been returned from the hotel laundry. The basket is covered with a piece of paper on top of which sits a pair of freshly shined Italian loafers.

The door to the public corridor is upstage center. After a moment, it is unlocked from the outside. It is a bolt of the European variety, which requires several revolutions of the key. Presently, two male figures enter, silhouetted to the audience by the light spill from the hallway. Even in the chiaroscuro, it is apparent that the FIRST MAN *is in dark apparel, the* SECOND *in light-colored clothing, and that both are wearing sunglasses. The* SECOND *is laden with shopping bags from smart stores on the Via Condotti.*

265

It is just after six p.m., and a nearby church bell is ringing the Angelus.

FIRST MAN
[*Crossing to balcony, with enthusiasm*]
—*Dio mio*, as they say, just look at that view!— Oh, I was hoping your room
would be on the front of the hotel and have a view of the steps and piazza!
[*He parts the sheers, widens the doors, and scans the view. A long shaft of
cool, purplish light bisects the room. Street sounds rush in. The bells louden.
The second man closes the entry and goes through the shadows to deposit the
shopping bags on the bed*]
Magnificent! Is that the dome of St. Peter's in the distance?— What am I
saying—of course it is!
[*Pointing*]
I'm staying just to the right of it.— My God, that's a heavenly sight!
[*The SECOND MAN stands silently observing the FIRST MAN for a moment
before snapping on the lamp on the night table, introducing a small pool of
warm, rosy light to the area surrounding him. In spite of his dark glasses, he
is revealed to be in his early forties, trim and average-looking, but well-
groomed in a creased ecru linen suit and soft white shirt without a tie*]

SECOND MAN
—Yes. And magic hour, to boot.— Very picture-postcard, don't you think?
[*The FIRST MAN, at the balcony window, observing the view (through his sunglasses), turns inside to reveal that he is in his late fifties, dressed in the black
garb and Roman collar of a priest*]

FIRST MAN
Oh, if only I could stamp and mail this moment!
[*Turns back to react to bells tolling*]
—And just listen, Patrick…the Angelus, so *near* you can almost touch it!

PATRICK (SECOND MAN)
Mmm.— Almost, but not quite.

FIRST MAN
—Is it coming from Trinità dei Monti next door?

PATRICK
Too far away for that, Father.

FIRST MAN
[*Faces Patrick again*]
Now, please, do call me Conrad. Father sounds so…

PATRICK
Paternal?

CONRAD (FIRST MAN)
—*Respectful!*

PATRICK
[*Putting room key in side jacket pocket*]
You must take off your sunglasses so you can really get the full-tilt
"schmear."

CONRAD
[*Re sunglasses*]
Ohh! Had them on so long I completely forgot! Wear them all the time in
California. I really don't like the sun much.

PATRICK
Well, then, you live in the wrong place if you don't like to be sun-kissed.

CONRAD
—Maybe it's something I inherited from my mother. She never liked the
sun. Said she couldn't see for the light!
[*Picking up from before*]
The full-tilt *what?*

PATRICK
Schmear. The whole deal.

CONRAD
[*Comprehending*]
Oh.— That's not Italian, is it?

PATRICK
Yiddish.

CONRAD
Oh.
[*Removes his glasses, turns back to luxuriate in the view*]
—Oh, oh, oh, oh, *ohhhhh!*— Well, yes, that *does* make a difference! Now I can
really see what's going on!
[*Turns back to PATRICK, who now slowly takes off his glasses*]

PATRICK
—And now we can see each other too.
[*Dryly*]
And not through rose-colored glasses.

CONRAD
[*Laughs*]
Yes, finally! I couldn't make out your eyes behind your shades at lunch.
From here they look blue. Very, very blue.

PATRICK
—They're green. It's the light playing tricks.
[*Looks away*]
And *your* eyes are...

CONRAD
Bloodshot, probably, after all that wonderful wine!

PATRICK
[*Staring off*]
—Brown. Dark, dark brown.

CONRAD
—It's the black Irish in me. I must say, you have better sight than I do.
[*Re bells*]
—Ahh, just listen to that!— Such a clean sound.
[*Turns out, listens; after a moment*]
—Where do you think it's coming from, San Silvestro?— Or one of the
churches in the Piazza del Popolo?

PATRICK
Who knows? In this town church bells ring like telephones.
[*PATRICK moves around to the other side of the bed as CONRAD steps back into
the room. PATRICK begins to empty the shopping bags and put the contents
away (Armani trousers, Gucci agenda boxes, brand-name cologne bags, and
a Cartier watch case)*]

CONRAD
Such a treat, isn't it?—coming from Los Angeles, where you never hear
church bells at all!

PATRICK
[*Aside*]
Mmm. The lost Angelus of Los Angeles.

CONRAD
[*Chuckles*]
Isn't that odd?

PATRICK
[*Wryly*]
One more odd thing.

CONRAD
You mean about L.A.?— Or our both *being* from L.A.?

PATRICK
That too.

CONRAD
Absolutely incredible! Imagine, meeting each other halfway round the
world!
[*Turns to the open window, listens*]
—Such a reassuring sound! We're really cheated in L.A. It's so spread-out,
we can't even experience one of the most reassuring things in the world.

PATRICK
For me, one of the most reassuring things in the world is a plate of pasta.

CONRAD
[*Hesitates, then laughs*]
Well, then, you're in the *right* place!

PATRICK
And so are you if it's ding-donging that you find reassuring.
[*CONRAD becomes aware that PATRICK is staring at him, turns toward him as
they both listen to the bells for a moment*]

CONRAD
There's that faraway look of yours again. What are you thinking, if I may
ask?— You seem lost.

PATRICK
[*Focusing*]
Forgive me.
[*After a moment, agreeably*]
—I must admit, I too love to hear bells tolling.— But for some reason the
sound always makes me sad.

269

CONRAD
Sad?

PATRICK
It's a melancholy sound. But, at least, a bell is something civilized man has made when he's made so many terrible things.

CONRAD
The call of angels.

PATRICK
A bell is an elegant…noble creation—as admirable as the quaint little rituals man's invented for ringing his brainchild.

CONRAD
[*Amused*]
You mean a "quaint little ritual" like the Angelus.

PATRICK
That too. The Angelus, the time of day, New Year's. All ring-out-the-news occasions are all the same to me, no matter what. And no matter how joyous—even if it were the end of a war—I don't know, it's a plaintive sound.

CONRAD
Funny—I think just the opposite. Even a bell tolling at a funeral is a joyous sound to me. I remember that, when my mother died, thinking that she was so much better off.

PATRICK
Well, I do find a death knell joyous! You think it's just the beginning of something. I think it's joyous because it's the end.— *Finally!*— Over!— Hallelujah!—I *hope!*

CONRAD
Now, don't tell me you don't believe in the hereafter.

PATRICK
Let's just say, I believe in the *future*.

CONRAD
And when we die?

PATRICK
I can't conceive of what might be in store, but I hope that when this is over, *that's it.* I don't want any more. Bad or good.— And how good can it get? I can't think of anything more maddening than an eternal orgasm.
[*CONRAD chuckles a bit self-consciously.* PATRICK *snaps on the left bedside lamp, widening the warm circle of light*]

CONRAD
—Nice little room you have here!

PATRICK
It's majestic. But I call it home.
[*The Angelus ceases as* PATRICK *comes around the bed and crosses to the panel in the upstage wall, right of the corridor door...* Indicates]
Please...sit anywhere you like.

CONRAD
Thank you.

PATRICK
[*Re suit and basket on the settee*]
That is, anywhere you can find a seat. Here, let me get the laundry out of the way.

CONRAD
It must cost a fortune to stay here.
[*CONRAD crosses from the window toward the settee...*]

PATRICK
Well, I'm not paying for it, the brothers Warner are.— And, *yes*...it costs a *fortune* to stay here.
[*CONRAD laughs as* PATRICK *snaps on a wall switch, illuminating the sconces, which infuse the stage right sitting area with the same rosy glow as stage left. Crossing down behind settee*]
Sorry things are messy.
[*CONRAD has reached the chair first, picks up the hanger with the pale linen suit...*]

CONRAD
Such beautiful clothes.

PATRICK
As you've probably heard—they make the man.
[*PATRICK leans over the settee to pick up the wicker basket of laundry with the shoes on top and takes the hanger from CONRAD*]

CONRAD
Such beautiful shoes.

PATRICK
If the shoe fits, charge it!
[*PATRICK goes to the bed, puts down the wicker basket, picks up the shoes and takes them to the upholstered dressing stool, drops them on top of it, and takes the suit of clothes into the bathroom*]

CONRAD
[*During the above*]
You should see *my* room!— Like the inside of a crashed plane! Compared to me, you're the very soul of immaculacy.

PATRICK
[*Offstage*]
"The soul of immaculacy!" That sounds so Catholic—when all I am is anal-compulsive.— Anyway, it's all show. Inside, I'm...well...

CONRAD
What?

PATRICK
[*Offstage*]
Like the inside of a crashed plane.— You say you're staying on the right side of St. Peter?
[*CONRAD settles on the left arm of the settee*]

CONRAD
Well, I always try to stay on the right side.
[*Chuckles*]
A big old palazzo which is a convent now. The nuns are away for the summer.— Of course, my room is nothing grand like this.
[*PATRICK reenters, goes to pick up the pair of loafers on top of the dressing stool, and sits down on it. He starts to take off his shoes and put on the loafers*]

PATRICK
The first time I came to Rome I stayed in a place laughingly called the Grande Hotel—not the famous, fancy one near the Piazza della Repùbblica—a little dump in Trastevere. It was so awful, in fact, that I stumbled home pissed-out-of-my-mind one night, took a Magic Marker, and in front of the name, I printed the words "Not Very." The *padrona* wasn't at all thrilled I'd rechristened his establishment the "Not Very Grande Hotel."
    [*CONRAD laughs. PATRICK finishes changing shoes*]

PATRICK
    [*Re loafers*]
Ouu, does that feel better! *My* mother always used to say there's nothing that relaxes you like changing your shoes.— Would you like a pair of slippers? I just charged some very smart velour ones the other day. We look to be about the same size.

CONRAD
    [*Hesitantly*]
Oh, no, I don't think...

PATRICK
    [*Gets up*]
Please.— Get comfortable and stay awhile.

CONRAD
    [*Relenting*]
Well, I have been on my feet since dawn. You walk much more in Rome than in New York even. And, of course, in L.A. you never walk anywhere at all.
    [*PATRICK exits into the bath, taking his original pair of shoes with him as CONRAD crosses to the dressing stool...*]

CONRAD
—If you've been here three months and the movie studio is paying for it, why haven't you rented a place?
    [*PATRICK returns with a pair of black velour slippers. CONRAD starts to take the slippers from PATRICK, but PATRICK puts his hand on CONRAD's shoulder and gently pushes him down on the stool, then kneels before him and begins to unlace his shoes...*]

PATRICK
    [*During the above*]
I'm a hotel boy. Love hotels. Lived in the Algonquin for four years.

273

CONRAD
The Algonquin? Oh, yes. The place with the famous table.
[*PATRICK removes CONRAD's shoes and puts the slippers on his feet*]

PATRICK
Checked in one night when a play of mine was in rehearsal. The play closed,
but I stayed on. And on and on. Till the money ran out. To me, being in a
hotel is like being in a wonderful hospital where all the doctors and nurses
are dressed up in disguise as waiters and maids. Room service is my idea of
therapy!

CONRAD
[*Re PATRICK's action*]
You make a pretty good valet!

PATRICK
[*Wryly*]
You're a servant of the Lord, and I'm a servant of the servant of the Lord.
[*Finishing*]
—There now. Isn't that better?

CONRAD
Ohh my, yes!

PATRICK
Good.

CONRAD
[*Re slippers but also glancing at PATRICK*]
Very handsome, indeed.

PATRICK
Yes, I liked them so much I took them in every color, but the black seems to
suit you.— And speaking of room service—what can I offer you?
[*PATRICK takes CONRAD's shoes, stands, and crosses to place them neatly
beneath the luggage rack. CONRAD rises and walks around in a circle, getting
the feel of the slippers, ending up down right*]

CONRAD
I really shouldn't have any more.

PATRICK
Not even a coffee?

CONRAD
Well, I wouldn't say no to a coffee before I go.

PATRICK
I never say no to a coffee when I'm in Italy. It never tastes the same anywhere else in the world, I don't know why.

CONRAD
Well, you're a connoisseur. Man about several towns.

PATRICK
I'm just a country boy. Shucks, what do I know?

CONRAD
Some country boy!— You like your Italian coffee in Italy, your French fries in France...

PATRICK
[A droll sigh]
My Turkish baths in Turkey.

CONRAD
You say that so wearily.

PATRICK
I say that nostalgically.
[Changing subject]
—Now, about that coffee.

CONRAD
[Looks at his watch]
—You're sure you have the time?

PATRICK
I have nothing but time. That's why I invited you back.— You said you like Sambuca?

CONRAD
[Relenting]
Yes, I do.— I probably shouldn't have any more, but—well, yes, an espresso will send me on my way. And a *liquore*.— Is that how you say it?
[PATRICK *starts to cross to the panel of service buttons on the stage left bedside table*]

PATRICK
[*En route*]
Sounds good to me.— I'll ring for the floor waiter.

CONRAD
In a moment, if that's all right.
[*PATRICK stops, looks at CONRAD. CONRAD moves back to the window.*
Re view]
—I'd just like to take all this in a bit longer.

PATRICK
No rush. We'll just go *piano-piano*.

CONRAD
Did you learn to speak Italian just by being here?

PATRICK
Oh, I don't speak it. Even after years of coming here.

CONRAD
You did very well at lunch.

PATRICK
Menu Italian, that's all. I have no talent for languages. I put the sin in syntax.

CONRAD
[*Smiles*]
—But it's obvious you have a talent for living.— Thanks again for the extravagant meal! I like eating late. So long and leisurely. And for the drinks on the way back at the Caffè Greco.

PATRICK
Meals are included in the deal.

CONRAD
Lunch was on the brothers Warner?

PATRICK
[*Nods*]
Mmmm.— And it cost them a *fortune!*

CONRAD
[*Chuckles*]
Well, I thank you anyway. You're very gracious and hospitable. You spare no expense.

PATRICK
It's almost impossible for me to do anything cheap.— Almost.— Especially with other people's money.

CONRAD
[*Laughs*]
God bless that expense account!

PATRICK
[*Grimly*]
Believe me, Father, it's small compensation for what one is put through.

CONRAD
Please. Call me Conrad.
[*PATRICK doesn't respond.*
Expansively]
—Seriously, this has all been such a treat! And all in Rome. As close as you can get to heaven!— The Holy City, the holiday, the high life!

PATRICK
A real summer cruise.

CONRAD
Oh, and am I dreading when the boat docks. I'll never forget this trip. It's made such an impression on me.

PATRICK
Funny how some things make an impression and others make no impression at all—like, do you remember where you were when Reagan was shot?

CONRAD
—I must admit, I get excited by all these luxuries which seem to exhaust you.

PATRICK
Please, don't misunderstand. It's writing to the dictates of a committee that gets me down. It's the traditional, time-honored, fraudulent, formulaic bull-shit of Hollywood that wears me out.— Not what it can pay for.

CONRAD
[*Chuckles*]
No respect for writers or the written word?

PATRICK
—Hollywood: nothing but brilliantly packaged lies.

CONRAD
Hollywood must package what it packages for a reason.

PATRICK
Lies sell tickets. Shit sells.

CONRAD
If it upsets you, why do you stay in such a profession?

PATRICK
[*Gestures about the room*]
I make a very good living selling shit.

CONRAD
You sound bitter.

PATRICK
[*Wryly*]
As bitter as that Campari you had before lunch.
[*After a moment*]
Funny how everything you place your trust in turns around and dumps on you.

CONRAD
I hope you don't believe that's always the case.

PATRICK
Sorry if it sounds a tad self-pitying, but I think it's been the case for me.

CONRAD
I'd say it sounds more cynical.

PATRICK
I'm not ashamed of being cynical. I think being cynical is just being realistic.
[*Sits on the edge of the bed platform; with a heaviness*]
—I must say, I'm bone-tired of the grind-of-it-all. Exhausted by the last go-round with this script. Believe me, it takes a velour slipper now and then to keep one's spirits up.

CONRAD
Of course, I don't know anything about how true show business is—but from the outside, it always *looks* and *sounds* glamorous.

PATRICK
I suppose it can be, but most of the time it's just like anything else—very hard work.— People in the entertainment business work hard at putting on a show for those who've worked hard all day and need to be entertained. And them that totes the weary load see a show and look at all the so-called glamorous entertainers having what looks like a lot of fun. And these glum folks with their noses pressed against the glass think they're missing out on something—when all they're missing out on is the very thing they're sick and tired of—hard work. In the end it's a joke all the way round. Everyone working hard and, most of the time, not having much fun. And everyone fed up and longing for something that doesn't exist. That's show business, and that's life.

CONRAD
You *are* cynical. But life can be wonderful. This day has been wonderful for me. And I wish it had been for you too. After all, we have a lot in common.

PATRICK
Such as?

CONRAD
—When the weary come to me, I don't entertain them, but I try to send them off refreshed…and not with lies, of course, but with the truth.

PATRICK
There's a market for everything. You sell your brand of shit, and I'll sell mine.
    [*Silence. After a moment, CONRAD stands…*]

CONRAD
—May I indulge in my little vice?

PATRICK
What?
    [*CONRAD takes a pack of cigarettes from a side pocket of his jacket…*]

CONRAD
May I smoke in here?

PATRICK
Of course.
[PATRICK *gets up off the bed platform, goes to pick up an ashtray from the* *chest of drawers and crosses to* CONRAD, *placing it on the low table*]

CONRAD
[*Re ashtray*]
Smoking in the restaurant—well, in that little enclosure of hedges on the street—that was one thing, but in your bedroom…

PATRICK
Oh, I don't care. When in Rome…
[CONRAD *laughs.* PATRICK *takes a matchbook from the ashtray, lights* CONRAD's *cigarette*]

CONRAD
[*Re the light*]
Thank you.

PATRICK
—Living in L.A., I think it really would be hypocritical of me to get all bent out of shape about the quality of *air.*

CONRAD
Oh, but you know how people can be about secondary smoke. Actually, we're back where we started—fifty years ago we had to go behind the barn to do it, and that's where we have to go again!
[PATRICK *goes to the bed to remove the paper from the wicker basket and gather up a few shirts. He crosses down left to open the top of the suitcase on the luggage rack and begins to pack them.* CONRAD *takes a long drag on his cigarette*]

PATRICK
Do sit down and make yourself comfortable.— I'm sorry, but did you tell me why you're in town?

CONRAD
In town? You mean the *Vatican?*

PATRICK
And environs.

CONRAD
You know, there were times at lunch when I believe I completely lost your attention.

PATRICK
I apologize if I drifted off. Staring into space is one of my favorite things.

CONRAD
No need to apologize, you weren't rude at all. I just had the impression that sometimes we weren't really connecting.

PATRICK
Actually, my thoughts never left you for a moment—even when I got lost in them.

CONRAD
I hope you don't mind my saying so, you struck me the same way when I approached you on the street and spoke to you.— You seemed to be just standing there in your own world.

PATRICK
    [*After a moment*]
Yes, you sort of woke me up—I couldn't have written a better scene.

CONRAD
It *was* a bit like a movie, wasn't it?

PATRICK
Mmm. A real meet-cute.

CONRAD
A *what*?

PATRICK
Meet-cute. I suppose the classic example is when Claudette Colbert meets Gary Cooper shopping for pajamas. She only sleeps in the tops, and he only sleeps in the bottoms, so they buy one pair and split them. They meet-cute. And, it goes without saying, live happily ever after.

CONRAD
Ohh.— And *our* scenario?

PATRICK
Let's see.— Ohh, American religious, lost in the Holy City, looking for God or whatever—and along comes Godless American, lost in his head, looking for God knows what.

CONRAD
    [*Chuckles*]
I see. We met-cute.

281

PATRICK
Well, close but no pajamas. And who knows where the story goes from there.

CONRAD
Well, I, for one, hope we know each other happily ever after.— Imagine!
The first person I stop in that maze of little alleyways to ask directions was
another American from Los Angeles who knows his way around like a
native! What are the chances of that?

PATRICK
Slim.

CONRAD
Just imagine!

PATRICK
—But the *world* is just a maze of little alleyways, isn't it? We might have
bumped into each other anywhere.

CONRAD
—Or we might not have.

PATRICK
Or we might not have.

CONRAD
Now that I've met you, Patrick, I do hate to think of that.

PATRICK
Who can fight fate?— Now, remind me why you're here.

CONRAD
Well, actually I'm here on business, but it's been a lifelong dream to see this
city. St. Peter's city—the rock upon which the church is built. But no harm
in mixing a little business with pleasure.

PATRICK
Oh, yes, pleasure. I was focused for that part.— And the business?

CONRAD
I'm attending a conference.

PATRICK
    [*Groans*]
Ohh, conferences. I must have been staring into space for that part.
    [PATRICK *turns his attention to the laundry on the bed, goes to it*]

282

CONRAD
—A series of lectures, actually.

PATRICK
Contraception, women priests, gay rights, that sort of thing?

CONRAD
[*Laughs*]
Well, not quite. Not yet!

PATRICK
Maybe on your next trip.

CONRAD
If I ever come back.

PATRICK
Maybe by then celibacy will be out and priests will be married.— If that's
their bent.

CONRAD
I must admit I'm more for tradition. I'm one of those who even wish it were
all still in Latin.

PATRICK
Well, lots of luck and *Dominus Vobiscum*.

CONRAD
In my opinion, celibacy isn't going to go so easily. Because in many ways, I
think it is a good thing.

PATRICK
Name one.

CONRAD
Well...it keeps a man from having to think about so many things that have
nothing to do with his vocation.

PATRICK
Oh, come on, Father. Celibacy never stopped one human being from thinking about things he shouldn't be thinking about.
        [CONRAD *gets up, stubs out his cigarette in the ashtray on the low table and
        crosses toward* PATRICK. PATRICK *takes part of the stack of shirts and moves
        away from the right side of the bed before* CONRAD *reaches him.* CONRAD *studies
        the contents of the wicker basket.* PATRICK *crosses from the suitcase back to the left
        side of the bed, standing opposite* CONRAD, *and scoops up the rest of the shirts*]

283

CONRAD
Beautiful shirts. Like so many Easter eggs.

PATRICK
I try to get a little color in my life.

CONRAD
Beautifully finished.

PATRICK
They're brilliant at washing and ironing in this country. It's still done the old-fashioned way with such care and thoughtfulness, it's almost like forgiveness!

CONRAD
Extraordinary undershorts.

PATRICK
[*Smiles, crosses back to suitcase*]
They're lavish.

CONRAD
—Silk?

PATRICK
Mmm, pure silk.— *Seta pura.*

CONRAD
Italian, of course.

PATRICK
[*Nods*]
Local threads.
[PATRICK *takes a handful of the silk shorts and goes back to the suitcase.* CONRAD *comes closer to the bed and extends a hand to finger the edges of a remaining pair of silk shorts*]

CONRAD
Custom-made?

PATRICK
Just the shirts.— The shorts are from the shirtmaker's marvelous little haberdashery. Wonderful robes and scarves—*slippers*, of course, and…oh, I don't know, odd things.

CONRAD
Beautiful.
[*CONRAD withdraws his hand as* PATRICK *returns and collects the rest of the shorts and transfers them to the suitcase.* CONRAD *turns and begins to slowly circle the sitting area of the suite, up right behind the settee.* PATRICK *closes the suitcase and goes to take the empty wicker basket off the bed and put it on the top of the chest of drawers. He looks up into the mirror to watch* CONRAD *as he takes out his pack of cigarettes, removes one, and lights it, stopping at the window to blow out the match and toss it over the balcony. He puts the pack in his inside breast pocket*]
The Italians really know how to do it, don't they?

PATRICK
They do, indeed.

CONRAD
Wonderful style in everything.

PATRICK
They're really with-it about the general *presentation* of life.— Which is *love*, I suppose.

CONRAD
[*Looks out at the city*]
Yes, it seems to be in the air here.

PATRICK
Sort of secondary, you might say. You just breathe it. Good for every organ.
[*CONRAD laughs, turns back, and goes to the ashtray on the lower table.*]

CONRAD
[*Crushing his cigarette*]
Enough of this self-pollution! I think I'll just get used to inhaling *amore*.

PATRICK
Ah, yes, *amore*. I suck up as much as I can.

CONRAD
—That restaurant really did it with love. You could breathe that. It was palpable.

PATRICK
It was the garlic. A little too much garlic, actually. That restaurant really used to be much better. It's changed over the years.— Like everything.

CONRAD
[*Jovially but a bit sadly*]
And every*one*.

PATRICK
[*Looking at CONRAD*]
Exactly.
[*Turns to look at himself in a mirror*]
—Getting old is the worst.

CONRAD
You're not old. *I'm* old.

PATRICK
[*Turns away from mirror*]
The truth is, I've always felt like I was never young.

CONRAD
Really? Why?

PATRICK
—Ohh, my childhood was sort of short-circuited by…circumstances.
[*Turns back to mirror*]
But now I can actually see myself falling to bits. It's the visual-of-it-all that's so disconcerting.
[*PATRICK now turns from the mirror as if he cannot bear to look at himself. A pause. CONRAD goes to the window again and looks out*]

CONRAD
Things can be beautiful *because* of their age. Just look at this city.

PATRICK
When *I'm* three thousand years old, *I* should look so good!— I heard an Englishwoman on the street the other day, looking up at the Villa Medici and saying quite forlornly, "It wants a coat of paint."
[*CONRAD laughs pleasantly, looks at PATRICK, who again looks at himself in the mirror*]

PATRICK
—*I* could use a coat of paint.

CONRAD
Are you talking about covering up the truth?

PATRICK
What's the point?— Not worth it.
[*CONRAD turns to study the view out the balcony window*]

CONRAD
[*Turns to PATRICK*]
I really don't know what I'd have done if you hadn't come along this afternoon.

PATRICK
[*To CONRAD, thoughtfully*]
I don't know what I'd have done if *you* hadn't come along.— Just carried on with my life in the same old way, I guess.

CONRAD
You didn't have any plans?—

PATRICK
—Still don't.
[*CONRAD crosses to the armchair but does not sit*]

CONRAD
Surely you must have many friends here. Surely, you're not…well, you're not lonely.— Are you?

PATRICK
Lonely?

CONRAD
—For companionship.
[*CONRAD takes a step toward the dressing stool. Then takes another. PATRICK immediately gets up and crosses in a slow straight line across the stage, up behind the settee, until he reaches the balcony…*]

PATRICK
[*On the move*]
—I'm never lonely when I'm in this city. Even when I'm alone. Even when I'm lost in a labyrinth of streets. This is one of my favorite places on earth. I've always felt secure here. Solo, but surrounded by love. I never feel more whole than when I'm in Rome.

CONRAD
I'm afraid there's a lot of the tourist in me. My first days here—whenever I was out alone and I heard someone speaking English, I'd always say hello.

PATRICK
I usually run for the nearest exit when I hear anyone speaking English.
[PATRICK *turns from the window and crosses to the back of the settee, sits on it, one leg hiked up, facing* CONRAD...]

CONRAD
But you didn't run when *I* spoke to you.

PATRICK
[*After a moment, directly*]
You interest me.

CONRAD
—You're an intriguing fellow yourself, Patrick.

PATRICK
[*Flatly*]
I'm strange.— And I know it.

CONRAD
[*Chuckles*]
I think all of us are stranger than we let on.

PATRICK
I'm stranger than you'd think, Father.

CONRAD
You'd never know it to look at you.

PATRICK
Or to look at *you.*
[CONRAD *laughs uncomfortably*]
I told you, what you see is what you *don't* get. It's all just show. If I were turned inside out, *you'd* run for the nearest exit.

CONRAD
[*Sits on the arm of the armchair*]
Now, that's hard for me to believe.

PATRICK
I'm as creepy as the creepiest person you ever saw on a street and wouldn't dare ask directions even though you were hopelessly lost.

CONRAD
Why do you usually run from people when you hear them speaking English?

PATRICK
Don't like familiarity, I suppose.

CONRAD
You hear so much about fear of intimacy these days. Self-help books, TV talk shows, the Internet.

PATRICK
[*Dryly*]
Everything but semaphore.
[*CONRAD laughs. PATRICK moves to the window, looks out*]
Solitude not only makes me content, in some strange way it exhilarates me.
[*After a moment*]
—Even in the American cities I've lived in, I'd sometimes get in a taxi or get in my car and go to parts of town that were foreign, so to speak. Unfamiliar territory. And when I finally traveled to real foreign towns in real foreign countries, I felt that familiar, safe freedom of being a stranger in a strange place. I *wanted* to be lost. I didn't *want* to understand what was going on. And whenever I'd learn the language a little, I'd move on. To other countries with more difficult, more *arcane* languages which I could not possibly pick up.— I tried that in Finland, once. Forget it.

CONRAD
Maybe that's why you've never learned the language in this country.

PATRICK
Yes, I don't want to spoil it for myself. I don't want to be disappointed by the banality of it all. I prefer the mystery. In my hometown, there were these wild Sicilians I adored but whose lingo I resolutely refused to pick up. A widow and her three children who became sort of my surrogate family. Of course, I always felt like a fifth wheel, but it didn't matter. They were so full of life—just a great big cliché, really—lots of loud and passionate squabbling, lots of tears, lots of love...and, of course, lots of *pasta*.

CONRAD
Which was reassuring.

PATRICK
Exactly.

CONRAD
It's a wonder you don't prefer Palermo to Rome.

PATRICK
[*Dryly*]
Palermo is *too* Sicilian! Palermo is meshuga!

[*CONRAD looks blankly at* PATRICK]
Pazzo! Crazy!

CONRAD
Why were the Sicilians your surrogate family? Your parents were there for you, weren't they?

PATRICK
Well, they weren't there for each *other,* so, yeah, they were all over *me* like the mange.

CONRAD
What do you mean? I don't mean to pry.

PATRICK
[*Wave of the hand*]
Fa niente. I just mean, divorce was out because of the Church, so I was a kind of excuse to keep their unhappy marriage together.— I was coddled and coached and clocked to be a success, because my success would be *their* success. Of course, the stakes were so high, I was like something let out of a burning barn! I guess I would have flipped out for good if it hadn't been for the Sicilians and for...

CONRAD
Someone special who got you through? A teacher?

PATRICK
No, not a teacher—the movies.— That bright ray of light from a projection machine very definitely dazzled me.— It offered hope...and a way out.
[*Silence. A slight pause*]

CONRAD
I felt that way about the priesthood.

PATRICK
It offered a way out?

CONRAD
I think so.

PATRICK
A way out of what?

CONRAD
—Ohh, life. As I knew it.— My family life, I suppose. That, and I wanted to
be in touch with man's suffering. I wanted to make a difference. When I was
in school and a priest passed through the playground, there were no more
fights, no more resentments.— The face of the nastiest kid became angelic,
everything changed. At least, for me. Oh, there are so many reasons why I
became a priest.

PATRICK
Personally, I'd have only done it for the robes.

CONRAD
[*Incredulous*]
The vestments?

PATRICK
I used to be crazy about dressing up as an altar boy—all that lace! It made
me feel above the congregation.

CONRAD
Ritual is a powerful thing.

PATRICK
And it gives power.

CONRAD
Yes...but, when I was young I felt...

PATRICK
What?— Powerless?

CONRAD
Well...incomplete.— Fragmented. Not whole. The love of God and some
contact with Him seemed to be the one thing that gave me strength. I
remember when *I* was an altar boy...one morning no one showed up for six
o'clock mass, and when the priest gave me communion—just to me and no
one else—I never felt so special. I felt so...

PATRICK
What? Powerful?

CONRAD
Well, I found something that gave me the strength to pull myself together
and have hope. It almost made me sick with joy to know that devotion
afforded a way out.

PATRICK
Was your family religious?

CONRAD
My father died before I knew him. But my sister was, although she was
quite a bit older; I never knew her much until I had to move in with her
while I finished high school.— Just before I went into the seminary.

PATRICK
Why did you have to move in with her?— Did your mother die too?

CONRAD
Oh, no.— I just couldn't live with her anymore. Things were just
too...tense...and, well, unhappy.

PATRICK
Your mother wasn't a religious person?

CONRAD
Yes and no. She was like anybody else, I suppose—you know, commit...
transgressions...and then go to confession, get absolution, and do her
penance. She always said going to confession made her feel like a brand-new
human being. Of course, as soon as she got home she would start all over
again.
[CONRAD *takes a handkerchief out of his outside breast pocket and starts to
wipe his hands*]

PATRICK
What's the matter?

CONRAD
Oh, nothing.— My mouth is just dry.

PATRICK
[*Looking at* CONRAD'*s action*]
And your hands are wet.

CONRAD
[*Laughs, chagrined*]
Yes! So they are!

PATRICK
Are you ready for the *caffè*?

CONRAD
Oh, my, yes!— And maybe a little *acqua minerale*.

PATRICK
There's some beside the bed. Help yourself.

CONRAD
Grazie.
[*PATRICK goes to press the service panel on the night table stage left of the bed. Lightly*]
Maybe we should have doubles! I must be putting you to sleep.
[*CONRAD puts the handkerchief back in his breast pocket*]

PATRICK
On the contrary. I'm riveted.
[*CONRAD goes to the night table stage right of the bed and pours some mineral water into a glass, drinks it, and replaces it on the tray. PATRICK closes the suitcase, snaps it secure*]

CONRAD
Are you packing to leave?

PATRICK
In the morning.

CONRAD
[*Surprised*]
Really?! I don't know why, I got the impression your work on the movie was going to keep you here much longer. I thought that's why you "drifted off" in the restaurant—I thought you were thinking about your work.

PATRICK
No, my work, such as it is, is finished.
[*Looks at Conrad*]
—Give or take a loose end or two.— And you're here just till the end of the week? Then it's back to Los Angeles and to teaching?

CONRAD
Why? Do I look like a teacher?

PATRICK
Yes, you do.

CONRAD
Well, I did teach once, but I don't anymore.— Now I'm...

PATRICK
Why is that?

293

CONRAD
    [*Evasively*]
Oh…it's a long story.

PATRICK
Do you miss it? Teaching?
    [*PATRICK settles on the dressing stool*]

CONRAD
I do. I always got a great deal of satisfaction out of it. Seeing them learn and grow up and go out in the world. It made me feel I'd touched their lives.

PATRICK
It must have filled you with a great deal of pride.

CONRAD
Oh, it did. Because I was crazy about it—doing what I really wanted to do. And it went beyond the classroom. I had a nice car, and I'd pick up the kids and we'd drive to the country, take hikes, swim, have pillow fights, and I'd let them stay up as late as they'd like. There was nothing like helping those boys to believe in themselves, because a lot of them were from troubled backgrounds and really didn't know…

PATRICK
Love?

CONRAD
    [*Nods*]
—They really didn't know what it was to have anyone take an interest in them. Oh, we had some terrific times!

PATRICK
They must have worshiped you.

CONRAD
Oh, it was so rewarding. For them. For me.
    [*Adds, lightly*]
—Of course, I'd always let them win!

PATRICK
You sound like you were just a big kid yourself.

CONRAD
Maybe so. Sometimes I got into trouble with my superiors because I was rather lax with the paperwork.

PATRICK
The grown-up stuff.

CONRAD
Yes, you might say that. Kids never give a damn about paperwork.

PATRICK
You don't deal with them at all anymore?

CONRAD
No.

PATRICK
That must be very hard on you.

CONRAD
—Now I'm chaplain in a hospital. For a while I was in school administration—picking out textbooks, that sort of thing. Then I did a short stint as an adviser to Catholic charities. Then when parish work didn't pan out, I became a chaplain.

PATRICK
What hospital?

CONRAD
Oh, I move around a lot within L.A.— Go where the job is.
    [*Lightly*]
—Kinda like being in show business, I would imagine.

PATRICK
    [*Not responding*]
You must deal with a lot of AIDS.

CONRAD
What?

PATRICK
People with AIDS.

CONRAD
Oh, well, naturally.
    [*Changes subject*]
—Anyway, the only thing I was really good at was teaching. I enjoyed it.
    [*Thoughtfully*]
—Yes, I enjoyed it so much.

[*Slight pause*]
And you?— Back to L.A.?— Or is it New York?

PATRICK
Both, eventually. First, I'm going to stop in London and have a meeting with a producer. I have a play in mind, and he's offered to put it on if I can just write it.

CONRAD
If you can just write it?

PATRICK
Yes, I've had this play in mind for years, but I can't seem to get at it.

CONRAD
Not enough time?

PATRICK
Oh, no, not that.— The famous writer's block.

CONRAD
The creative process! It's always fascinated me.

PATRICK
And eluded me.

CONRAD
Do you have any idea as to why you're blocked?

PATRICK
Well, I know I'm only blocked when it comes to writing something personal. Something of my own. So that's why I'm in Hollywood selling shit.

CONRAD
What a pity that you can't get in touch with your true feelings.

PATRICK
It's hard, don't you think, getting in touch with your true self?

CONRAD
Maybe I'm blessed, but I don't know that I've ever had that problem.

PATRICK
Oh, well, then you *are* blessed.

CONRAD
Oh, I may have had a crisis—a spiritual crisis in my time, but I've always
managed to pull through. I think prayer saved me. I'm very devoted to the
Blessed Mother. What a pity you can't...

PATRICK
Ask Her to get me out of the fix I'm in? Place my faith in God?

CONRAD
I think you already have faith, Patrick, no matter what you say.

PATRICK
[*Shrugs*]
Faith is personal and easily misunderstood.

CONRAD
God understands.

PATRICK
[*Sardonically*]
You can swear to that on a stack of Bibles?

CONRAD
There are so many issues on which the Church seems adamant, but...well...
I mean, there is an official position, of course, and these days particularly I
have to take that position in the pulpit, but there can be mitigating circum-
stances.

PATRICK
You can bend the rules to stay in the club?

CONRAD
—Well, no, but for instance, in the context of one couple to one counselor
regarding, say, contraception...we can...

PATRICK
Do lunch.

CONRAD
Well, there is always the official versus the unofficial.

PATRICK
Just a tad hypocritical around the edges, isn't it?

CONRAD
[*Defensively*]
Well, life is not black-and-white! Life, I'm afraid, is endless shades in between!

PATRICK
[*Controlled*]
You're talking out of both sides of your mouth!

CONRAD
[*Mounting ire*]
Talk about hypocrisy after what you've said about your profession as a writer!

PATRICK
I don't defend *my* profession!

CONRAD
It's the same in all institutions, religious and secular!

PATRICK
[*Drolly*]
Yeah, who's ever heard of a politician who's even masturbated.
[*CONRAD is somewhat embarrassed, and the moment is defused*]

CONRAD
[*Covering his discomfort*]
—If I had your quick wit, just imagine the sermons I could write!

PATRICK
Would you practice what you preached?

CONRAD
[*Getting back to the original subject*]
At lunch you told me you've written very personal work in the past.

PATRICK
Oh, yes, I've bared my soul, so to speak. All fired up with ambition and productivity. And I don't understand how I did it one bit. I think if I can ever rediscover my imagination, I'll find myself.

CONRAD
Imagination can be more revealing than the truth.

PATRICK
Exactly. I once had an analyst in Beverly Hills who never wanted to hear the
mundane particulars of my daily life. She'd say, "Just bring me a big, fat,
juicy dream."
[CONRAD *laughs*]
Anyway, I have an idea for a play— I know how it starts now, how it pro-
gresses up to a point—it's kind of a dream.

CONRAD
A big, fat, juicy one?

PATRICK
Mmmmmm. Quite tasty.

CONRAD
But you don't know how the dream comes out yet? Is that it?

PATRICK
Well...it's getting there.

CONRAD
What's it about?

PATRICK
[*Avoiding the question*]
You know, when I was a child I could draw picture after picture and never get
tired or bored or exhaust my imagination. At Christmas I could wrap gift after
gift—each different, more charming, more original. And when I started to
write, I was tireless at writing sketches and playlets and, finally, plays one after
another. But I cannot write plays anymore. Not even the one floating around
in my head. Why can't plays come out of me like pictures and presents?

CONRAD
In my own way, I know what you mean. In the hospital, I find it very difficult to counsel grieving families. It's one thing to console the dying but
quite another to know what to say to the living!— Because when someone
dies, those left behind feel...responsible. How do you give them hope and
strength to go on? I'm afraid that's something not in my power.— What are
you thinking?

PATRICK
I hope we both find our way.

CONRAD
We'll find a way. I know we will. If we just go *piano-piano*.

PATRICK
From your mouth to God's whatever, Father.

CONRAD
Conrad.— Your friend.

PATRICK
Conrad.
> [*Silence, for a moment, which is broken by the room service* WAITER *unlocking the door with his keys. He enters. He is about* PATRICK's *age*]

WAITER
> [*Entering*]
Permesso.

PATRICK
Sì, avanti.

WAITER
Prego, signori?

PATRICK
> [*To Conrad*]
Coffee and a *liquore?*

CONRAD
That would be very nice.

PATRICK
Do you want Sambuca, or would you like to try something else?

CONRAD
You mean like grappa?

PATRICK
> [*To* WAITER]
Do you have any Genepy?
> [*Note: Pronounced in English and Italian GEN-a-pee*]

WAITER
I will ask the barman downstairs.

PATRICK
If so, we'll have that. And two coffees.

WAITER
Due Genepy. *Due caffè.*

PATRICK
Solo uno Genepy *e due caffè, per favore.*

WAITER
Grazie.
[*PATRICK goes to retrieve the laundry basket and hands it to the* WAITER]

WAITER
Everything was nice and clean?

PATRICK
Sì, sì. Era limpida come la pipi di un' bambino.
[*The* WAITER *laughs wickedly and goes out*]

CONRAD
I couldn't understand that, but from the way he laughed, it must have been something dirty.

PATRICK
Not really. Just an expression. I said everything was as clear as baby piss.

CONRAD
[*Chuckles*]
What is Genepy?

PATRICK
Something from the Dolomites. Made from juniper berries. Rome's a little far south to have it.

CONRAD
I'm sure a hotel like this has everything. But even I understand enough Italian to know you didn't order one for yourself. You said, "*Solo uno...*"

PATRICK
I don't drink.— That is, I don't drink *anymore.*

CONRAD
When you refused the wine this afternoon, I thought maybe you just didn't imbibe at lunchtime.

PATRICK
I used to imbibe at lunchtime. Cocktail time, dinnertime, and stay up all
night and sing 'em all! Now…I don't *drink* at all. Or, rather, I struggle not
to.— I'm an alcoholic. An alcoholic blocked writer—how's that for original?

CONRAD
An *ex*-alcoholic.

PATRICK
Well, I'm what we call in the program a "recovering" alcoholic.
[*CONRAD stands, takes his pack of cigarettes from his side pocket, and lights one.*
CONRAD moves to look out the window.]

CONRAD
If you ever had a serious drinking problem, I think you must be some kind
of miracle.

PATRICK
There you go getting religious again.

CONRAD
But these twelve-step programs are all *about* spirituality.

PATRICK
Yes, and that's not to be confused with religion. Religion is what people get
when they're afraid of going to hell. Spirituality is what they get when
they're on their way back from there.
[*CONRAD laughs*]

CONRAD
Are you on your way back?

PATRICK
I'm in transit.

CONRAD
If you're…agnostic, what do you make your Higher Power?

PATRICK
The group.

CONRAD
The power of the collective.

PATRICK
For me it's the humanity of the group. There's something very poignant
about the *humanity*. And very compelling. Something about the frailty of a
group of vulnerable human beings, struggling valiantly against their darker
instincts.

CONRAD
I wouldn't have any problem whatsoever turning myself over to God. I
never have— And you wouldn't either, if you saw what I see in a hospital.
Yes, you were right…I see so many who die of AIDS.

PATRICK
I thought you must, but you didn't seem to want to talk about it.

CONRAD
I don't know why I didn't before.
   [*After a moment*]
—Anyway, there was one young man whose family rejected him.— He was
near the end, and I came by to give him what I still call Extreme Unction
and was shocked to find him in the best spirits I'd ever seen! He said it was
because, at last, his friends had come to say good-bye. The room was empty,
and he was blind, so I asked, rather carefully, who was there. "Don't you
see—there's Violetta and Lucia and Mimi." Well, I don't know the first
thing about opera, but he introduced me to the three of them and said, "You
know, I'm blind, but I can really see them, so this must be a miracle." And I
said yes, it sure is, and took it as a sign that it was time to give him the last
rites. When, suddenly, he sat bolt upright and gasped some strange word—
"*Ree-na-chee!*" —and then fell back on the bed as dead as dead can be.—
Well, after all *that*, I didn't need a drink—I needed the comfort of God. And
I went to the chapel, and I prayed. Prayed for that young fella's soul. The
whole *idea* of a power higher than myself was very comforting to me.

PATRICK
Rinasce.

CONRAD
I didn't know what the hell he was talking about.

PATRICK
Violetta's last line in *La Traviata*. She's Italian, so naturally she goes on a bit
longer. "*In me rinasce*, yadada, yadada, yadada, *oh, gioia!*" It means, "In me,
there is rebirth.— Oh, joy!"
   [*Pause*]

CONRAD
I suppose you know a lot about opera?

PATRICK
No, I don't. What I know a lot about are those long, long intermissions. I always enjoyed them so much more than I did the opera itself. It was my favorite time to get shit-faced on champagne. And I didn't even *like* champagne! I much preferred the comfortable haze of the first dry martini.

CONRAD
You only went to the opera to drink between the acts?

PATRICK
To get drunk, really.

CONRAD
Well, there must have been a less expensive way.

PATRICK
Well, yes, but as you put it about praying to God in the chapel—the whole *idea* was comforting to me, the romance-of-it-all, the glitz, the glamour— long-stem glasses and more than a bit of the bubbly in a splendid crush bar or some dead-assed Founders' Circle— That and a lot of *posing*, no doubt. *Heavenly.*— Except when it turned hellish.

CONRAD
[*With private interest*]
It could turn on you?

PATRICK
Could, and finally did. I once flew to Paris with a friend for *La Bohème* on Christmas Eve. Well, now, the very *idea* of an opera taking place on Christmas Eve and seeing it that very same night, and *Paris*, and *Puccini*, and the *interminable* intervals, and all the chilled champagne in the whole of France was too much for me! I drank so excessively after the first act that I passed out and snored all through the Café Momus scene in the second. Then woke up and threw up. Ruined my new dinner jacket. My friend had to get me up the aisle and out. By this time, I was singing along. Needless to say, I was not a hit at the Paris Opera.— And my friend hasn't forgiven me to this day.

CONRAD
Talk about "bottoming out" in style!

PATRICK
Oh, so you know about bottoming out, do you?

CONRAD
[*Quickly*]
Well, I know what's meant by it.
[*Moving on*]
I envy you.— In your own way you've redeemed yourself. In the end, I
hope I'm redeemed. And delivered.

PATRICK
Are you guilty of something?

CONRAD
Who among us is not?

PATRICK
Is that why you've come to Rome?

CONRAD
Of course not. But it is inspiring here. I feel...*cleansed* here.

PATRICK
[*With an edge*]
Purged?

CONRAD
That's a good word.

PATRICK
[*Heating*]
Absolved? Pure as silk? Clear as baby piss?!

CONRAD
[*Evenly, but with an effort*]
You penetrate with words, Patrick. It's obvious you're a writer.

PATRICK
And an ex-Catholic. Guilt is an old friend of mine. As the joke goes—the
Jews may have invented guilt, but the Catholics perfected it.

CONRAD
[*Testily*]
You're not an ex-Catholic, you're a fallen-away Catholic.

PATRICK
[*Adamantly contrary*]
Maybe I should say, a *recovering* Catholic.

CONRAD
[*Not conceding*]
But once you are baptized, you are *always* a Catholic!
[*Flippantly*]
Something like being an alcoholic, isn't it?

PATRICK
[*Sarcastically*]
Once a Catholic, always a Catholic. Once a priest, always...safe.

CONRAD
[*Testily*]
I'm not ashamed to say God keeps me safe—that the priesthood is, for me, like a haven.

PATRICK
[*Tauntingly*]
Like a cover?

CONRAD
[*Thrown*]
A cover?
[*Forced lightly*]
—You mean like a security blanket or like...

PATRICK
[*Bluntly*]
I mean like a *mask*. Like something safe to *hide* behind.

CONRAD
[*Heatedly*]
Now, just one minute, my son.

PATRICK
[*Snidely*]
I am not your son, Father.

CONRAD
[*Angered*]
But I am still a priest!

PATRICK
And a priest is still a human being! He's still a man, and the Church is no haven, no "safe house" in which a man can hide out from temptation.

CONRAD
[*Pointedly*]
No, and in order to resist the more insidious temptations of this world, most human beings place their faith in God! In the end you'll believe in God. Mark my words, you'll call out for Him, and it's going to be such a powerful epiphany, your tongue is going to rot in your mouth!

PATRICK
[*Bitterly*]
In the end, this fugitive from the premises of God only prays he has the courage to meet the unknown and die without screaming for a priest!

CONRAD
[*Violently*]
Enough of this!

PATRICK
OK!— *Basta.*
[*Slight pause. Silence.*
Deliberately]
—I once heard someone say in a meeting that the three requisites for being alcoholic were, one—being an orphan, two—being a survivor of child abuse, or three—being a Catholic.— I thought they had a point. I qualify on two of those counts. I'm not an orphan.
[*CONRAD is silent. The sound of a key enters the lock. The door opens, and the FLOOR WAITER enters*]

WAITER
Ecco, signori!

PATRICK
[*Re liquore*]
Ah, you *do* have Genepy!

WAITER
I have brought you the whole bottle!

PATRICK
Bravo!

WAITER
Salute!
   [*The* WAITER *sets the tray on the low table*]

CONRAD
   [*Crossing*]
May I have a look at the label?
   [PATRICK *picks up the bottle of liqueur and hands it to* CONRAD, *who studies it
   as* PATRICK *takes the bill from the* WAITER]

CONRAD
What a color! As green as your eyes, Patrick.

PATRICK
Help yourself.

CONRAD
—Thank you. I do want to try it.
   [CONRAD *opens the bottle and begins to pour himself a pony of Genepy as*
   PATRICK *signs the bill*]

PATRICK
Among its other powers, it's great as a *digestivo.*

CONRAD
Then it's heaven-sent.

PATRICK
   [*To* WAITER, *handing him the bill*]
Grazie.

WAITER
Prego, signor. Grazie a lei. Buona sera.
   [*Deferentially*]
—*E buona sera, Padre.*

CONRAD
   [*Nods pleasantly*]
Buona sera.
   [*The* WAITER *goes out.* PATRICK *follows him to the door as* CONRAD *tastes the
   Genepy.*
   Re liquore]
Oh, my, that *is* delicious.
   [*Aspirates*]
—But strong!— My God!

PATRICK
[*Rolls his r's in mock exaggeration*]
Forte! Forte!
[*Suggestively*]
—It'll put starch in your collar, Padre.
[*CONRAD is a bit thrown by the vulgarity of the remark but laughs feebly*]
Just put on a Roman collar and people automatically have respect for you,
don't they?

CONRAD
Or contempt.

PATRICK
Does that happen in America the way it does here? I mean that little tacit
courtesy?

CONRAD
Sometimes.

PATRICK
Anyone could dress up in that costume and get respect, couldn't they?

CONRAD
Or contempt.

PATRICK
Sometimes contempt can be more exciting than respect. Too much respect
can be paralyzing.
[*PATRICK has picked up the espresso pot and poured two cups*]
—Sugar?

CONRAD
Just black, please.
[*PATRICK hands CONRAD a demitasse*]
Thank you.
[*CONRAD takes his cup and sits on the left end cushion of the settee. PATRICK
goes to sit on the right end cushion, then hesitates a moment before deciding,
instead, to turn and settle into the armchair.*
Re espresso]
I need this.
[*After a moment*]
—I really shouldn't drink, either.— One or two's my limit—three tops.

PATRICK
Just to put the stopper on, so to speak?

CONRAD
Well, I will admit I used to be able to handle it better.— I just have to exercise a little more control these days.

PATRICK
Control's always a good thing to exercise. Control and one's abdominals.

CONRAD
[*Smiles, pats his stomach*]
—Oh, no dinner for me tonight! Just very early to bed.
[*Re Genepy*]
I'll be ready after this.— Delicious.

PATRICK
[*Re Genepy*]
Yes, I have fond memories of it.

CONRAD
It's not a problem if I drink this in front of you?

PATRICK
You could swing from the chandelier if we had one, and it wouldn't faze me.

CONRAD
You mean you never even think of it anymore?

PATRICK
Oh, it's always on my mind—like death.

CONRAD
[*Laughs, sips Genepy. After a moment*]
—Do you know why you drank?

PATRICK
To get some feeling going. And to stop any feeling.

CONRAD
Can you run that by me again?

PATRICK
It all boiled down to that—to fill one's system with *anything*—anything just to stop *feeling* something—or anything to *feel* something.

CONRAD
[*Reflectively*]
I see you've given this some thought.

PATRICK
Sometimes I wanted to feel as bad as I could and would smoke or snort or
swallow anything to make me feel just as rotten as possible because, at least,
I *felt something*. To feel *bad* is, at least, to *feel*.

CONRAD
I grew up with a family of drinkers. Working-class people from Ireland.—
Both my parents were big, big drinkers. My father used to say he didn't trust
a man who didn't drink.— You've heard that one.

PATRICK
[*Dryly*]
Yes, and from no one I admire.

CONRAD
My father was banned from every pub in Galway, no mean achievement. So
he came to America and started all over.

PATRICK
Do you know what an Irish queer is?— A fellow who prefers women to drink.
        [*CONRAD laughs hollowly. There's a slight pause*]

CONRAD
—My father died of cirrhosis when I was just a boy, and although my mother
died years later of heart failure, it all was brought on by years of drinking
too. Slow drinking.— I somehow wish she'd have gone first. It would have
spared me so much...so many...
        [*Breaks off*]
—It's one reason I think I went in the priesthood as soon as I could.

PATRICK
What is?
        [*Slight pause*]

CONRAD
[*Rationalizing*]
—She was a good person, basically.— But, like anybody—human. With
human flaws.
        [*Directly*]
—Forgive me, for rattling on. I don't know what got me started.

PATRICK
Tell me more. Dump the cargo and fly low.
        [*CONRAD smiles, takes a deep sip of Genepy*]

CONRAD
It's something I never talk about—my family. My mother.

PATRICK
Why's that?

CONRAD
[*Forced lightly*]
I suppose you might say I'm blocked.

PATRICK
—It's not easy being numb.
[*Silence.* CONRAD *takes another sip of Genepy*]

CONRAD
[*After a moment*]
—Let's just say my parents weren't happy people.

PATRICK
That's something we have in common.
[CONRAD *is silent, takes an even bigger swig of Genepy*]

CONRAD
[*Motioning to Genepy*]
May I?
[*As Patrick nods*]
—It's really and truly funny to think of us both as blocked.

PATRICK
Well, not *too* hilarious.

CONRAD
You're a bit of all right.

PATRICK
Am I?

CONRAD
You're a "cozy" person—like the dark snug of a pub. I feel I've known you forever.

PATRICK
Maybe it's my Southern charm.

CONRAD
You're from the South?!

PATRICK
Is the Pope celibate?

CONRAD
But you don't have an accent.

PATRICK
I had one once that you could cut with a sugar cane machete.

CONRAD
Sugar cane...let's see—Louisiana?

PATRICK
Mississippi.

CONRAD
[*Stunned*]
Mississippi?! You're *joking!* You didn't tell me that at lunch!

PATRICK
I was too busy impressing you with all the celebrities I've known.

CONRAD
—But I assumed you were from New York!

PATRICK
No.

CONRAD
Where in Mississippi?

PATRICK
Oh, just a little cow track.

CONRAD
—Well, that *is* interesting.

PATRICK
[*After a moment*]
Is it?— Why?

CONRAD
—Well...for one thing, you certainly don't sound it. I'd never have guessed.
How did you get rid of your accent?

PATRICK
I was a speech and drama major in college—and I took lessons to get rid of it.

CONRAD
Whatever for?! Southern accents are so charming.

PATRICK
I thought a regional twang made one sound like a hick. Appear stupid.— Of course, that's just what I was—a stupid hick. But I didn't want to *sound* like one!
[*Pensively*]
—Also...

CONRAD
Yes?

PATRICK
—I saw it as a kind of failure. Something imposed on me without my consent.— One *more* thing, I should say.
[*Deliberately*]
I once felt that way about my homosexuality.
[*Slight pause.* CONRAD *tries not to appear thrown by* PATRICK's *remark.* CONRAD *reaches for the Genepy bottle and pours himself another drink*]

CONRAD
[*A bit uncomfortably*]
You didn't tell me that, either.

PATRICK
I didn't think I had to.

CONRAD
[*Lightly*]
If you'd drunk as much of that Pino Grigio as I did, Patrick, I'd say it was the vino talking now.— But, then, all you had was mineral water.

PATRICK
—So maybe it's just the gas talking.

CONRAD
[*Laughs nervously*]
Con gas!— That's about all the Italian I've picked up.— *Acqua minerale.*— *Con gas o senza gas!*
[CONRAD *chuckles feebly at his own joke.* PATRICK *doesn't. Silence.* CONRAD *rummages nervously through his pockets...*]

PATRICK
—Have you lost something?

CONRAD
I...I...
[*Quickly*]
I don't know what I did with my cigarettes.
[*Gives up search*]
—It doesn't matter. Better if I don't find them, anyway.

PATRICK
They're in your left side pocket.

CONRAD
You'd make a good detective.
[*CONRAD takes out the pack of cigarettes as* PATRICK *picks up the matches and strikes one.* CONRAD *puts a cigarette in his mouth, and* PATRICK *gets up and lights it for him*]
Thank you.

PATRICK
[*After a moment*]
—Didn't it cross your mind?

CONRAD
[*Quickly*]
What?— No. It didn't.

PATRICK
Really?

CONRAD
[*After a moment, lightly offhanded*]
You certainly are very candid.

PATRICK
There's no point in being anything else. It takes too much effort to lie. All that keeping track of the "official" story. Not worth it. Unless, of course, I get paid for it.

CONRAD
Well, telling the truth is indeed a great virtue.
> [*PATRICK is silent.* CONRAD *takes another long swig of Genepy, then becomes more serious*]
—You say you considered your…sexual proclivity…some kind of failure?

PATRICK
I guess I did. I tried to get rid of that too.

CONRAD
And you didn't succeed?

PATRICK
Well, let's just say, the attempt was less successful than with my accent. I knew I was gay from the time I was six, and I wasn't very happy about it. But I no longer feel that way.

CONRAD
—If *I* may be candid—exactly how did you try to go about getting rid of it?— Your…homosexuality. Therapy of *another* sort?

PATRICK
Exactly.

CONRAD
The psychiatrist in Beverly Hills?

PATRICK
> [*Turns to* CONRAD]
Psychoanalyst. She was one of several. All women. Most all of whom were of some note. Maybe I should have dropped their names at lunch too.

CONRAD
You do everything first-rate.

PATRICK
As I said, it's almost impossible for me to do anything cheap.— *Almost.*

CONRAD
> [*Expansively*]
Of that, I'm convinced!

PATRICK
So far I've simply chosen to tell you one side of the story. The safe side.
The cozy, snug side. I don't think you'd want to hear about my nostalgia for
the gutter. The cheap side. However, in its way, that was always first-rate
too, inasmuch as you couldn't get any lower.

CONRAD
I doubt that I'd be shocked. I've heard a lot in my time.

PATRICK
In confession?

CONRAD
Well, yes, of course. But I *am* a man of a certain age. I may have been born
yesterday, but I wasn't born *late* yesterday.

PATRICK
    [*Laughs*]
I like that. I think the Genepy has knocked the edges off.

CONRAD
    [*Raises his glass of Genepy*]
Cheers!—and *buona notte!*
    [*PATRICK doesn't laugh, just looks at* CONRAD. *Slight pause*]
I know a priest who works with homosexuals.

PATRICK
"Works with"? That sounds arduous. Like it might even smart.

CONRAD
There are some, Patrick, who would like to reconcile themselves with the
Church.

PATRICK
And what if they just can't pretend they're something they aren't?

CONRAD
Well, off the record, and admittedly it's becoming more difficult, but I
suppose if there's a consensual, nurturing, monogamous relationship…

PATRICK
You can work out a deal. Forgive me for saying the obvious, but who wants
to be a member of that cockamamy club? *Cockamamy*—that's Yiddish too.

CONRAD
[*Chuckles*]
Why do you keep using Jewish words? You're not Jewish.

PATRICK
I might as well be—show business and psychoanalysis are my life!

CONRAD
Of course, Jesus was Jewish.

PATRICK
No, He wasn't. He was Irish.

CONRAD
What?

PATRICK
Consider the facts—on the last night of His life, He went out drinking with the boys.— He thought His mother was a virgin, and she thought that He was God.

CONRAD
[*Laughs, holds up glass*]
—What's the name of this?

PATRICK
Genepy.

CONRAD
Genepy. Great stuff. I wouldn't have missed it for mass!
[*Looks heavenward*]
—Just kidding, Lord!
[*Another slight uncomfortable pause.* CONRAD *gets up, goes to the balcony window, looks out, and sips his Genepy thoughtfully...*
After a moment]
Whoever said "small world" really knew what he was talking about!

PATRICK
What do you mean?

CONRAD
[*After a moment*]
—I once taught school in Mississippi.

PATRICK
Now, that's something you didn't tell *me*.

CONRAD
I'm telling you now.

PATRICK
Why didn't you mention it before?— When I said I was from Mississippi.

CONRAD
[*Evasively*]
—Well…

PATRICK
Well, what?

CONRAD
[*Uncomfortably*]
Well, suffice it to say I *did* teach there.— Isn't that another unbelievable coincidence?

PATRICK
[*Casually*]
—Small world. Enormous fate, I guess.

CONRAD
Amazing!

PATRICK
Life *is…amazing* sometimes.

CONRAD
Yes, imagine! Each of us now living in the same random American city, never knowing the other existed within that city or state or space—and having also existed within another state and space at the same time, sometime in our pasts. And now, our paths cross in a distant, foreign place!— What are the chances of that?!

PATRICK
Slim.

CONRAD
—Of course, I'm not from L.A. originally. I'm from…

PATRICK
[*Evenly*]
Boston would be my guess.

CONRAD
[*Dumbstruck*]
You do have a sharp ear for accents!— And I never even said, "I pahked the cahr in Hahvahd yahd!"
[*CONRAD laughs at his own joke. PATRICK does not*]
—Actually, I'm from South Boston. I'm a "southie." Went into the seminary outside Brookline and taught for a while in Beverly, Mass.— Then I was sent to one of our schools in Mississippi.

PATRICK
And how did you wind up in L.A.?

CONRAD
[*Evasively*]
—I was…unhappy…in Mississippi…in that small town, so I asked to be transferred to a city. Any city anywhere that needed someone. I needed to be…swallowed up.
[*Re Genepy*]
—May I?

PATRICK
But of course.
[*CONRAD refills his glass, takes a long sip. Pause. CONRAD takes another sip, looks to see PATRICK staring at him*]

CONRAD
—You're so silent. You're not falling asleep, are you?

PATRICK
I'm not even staring into space.

CONRAD
—What are you thinking?
[*PATRICK looks at CONRAD a moment longer, doesn't answer, gets up, and goes to the window to look out*]
Something you don't want to say?
[*PATRICK is silent. After a moment, CONRAD gets up and crosses to stand beside him. Silence. Some street noises. Someone somewhere is singing and whistling a snatch of "Non Dimenticar." Pause.
Looking out*]
Ah, *bella Roma!*— The Eternal City.

PATRICK
[*Looking out*]
Maternal, paternal, eternal.

CONRAD
What a fantastic night. I've always preferred the night. The night always exaggerates things—there's a kind of heightened reality, isn't there?

PATRICK
Yes, it's like drink or a drug. I was a night person too, all my life. I used to feel alive *only* at night.— Now I quite appreciate the day. There's nothing more beautiful than light—and what it does to things. Light and shadow are something to consider. I envy painters.
[*CONRAD puts his hand on PATRICK's shoulder and looks out at the city...*]

CONRAD
—This has all been so extraordinary, I shall never forget it. Meeting you. Becoming friends. Imagine—just hours ago we were two strangers in a foreign country.

PATRICK
I have always been a stranger in a foreign country—always. There and then as a child in the South—and here and now in this Holy City.— Excuse me.
[*PATRICK gently slips out from CONRAD's grasp, moves away, crossing to the back of the settee, where he sits, his back to the audience. CONRAD doesn't leave the window, but turns from it to face PATRICK*]

CONRAD
—What's the matter, Patrick? Don't like being nostalgic?

PATRICK
I'm a person who dwells on yesterday to the point of pathology.

CONRAD
In some cases I think it's better to forget and move on.

PATRICK
The past, for me, is not a darkened stage whose players have vanished and are forgotten.

CONRAD
[*Almost as if he's seeking advice*]
Do you really think you can resolve the troublesome things of the past?

321

PATRICK
Some things. But it's hard to confront the big time.

CONRAD
[*Re the Genepy*]
—You know, it's really *Kelly* green!

PATRICK
[*Drolly*]
You mean it's user-friendly.

CONRAD
[*Warily*]
—Did you go to a Catholic school in Mississippi?

PATRICK
Mmm.— I wonder if you can guess which one.

CONRAD
Well, there are so many!— Isn't it amazing how many Catholic schools there
are in a hard-core Baptist state?
[*Picking up the Genepy bottle*]
—May I have a tiny drop more?

PATRICK
Be my thirsty guest.— I not only went to Catholic grade school and high
school but even a Catholic university. My father was rather cracked on the
subject of religion.

CONRAD
And your mother?

PATRICK
Oh, she converted just to keep peace. She only went to church on Sunday to
show off her fur coat.
[*PATRICK gets up, moves away to the chest of drawers. He starts to place the
toilet articles—cologne and talcum—into the zipper case lying on the top of
the chest*]

CONRAD
[*Settles into the armchair*]
—The older I get, the more I find myself doing things just the way my
mother did.

PATRICK
Such as?

CONRAD
Ohh, little things like...tucking my handkerchief in the sleeve of my cassock or checking things several times before I can go out—the light in my room, the front door, the back door.— Sometimes I lock and unlock and *re*lock the doors three or four times before I can leave.

PATRICK
Just as she did.

CONRAD
Yes.
    [*Hesitantly*]
—And in the last couple of years I've noticed something else—something I hated as a child—something I never thought I'd be doing.

PATRICK
—Like?

CONRAD
Like...taking to bed in the middle of the afternoon when I've always been so on the go, so active. I've always hated lying around. But sometimes I get depressed—just like she used to get depressed.

PATRICK
What about?

CONRAD
Things I thought I'd left behind so many years ago in South Boston.

PATRICK
—And why did you leave?— Mississippi, I mean. Not Massachusetts.

CONRAD
    [*Carefully*]
As I say, I was transferred.

PATRICK
You said you *asked* to be transferred.

CONRAD
—Yes, that's right.
    [*Lightly*]
—Are you taking this down?

PATRICK
I'm a good listener, Father.

CONRAD
You certainly are.

PATRICK
And an even better scopophiliac.

CONRAD
What's that?

PATRICK
The morbid urge to observe.— You were saying?

CONRAD
—I came to love the South, but...well, it got to be too...

PATRICK
—What?
[*Playfully*]
—Too humid? too hot?

CONRAD
[*Seriously*]
Too painful...for me to stay there.
[*With a certain difficulty*]
—I had a bad experience—got myself into a...troublesome situation there,
so it was somewhat of a relief to get out.

PATRICK
Then it *did* get too hot for you?

CONRAD
[*Tonelessly*]
Well, you might say that.

PATRICK
—And sticky?

CONRAD
[*Grimly*]
—Yes.—I guess you might say...

PATRICK
—The heat was on?

CONRAD
Believe me, it was no joking matter.

PATRICK
I believe you.
> [*Pause.* CONRAD *puts down the coffee cup on the low table, picks up the pony of Genepy, and drains it. He pours himself another, settles back in the armchair.*
> *After a moment*]
—What's the matter, Conrad?— Are *you* nostalgic now?

CONRAD
> [*Evasively*]
Just very mellow. This Genepy is making me very, very sleepy. I must get up and stretch.
> [*Stands, yawns*]
—Ohh, my, your bed looks so inviting.
> [PATRICK *looks at* CONRAD *reflected in the mirror. He doesn't turn to face him.* CONRAD *puts down the empty Genepy glass on the low table and comes up to the left head of the bed*]
The sheets! Real linen, are they?

PATRICK
Mmm. I love that about good hotels in Europe.

CONRAD
> [*Extends his hand*]
May I?

PATRICK
Go ahead. Give it a feel.

CONRAD
> [*Touches the pillow*]
Soft and smooth—
> [CONRAD *then sits carefully on the bed.*
> *Reacting to the comfort*]
Oh, my! How luxurious. I'd better not go any further or I could curl up and spend the night!

PATRICK
Could you?
> [CONRAD *slightly bounces up and down on the mattress*]

CONRAD
I could indeed.
> [*There is the sound of a key in the door as the* FLOOR WAITER *returns*]

WAITER
    [*Entering*]
—*Permesso.*

PATRICK
Sí, avanti.
        [*CONRAD immediately gets off the bed...*]

WAITER
Are you finished with the tray?

PATRICK
We're finished with the coffee.
        [*The WAITER crosses to the low table*]

WAITER
I will leave the Genepy.

PATRICK
Thank you.

WAITER
Mi scusi, Padre, you like the Genepy?
        [*Picks up bottle, looks at contents*]
—Oh, I see you like it very much.

CONRAD
Yes, it's very soothing.

WAITER
It is good in the wintertime—for "After-ski."

CONRAD
Well, you might say I've been going downhill all afternoon!
        [*The WAITER doesn't really understand but smiles enigmatically and refills
        CONRAD's glass. He sets the bottle on the low table and picks up the tray with
        the coffeepot and used cups and starts to go*]
Grazie.

WAITER
Grazie, a lei, Padre. Buona sera.

CONRAD
Buona sera.

WAITER
[*To Patrick*]
Buona sera, signor.

PATRICK
[*Pointedly*]
Grazie et buona notte.

> [*The* WAITER *goes to the door.* CONRAD *goes back to the low table and picks up the drink as* PATRICK *comes around the bed and follows the* WAITER *out.* PATRICK *casually locks the door (three revolutions) and puts the key in his side jacket pocket.* CONRAD's *back is to* PATRICK, *but he hears the sound of the door being locked. Whether he thinks anything of it or not, he doesn't react or comment on it.* PATRICK *doesn't move from the door.* CONRAD *goes to the window. Some car horns are heard from below and a few indistinct exchanges in Italian. A Vespa goes by. Pause.* CONRAD *turns to face* PATRICK, *who is looking at him*]

CONRAD
[*After a moment*]
—What are you thinking?

PATRICK
I'm thinking about your sitting on my bed.

CONRAD
Oh, I hope you don't mind, it just looked so…

PATRICK
—There was a time—not so very long ago, Conrad—that I'd have taken that as a come-on—if someone had come up to my room and patted my pillow and asked to give it a feel.

CONRAD
[*Lightly*]
Now, really, Patrick, are you trying to shock me?!

PATRICK
I'm not saying what was on *your* mind. I'm just telling you what was going through *mine*.

CONRAD
I just meant that...well...what I *mean* is, I'll definitely take a little nap as soon as I get back to my room.
[*Looks at his watch*]
—and I really have to think about going.

PATRICK
[*Looking at the bed*]
The difference between then and now is that I'd have been drinking like you've been drinking this afternoon.— Half-pissed and horny, I'd have picked up someone in a bar or off the street or in a pissoir and probably paid them.— That would have been the first-rate gutter side of me.— But not anymore. Those days are over. I'm too sober.
[*Grimly*]
—And the world's too sober today too.— The leaves are knee-deep in the pissoirs in the Borghese Gardens now. Sign of the times.

CONRAD
You know, Patrick, sometimes you go a bit too far.

PATRICK
—It could have been an afternoon like this afternoon, Conrad. After all, I did sort of pick you up on the street too, didn't I? And brought you back here with me?

CONRAD
[*Admiringly intrigued*]
You just don't care what you say, do you?

PATRICK
I just don't think there's any point in pretending.
[*Shrugs*]
Not worth it.

CONRAD
Actually, I wish I were like that.— I admire people who say what they think. People who have that power.

PATRICK
You mean it's tough for you to let down your hair. Expose yourself?

CONRAD
I don't think anything would shock you.

PATRICK
It'd take some doing. Try me.

CONRAD
You mentioned something earlier that made me think of something in my past.— It's been on my mind ever since.

PATRICK
What has?

CONRAD
I don't know what telling you would accomplish. I've never spoken to anyone about it—
   [*Waves his glass*]
—What is this, anyway?

PATRICK
Jet fuel.

CONRAD
   [*Lightly*]
You're going to have to roll me out the door and point me in the direction of the Tiber! And even then, I'm still bound to get lost.
   [*Re Genepy*]
What *is* it, anyway?! I know you say it's made from juniper, but it's like...

PATRICK
Truth serum!— In juniper veritas!

CONRAD
   [*Sits on the settee*]
I believe you may be right.
   [*After a moment*]
You've made me think of things that really have always been just out of mind.
   [*After a moment*]
—Funny, I feel so light-headed.

PATRICK
Take a few deep breaths and just go *piano-piano*.

CONRAD
   [*Chuckles*]
Yes. That might help.

PATRICK
It helps *me*.
[*CONRAD is silent. A slight pause... PATRICK sits on the foot of the bed. CONRAD sits next to him*]

CONRAD
[*Breathing heavily*]
—As I say, I've never talked to anyone about this, and I don't know if I'm prepared even to tell you. I'd like to.

PATRICK
[*Carefully*]
Would it help if you thought of me as your, well—as your...father confessor?

CONRAD
Are you being...

PATRICK
Tongue-in-cheek? No, for once.

CONRAD
[*Tentatively, re liquore*]
—I think this...this Genepy has loosened my tongue.

PATRICK
Do you always have to drink to loosen up?

CONRAD
Well, it always helps.

PATRICK
And are you relaxed now?— Are you comfortable with me?

CONRAD
Yes. You certainly know how to put a man at ease.

PATRICK
Thank you.

CONRAD
You have that power.

PATRICK
Thank you, again.

CONRAD
Power must be the most intoxicating thing in the world. Far more heady
than alcohol.

PATRICK
Maybe there's just something about me that encourages you to be intimate.
[*A loaded pause*]

CONRAD
[*Anxiously moves away*]
—I don't think I can. Speak of it. I'm sorry. Been bottled up in me too long.
[*Silence. A pause.* CONRAD *silently sips the Genepy.* PATRICK *gets off the bed*]

PATRICK
[*Flatly*]
I doubt if you could tell the truth about yourself to anyone.

CONRAD
[*Somewhat startled*]
What?

PATRICK
You have done nothing but pretend to me since I met you. Pretend to be
chaste, pretend to be celibate. And yet you sit on my bed and make seductive remarks. You can be had, Conrad.

CONRAD
What did you say?

PATRICK
Too intimate for you?

CONRAD
I don't know what you mean!

PATRICK
—And you're a drunk! That's one's choice, of course, but you lie about that
too—pretending "one or two's my limit—three tops!" You have no limit.
There is no top. Boundaries are a problem for you, Conrad.
[CONRAD *is unsettled, knocks over the glass of Genepy on the low table, and
looks up with apprehension*]

CONRAD
[*Flatly*]
Patrick, you're way out of line!

PATRICK
[*Drawing nearer, quietly*]
You're a failure at everything you set out to be—a teacher, a shaper of young minds, the bearer of the word of your God. With your lies you have betrayed the integrity of a tradition centuries old. You're a flop as a priest. You're a flop as a person.— Conrad, you are a *flop.*

CONRAD
And you are something evil!

PATRICK
If I am, I am your creation, dear Father!

CONRAD
What are you talking about?!

PATRICK
[*After a moment, directly*]
—I have a confession to make concerning that play that I can't seem to get at.— It's about a betrayal of trust. Emotional betrayal. Sexual betrayal.

CONRAD
[*Standing, anxiously*]
Give me my shoes!!

PATRICK
What's the matter, don't you like being in mine?!

CONRAD
I'm leaving!

PATRICK
I'm not finished telling you about the play.

CONRAD
I don't think I'm interested!

PATRICK
—It's about a teacher who sexually abuses a nine-year-old student.
[*Pause. CONRAD stands silently aghast, staring wide-eyed at PATRICK*]

CONRAD
[*Hisses weakly*]
—Who are you?!

PATRICK
[*Calmly*]
Don't you know?— I loved you once.

CONRAD
What?

PATRICK
I said, *I loved you once.*
[*CONRAD's jaw sags with recognition*]

CONRAD
[*After a long moment*]
—It's not possible!

PATRICK
Apparently, it is.— *Very* small world department!

CONRAD
[*Quickly*]
His name wasn't Patrick!

PATRICK
Yes, it was! His middle name was Patrick, but you called him by his first name. You called me...

CONRAD
[*A hushed gasp*]
—Ned!

PATRICK
Yes. You called me Ned.— Ned for Edward, which is my first name. Just like my father. You remember my father, of course.

CONRAD
Your father?

PATRICK
Your friend, *Eddie!*

CONRAD
[*Remembers*]
Of course, I remember your father.— Dear, kind Eddie. How...how is Eddie?

PATRICK
Dead. So he's just fine.

CONRAD
[*Compassionately*]
I am sorry to hear that. We were great friends.— I liked Eddie so much.

PATRICK
And he was impressed with you. Bright young Irish-American priest. What he probably always wanted to be himself.

CONRAD
Eddie probably did think he missed his calling.— Yes, I suppose he did look up to me.

PATRICK
He'd do anything for you. Give you anything. Anything you wanted. And you *wanted* the things my father could give you.— You loved the perks. The cigarettes. The liquor. The good wine. The gifts of money. The car. The Christmas-of-it-all!

CONRAD
I didn't ask for those things!

PATRICK
You didn't have to. My father was generous, and in that small town he thought you were special. Educated, cultivated, and *holy!* A man of God. Good for his boy.— And how did you pay him back? By molesting his son!
    [*CONRAD runs to grab his shoes from under the luggage rack. PATRICK races after CONRAD and snatches his shoes from him and hurls them across the room. CONRAD is suddenly terrified of PATRICK's unbridled wrath, collapses back onto the top of the closed suitcase on the luggage rack*]

CONRAD
[*Hysterically*]
Why have you come back?! To get even?

PATRICK
[*Hovering*]
Ask your all-knowing God that! Ask Him why, after all these years, He's permitted this curious little collision in the mad mix-up of streets in this ancient holy town!

CONRAD
Let me go! Let me out of here!
[*CONRAD starts to get up, and* PATRICK *shoves him back onto the suitcase*]

PATRICK
—And while you're at it, ask Him why He permitted you to sit beside me at my desk in the middle of a room of prepubescent students and put your arm around me and slip your hand down the sides of my overalls to fondle my...

CONRAD
Stop it! Stop it!

PATRICK
Why He allowed you to slip my hand into your cassock where your trousers were unzipped.

CONRAD
[*Covering his ears*]
Stop! Don't do this!

PATRICK
—Why He let you take me to your room after class to kiss me and suck me and have me kiss and suck you.

CONRAD
Please, for God's sake!
[*CONRAD pushes past* PATRICK, *races for the door.* PATRICK *doesn't move.* CONRAD *begins to tear at the knob...*]

PATRICK
[*Calmly*]
It's locked. Didn't you see me lock it when the waiter left?
[*Removes key from his pocket, holds it up*]
—Here's the key.

CONRAD
[*Rushing back to* PATRICK]
Give it to me!

PATRICK
[*Calmly puts the key back in his pocket*]
—No.

CONRAD
[*Pathetically*]
Give it to me. Please.

[*CONRAD breathes hard, backs away from* PATRICK, *stumbles on the raised platform, and falls onto it (downstage of the foot of the bed), panting.* PATRICK *looks at* CONRAD *contemptuously*]

PATRICK
[*Icily*]
You look a bit green around the gills. As green as that Genepy you've been lapping up. As green as my eyes.
[*Calmly*]
I remember a day, a day of dread and anxiety the likes of which I have never known again—although at nine years of age I didn't know what the unnamed thing in me was. I wonder if you remember that day?

CONRAD
[*Breathing hard*]
What day?— What are you talking about?

PATRICK
[*Without affect*]
A cold day one winter when you were colder than the day outside. I knew something was wrong the moment I saw your face that morning. The moment you looked away from me and never looked at me again. I thought I had done something. I thought something was *my* fault. I couldn't eat at the lunchtime recess—the smell of sausage in the cafeteria made me ill. I couldn't play in the playground. I couldn't even see clearly, even though there wasn't any bright sunlight—just a canopy of gray, that chilly, dull noon. All I could do was wonder and worry and wait for the bell to come back to class…when you finally spoke to me. Without looking at me you told me to stay after school—that you had something to talk to me about. What had I done? What had I caused to make you so cold?

CONRAD
You didn't understand.

PATRICK
The hours dragged by like days that day of dread until, at last, at three o'clock on that cold dreadful afternoon, the school bell rang again and the rest of the students left, leaving me alone with you. And you locked the door.

CONRAD
Please, I want to forget—

PATRICK
—You remember there was a mesh grating over the windows in that room—

CONRAD
Yes…yes, I remember.

PATRICK
And I remember how that day the mesh seemed like a cage to me. The moment you started talking, I wanted to get out of that room. I was going to suffocate. I asked you to unlock the door, and you said, "No, I have to talk to you."
[*PATRICK crosses to bed platform, stands over* CONRAD, *and addresses him directly.* CONRAD *avoids* PATRICK'S *gaze*]
—You didn't sit beside me at my desk this time—you sat on the one in front of me—you didn't touch me, you kept your distance. You couldn't look at me when you finally said, "What we have been doing has to stop. What we have been doing is wrong. What we have been doing is a sin."— Do you remember?

CONRAD
[*After a moment*]
Yes. Yes, of course. How could I forget?

PATRICK
You unlocked the door and let me go. And I've never felt free again.— After that—the hours, the days left in that year—the interminable anxiety of having to be near you in the classroom, hearing your voice day after day. Seeing you in the schoolyard at recess, playing with the other children—running into you on the stairs, in the corridors, never having our eyes meet again, never knowing what was going on in your mind.— Then, coming back after the summer and suddenly finding out you were gone.— Disappeared.— They said you'd been transferred. I never knew where, never knew what happened to you, never heard of you again.— Until this day.

CONRAD
I can't believe this day!

PATRICK
Believe it. You're good at putting your faith in things which stretch credulity far more than this day. Such is life and show business in a bewildering world.
[*PATRICK moves away, crossing unsteadily to lean against the back of the settee.* CONRAD *slowly gets up off the platform, begins a slow semicircle downstage around* PATRICK, *edging right to search for his shoes. The next exchanges are rapid-fire*]

337

CONRAD
[*Moving*]
How long have you been following me?!

PATRICK
I haven't been following you!

CONRAD
You followed me here to Rome, didn't you?

PATRICK
No. I didn't.

CONRAD
You tracked me down, haven't you?!

PATRICK
Running into you was just what it was—an accident.— A sort of *divine*
accident!

CONRAD
You planned this!

PATRICK
I had no plan!— But I do now.
        [*CONRAD has edged his way down left. He finds his shoes, picks them up, goes
        to sit in the armchair, takes off the slippers. PATRICK slowly comes around the
        settee, up to the armchair to loom over CONRAD, who finishes pulling on his
        shoes, leaving them unlaced. CONRAD panics and runs to the balcony as a
        Vespa grinds past on the street below, making a racket. PATRICK doesn't move
        from the door.— The sound of the Vespa loudens...*]

CONRAD
[*Yelling outside, over the noise*]
—Help!—*HELP!!!*

PATRICK
[*Without passion*]
The word in Italian is *aiuto! Aiuto!* It means "help."
[*After a moment*]
—What's the matter? Can't you say it?
[*CONRAD is frozen with fear, unable to utter a syllable. We hear the rasp of the Vespa fade in the distance. PATRICK calmly crosses to the balcony, steps around CONRAD, and closes the exterior shutters, then the glass doors, shutting out the exterior noises. He then draws the brocade portieres. CONRAD stumbles dizzily back to center stage, starts to moan and contract his arms about his midsection. He collapses on the floor.*
Turning, tonelessly]
Get up.

CONRAD
[*Moaning*]
I can't.
[*PATRICK calmly crosses to stand above CONRAD but does not touch him*]

PATRICK
I said, *get up!*
[*CONRAD starts to gasp and crawl across the floor toward the bathroom door*]

CONRAD
I'm sick!

PATRICK
What's the matter? Choke on your rosary?
[*CONRAD moans loudly, grabs his stomach with one hand, and covers his mouth with the other, as if he is about to vomit. He gets to his feet and stumbles the rest of the way across the stage into the bathroom*]

CONRAD
I'm going to be sick!!
[*We hear him retch offstage. PATRICK slowly approaches the open bathroom door, looks in. After a moment, he speaks…*]

PATRICK
[*With mild contempt*]
Pity. All that expensive expense-account lunch down the toilet.

[*The sound of the toilet being flushed can be heard offstage…* PATRICK *steps across the threshold to the bath, where he can still be seen by the audience, whips a towel off the warming rack, and hurls it off to where* CONRAD *would be.* PATRICK *steps back over the threshold, into the room. The sound of running water is heard offstage… Suddenly,* PATRICK *pulls the bathroom door shut and collapses against it, hyperventilating. He stands there gasping a few seconds, then forcefully pushes himself away from the door, propelling himself around, stumbles to center stage, where he stops, frozen for a moment, before he begins to shake violently…*
Desperately, to himself]
Pat, Pat, Pat, Pat, Pat, Paddy, Paddy, Paddy…
[*He gasps for breath*]
—Neddy, Neddy, Neddy, Ned, Ned, Ned, take a few deep breaths…take a few deep breaths… Hold on… Hold on… Hold on… *Piano-piano…*
[*A pause. He calms. And straightens. And smooths his hair… The sound of the running water in the bathroom is turned off. After a moment, the door to the bathroom is thrown open and* CONRAD *staggers out, looking ghostly pale. He has taken his suit jacket off and clutches it in his hand. His hair is wet, and a towel is around his neck…* CONRAD *moves unsteadily to hold on to the chest of drawers. He looks up at himself (and at* PATRICK*) in the mirror.* PATRICK *becomes aware of the eye contact, turns away to look straight out front…*
After a moment]
Do you recognize me?
[CONRAD *does not turn around—continues to look at* PATRICK *in the mirror*]

CONRAD
I didn't at first. You're older, of course… But now…
[*Turns to face* PATRICK]
—Well, yes, you are unmistakably you—
[CONRAD *turns back to the mirror, takes the towel from around his neck and wipes his face, picks up* PATRICK'S *comb and smooths his hair. He puts down the comb and the towel on top of the chest*]

PATRICK
[*Turns to face* CONRAD]
Even before I saw you, I knew. I heard your voice when you spoke to me, and I knew. Then I looked at you, and even behind dark glasses, I knew—

CONRAD
I'm older too. My hair…it's all salt-and-pepper.—

PATRICK
Not to worry. There's still more pepper than salt.
[*Out front, simply*]
I've seen your face in so many people through the years. Someone will look up and see me staring at them—on a plane or in a restaurant or a theater, and they'll never know that I wasn't looking at them at all. I was seeing you.

CONRAD
[*Not looking at PATRICK*]
Even though you're a grown man now, you still have the same sweet face, Neddy.

PATRICK
Don't call me that!!

CONRAD
That's who you are.

PATRICK
No. That's who you want.

CONRAD
[*Weakly*]
—I've got to lie down.

PATRICK
[*Coolly*]
You've been wanting to get in my bed since you got here, haven't you?
[*CONRAD stumbles to platform, steps up on it, and falls onto the bed...*
PATRICK goes to his suitcase, flings the top open, and scoops up all his pairs of
silk boxer shorts. He crosses to the bed, mounts the platform, and stands over
CONRAD, pelting him with the undergarments...]
Here. You've been wanting these too. Hold them. Feel them. Smell them.

CONRAD
[*Shrieks at PATRICK*]
You can't even it out! For God's sake, Ned!

PATRICK
I said, *Don't call me that!!*

CONRAD
All we can do is repent for the unthinkable monstrosity of what happened...

PATRICK
    [*Lashes out*]
Of *what you did!* Not *what happened.* There is nothing even in what happened! We're talking about the unspeakable monstrosity of *what you did!*

CONRAD
Do you blame me for everything that's gone wrong with your life?

PATRICK
—Do you have any idea how you changed my life?! And I don't mean you
made me homosexual. I mean, do you know how you fucked with my mind?!
    [*CONRAD doesn't respond. PATRICK turns to him.*
    Directly]
—Well, *do you?!!!*

CONRAD
I have paid for what I did!

PATRICK
You've *never* paid for what you did!

CONRAD
    [*Directly*]
How would *you* know! You don't know me. You don't know the way I've had
to live my life.
    [*Hysterically*]
You don't know the secrets of my heart!

PATRICK
Then SHOW me your heart if you have one!

CONRAD
    [*Lashes out*]
What do you want me to do?! I've confessed, I've been absolved, I've done
my penance. I've begged God over and over and *over* for forgiveness!

PATRICK
    [*Confronting CONRAD*]
I am the only one who can forgive you! *I* am the child you violated!

CONRAD
    [*Looking up at PATRICK, terrified*]
—What are you going to do?!— *What?*— Hurt me?!

PATRICK
[*Calmly but steely*]
Sorry, no bamboo shoots under the fingernails!

CONRAD
[*Stoically*]
—Are you going to kill me?
[*PATRICK straightens, very controlled, turns, and moves a little way left of CONRAD*]

PATRICK
Hold a linen-covered pillow over your face until you suffocate? Push you off the balcony and have you splatter your guts all over the Spanish Steps? Too predictable. No, this scene will not be written by the dictates of a committee. This scene will be of my own invention.
[*CONRAD gets up and runs for the door and begins frantically twisting the knob. PATRICK crosses to him, catches him by the back of his collar, and swings him round. CONRAD swings round and drops to his knees, center stage, sobbing*]

PATRICK
Listen to me!

CONRAD
[*Covers his ears*]
No!!

PATRICK
[*Takes him by the lapels, shakes him*]
I said, listen to me, goddamnit!!!
[*CONRAD tries to crawl away from PATRICK's grip. PATRICK jerks him around so forcefully that PATRICK himself is brought to his knees. CONRAD screams. Now they are both kneeling, face-to-face, CONRAD down on both knees, cowering—PATRICK on one knee only, slightly higher and above CONRAD, in the stronger position with more physical advantage. CONRAD sobs as PATRICK tightens his grip on CONRAD's jacket lapels...*]

CONRAD
Patrick, I'm an old man!!

PATRICK
A *dirty* old man! A filthy old pervert in a costume!

CONRAD
I'm a man of God!

PATRICK
Then ask your God why He permitted you to be the first person to teach me what I thought was love?! *Love!*— For the first time in my life! And for the last time in my life!

CONRAD
What are you saying? You didn't want me to end it?

PATRICK
You should never have begun it! What has love meant to me ever since? Humiliation and betrayal. I can have sex with strangers, but I can't make love with anyone who could love me or for whom I could feel one authentic emotion. And for that, I have you to thank.

CONRAD
I had to end it! It was wrong!

PATRICK
At the moment you *told* me it was wrong—that it was what you called a sin— at that moment you taught me the meaning of guilt.

CONRAD
Mother of God, I never meant to hurt you!
          [CONRAD *struggles with* PATRICK. PATRICK *stands and violently pulls* CONRAD *to his feet and hurls him across the room onto the bed, pinning* CONRAD *down*]

PATRICK
You wrecked me inside forever!— I was left with nothing but apathy, indifference, a detachment toward everything that is given any emotional credence in this world. The thought of a human being about whom I might genuinely care makes me ill. It makes *me* want to vomit. And left with that numbing emptiness, I fill it with a pathological commitment to luxury, a life of living beyond my means, an obsession for expensive, inanimate possessions of quality which cannot betray me. That is why I want nothing more than for my life to end. Certainly I want nothing after it is over. I despise life. I do not believe in anything beyond it. I have nothing but contempt for the idea of your God. I want you to live with that knowledge. I want you to live knowing that you are responsible for the *death of a soul of a human being.*
          [PATRICK *releases* CONRAD, *steps off the platform, and walks away to center. A pause.* CONRAD *weakly lifts himself up on his hands on the bed, looks at* PATRICK.]

CONRAD
[*After a moment*]
I often wondered if you'd even remember.

PATRICK
Remember!

CONRAD
I thought it might be something so shameful that you'd force yourself to block it out forever.

PATRICK
It doesn't work that way!

CONRAD
[*After a moment looks at* PATRICK]
—Did you tell your father?

PATRICK
I told my mother.
[*Slight pause*]

CONRAD
[*After a moment*]
What did she do?

PATRICK
Nothing. I think she was afraid to tell my father. But she didn't go to anyone else—your superior, for instance. She did nothing. All she said was "That dirty old son of a bitch. I always knew he was freaky."

CONRAD
—I thought about getting some treatment. I knew it was something dark for which I needed help, but it seemed easier to bury it. We should never do anything with the hope of forgetting.
[*After a long moment*]
—The irony is, it happened to me.— That's what I wanted to speak of but couldn't. What was so difficult to admit a few minutes ago now seems like nothing.— I was abused. All my young life— By my mother.
[PATRICK *looks at* CONRAD]
—After my father died, she made me share the same bed with her until I finally took it upon myself to get out and go live with my sister. I couldn't endure the...tension of it anymore, the cat and mouse of it...the unspoken *fact* of it.— In the winter months we'd sleep spoon fashion, and I remember

345

one night when I was twelve years old, lying there I felt the warm satin of her nightgown pressed up against me, rubbing me. I began to get excited, and I got an erection. At first, I didn't know whether she was asleep or not, but after a while...after she let me almost reach the point of ejaculation, she reached behind herself and pushed me away—I knew she knew.— I turned over...facing away from her...and I... This went on time after time, year after year, nothing was ever said—even though the sheets would be circled and slightly discolored the next morning.

PATRICK
It explains something, I suppose. Not enough. But something. But so what? Is that supposed to make what you did to me all right? It hasn't made me do it. It hasn't made me even think about doing it.

CONRAD
I never did it again either. If you can believe it—never with another child after you. Ever!

PATRICK
I don't know that I *can* believe it.

CONRAD
There've been adults.

PATRICK
Teenagers?

CONRAD
Consenting *adults!*

PATRICK
In California, the age of consent is *eighteen*.

CONRAD
You were the only child! The only one!

PATRICK
If that is true, it's a privilege I could have lived without.

CONRAD
I know that doesn't make it any less wrong—any less my fault!

PATRICK
No, it doesn't. Because *you* were an adult. I was a child.

CONRAD
Yes. A bright child. A seductive child. Alluring and dangerous. You were like a little spark of divinity, tinged with a shadowed side, some inner sadness, a melancholy I recognized and wanted to fix by touching you, holding you, making it all right. I could never get over how long you could sustain eye contact with me. You were never shy. You never looked away. You were bold.

PATRICK
Oh, I see. So *I* was the source of temptation! All children are seductive, but they are *children*. They are not the ones in control!

CONRAD
Yes. Yes, I know. I know better than anyone that children are helpless.

PATRICK
What did you think about what you were doing?

CONRAD
I knew it was risky. I knew it was against the laws of God and man, but at the time I must not have considered anything except...the excitement.

PATRICK
You didn't consider the consequences?

CONRAD
They made me sick with fear.

PATRICK
The consequences to *you*.

CONRAD
And to *you*. I never told anyone about it, except some unknown priest in a confessional. I finally got up the nerve and drove to New Orleans—no one would know me there. I didn't tell him that I was a priest, only that I was a teacher. He said he would grant me absolution only if the sin were never, ever repeated.

PATRICK
[*Snidely*]
And you felt like a brand-new human being.

CONRAD

—I can still hear his voice. He said the sin was mortal—that if I continued, I would be excommunicated, denied the sacraments, forbidden all contact with Holy Mother Church. He asked me if I thought I was fit to be a teacher and suggested I find another profession—remove myself from the near occasion of sin—the company of children. I promised I would, and he absolved me.— On the drive back I was in a stupor, but I knew I had to speak to you the next day and somehow get through the rest of that term. Leaving abruptly would've caused a scandal. When that year was finally over I asked to be transferred and prayed that would be the end of it.

PATRICK
[*Sarcastically*]
A simple moral failure, according to the club. Something calling for penance and plain old willpower. So it's five *Hail* Marys and out the door for ten *Bloody* Marys!— It would have been far worse if you'd have slept with a woman. That would have meant you'd broken your *vow!*
[*CONRAD, in an attitude of exhaustion, slowly, heavily swings his feet to the floor but doesn't seem to have the strength to get off the bed.*
Looking off right]
—You were a decent man, Conrad. Do you know why you did it?

CONRAD
[*Looking off left*]
I have no idea. The whole thing is something I've never understood. Why I did what I did to you—why I did what I did to myself. Teaching was my calling...and I ruined it. Now I am a minister to the comatose—giving sacraments to people who don't know if they're in this world or the next, let alone that I'm standing there, praying for their salvation. It's an empty task to say empty homilies over and over and over to a congregation that's long since stopped listening. Now, I'm surrounded by death. And when I think of my own death approaching, I don't even have my faith to comfort me.

PATRICK
All I want is to resolve the past so that I can go on, go on to God knows what. It's a joke, but some mysterious part of me wants to love and be loved— wants it in the mildest, most removed but most insistent way. In the end, none of it makes sense. Nothing tracks.

CONRAD
Like our having met the way we did after all these years.— It's all a mystery.

PATRICK
Exactly.— *Pazzo.*— Meshuga.

CONRAD
What I did is something I'll never forget or get over or comprehend.

PATRICK
You can try, and all you'll get is a giant explosion, like the first blast of the universe. Something you simply cannot explain. In the end, whatever you figure out, whatever you really *crack*, just reassembles into a question mark as soon as you turn your head.
> [*Silence. A pause.* PATRICK *goes upstage center, takes the key out of his pocket and unlocks the door (three revolutions) and leaves the key dangling in the latch.* CONRAD *slowly gets off the bed.* PATRICK *slowly moves downstage right, facing away from* CONRAD *as he goes to the door and stops...*]

CONRAD
> [*At the door, after a moment*]
—I want to ask something of you.

PATRICK
> [*Not turning, facing out*]
What is it?

CONRAD
—Would you please...put your arms around me?— Hold me for a moment?—

PATRICK
> [*Not looking at* CONRAD, *after a moment*]
I wouldn't be at all interested in that.

CONRAD
> [*Resigned*]
I understand.
> [CONRAD *opens the door.* PATRICK *hears the sound of the latch opening but still does not turn.* CONRAD *opens the door, starts to go, stops, shuts the door and turns back...*]
—Will you...
> [PATRICK's *body reacts to* CONRAD's *voice, having assumed that the sound of the door closing meant* CONRAD *had departed...*
> *Begs*]
...Will you please forgive me?

PATRICK
> [*After a moment*]
I don't know.
> [CONRAD *slowly comes beside* PATRICK *and kneels down beside him...*]

CONRAD
[*Quietly, begging*]
I want to atone for my sin. I want to be good—to be clean. Forgive me. Only you can make me clean. Make me—after all these years—pure. Restore me. Make me whole. I beg you.
[*PATRICK doesn't respond. CONRAD takes PATRICK's hand, presses it against his forehead…*]
—I confess to Almighty God and to you, my son, that I have sinned against you.— Forgive me, Patrick. Forgive me, Ned. I beg you to forgive me.
[*A church bell begins to toll somewhere in the distance… The sound is faint, as the doors to the balcony are shut*]

PATRICK
[*After a long moment*]
—I………I…………………forgive you.
[*After another moment, absently*]
Go in peace.

CONRAD
—God bless you.
[*CONRAD kisses PATRICK's hand. PATRICK does not pull away. CONRAD lets go of his hand, gets off his knees, and goes to the door. PATRICK does not look at CONRAD as he opens the door and leaves, closing the door softly behind him. A beat, as the church bell continues to toll. PATRICK turns toward the muffled sound, goes to the window, and with his two hands whips the portieres apart and pulls open the balcony doors. Suddenly, a surreal blaze of white light incandesces the room from outside as a strong wind blasts inside, billowing the sheers out, ruffling PATRICK's hair and suit jacket and trousers. Simultaneous with the blinding light and the blast of wind, the sound of the church bells louden to an earsplitting pitch. A beat… Black out*]

THE END